FORBIDDEN VALLEY

Center Point
Large Print

Also by Allan Vaughan Elston and available from Center Point Large Print:

Saddle Up for Steamboat
Timberline Bonanza
Treasure Coach from Deadwood
The Landseekers

FORBIDDEN VALLEY

Allan Vaughan Elston

CENTER POINT LARGE PRINT
THORNDIKE, MAINE

This Center Point Large Print edition
is published in the year 2019 by arrangement with
Golden West Literary Agency.

Originally published in the US by Lippincott.
Originally published in the UK by Ward Lock.

The text of this Large Print edition is unabridged.
In other aspects, this book may vary
from the original edition.
Printed in the United States of America
on permanent paper.
Set in 16-point Times New Roman type.

ISBN: 978-1-64358-305-1 (hardcover)
ISBN: 978-1-64358-309-9 (paperback)

19/08

Library of Congress Cataloging-in-Publication Data

The Library of Congress has cataloged this record
under Library of Congress Control Number: 2019941873

To Homer Loucks of Sheridan

CHAPTER I

RAIN PELTED us as Doug and I pushed on west toward Powder River. It wasn't far, but we'd be till nightfall getting there. You can't make time on soggy sod, leading a pair of lazy pack mules. Doug's dragged on the rope and he twisted in the saddle to give it a gentle cussing. The soaked brim of his hat sagged to hide half of his sandy, Scotch face. All I could see was his mouth and most of the time a good-natured grin was there. "Shucks!" he said. "What are we mad about, Harry? This rain's just what we need."

"It's a year too late," I said, nodding toward the bleached ribs of a steer. We must have passed fifty like it in the last dozen miles. For this was early July of the year 1887 and everyone knows what happened to Wyoming cattle in the winter of '86-'87.

"Just look at that grass!" Doug exclaimed. "Best grama stand I ever saw!"

"And nothing to eat it," I groused, "except antelope." It was a hard fact that last year's drought, followed by a winter of subzero blizzards, had wiped out most of the big stock outfits.

The spring roundup had showed winter losses running as high as eighty percent.

For the next mile the rain came down harder than ever, slapping the sagebrush, spanking the little muddy rivers that ran down the trail ruts. Doug's yellow slicker was too short for his height and it left his knees sticking out, his legs soppy wet from boots to thighs. But it didn't faze him any; nothing ever fazed Doug McLaren. Right now he wasn't riding hunched over, like I was, chin-down to duck the rain, but straight-backed like a cavalryman, holding the reins high, just like he'd ride down Main Street in Sheridan on a sunny Sunday. Sometimes it made me feel old just to look at him. He swept the prairie with his bright blue gaze. "There'll be plenty to eat it, Harry, before snow flies again."

I fumbled for the makings, mechanically, before remembering I couldn't smoke in the rain. "You mean new stuff from Texas?"

Doug nodded. "Eighty thousand of them, I hear, are heading this way up the Bozeman Trail."

"God help 'em," I said, "if we have another winter like we just been through."

"Trouble never lasts forever," Doug argued irrepressibly. "I had an old Scotch grandmother used to say that. 'Calamities,' she always said, 'like as not turn out to be blessings.' "

"Just name me one time," I said, "when losin' all his cows in a snowdrift ever blessed anybody."

Doug twisted toward me with that wide grin of his. "Okay, Harry. Remember the young fella they were talkin' about back at Sundance, as we passed through the other day? They said he came out from the east four years ago, in '83, and started a ranch right across the line in Dakota. Just as he got a nice herd built up, along came last winter's blizzards and wiped him out. So a couple of weeks ago he gave up and went back east."

"Which proves what?"

"Which proves a calamity," Doug said, "like as not turns out to be a blessing. Because when this young fella came out here four years ago he was a skinny, thin-chested invalid. When he left he was a hard-hitting top hand, and as tough as any he-antelope on the range. He lost eighty thousand dollars worth of cows and picked up a million dollars worth of health."

I'd missed that part of it. "Yeh? What did they say his name was?"

"Kind of a dudish name," Doug remembered. "Theodore Somebody. I got it—Theodore Roosevelt."

Suggsby's place, on the bank of Powder River, was a trailside store-saloon with a corral back of it. The only trees anywhere near were some half-dead cottonwoods on the riverbank. Under these a stranded covered wagon outfit had made camp and it didn't take long to see why.

"She's still a mile wide," Doug grinned, looking out over the river bed, "but she's plenty more than an inch deep!"

A mile wide and an inch deep! they said of Powder River. Powder River, let 'er buck! they said. We could see she'd been bucking some. Driftwood showed high on the banks but the flood had passed and right now there wasn't too much water except out in the channel. Mostly it was soft mud and sand. You couldn't blame the wagon outfit for waiting for a sunny day before crossing.

We rode into Suggsby's corral which had an open shelter shed along one side. Five jaded horses there looked like they'd been ridden too far and too fast. Somebody had broken open a bale of timothy for them. Doug and I off-saddled at the other end of the shelter. One of the mule packs had a feed sack with about twenty pounds of oats left. I put out four equal piles of it. Then Doug took two pair of dry socks from a duffle bag and we made tracks for Suggsby's kitchen door.

They were muddy tracks and a Chinese cook didn't like them. He had a bony face and eye sockets like caves. His tongue clacked. "Allatime muddy boot! Allatime sclub floor!"

We went on into a storeroom which had a bar on one side and a staples counter on the other. Suggsby was back of the bar and five customers were at a table. We were too wet to be interested in anything but a barrel stove at the front. "Mix up some hot rum and sugar, Suggsby," Doug sang out, "before we catch double pneumonia."

We peeled out of our slickers and boots. A minute more and we had on dry socks with the wet ones hanging by the stove.

A cork popped as Suggsby got busy with the drinks. He had a spirit lamp on the backbar and used it to heat the rum. He didn't say anything and that struck me as a little funny. He knew us well enough. We'd passed here last week on our way to deliver a bunch of Open 8 horses to Sundance. Right now he stood with his back to us, heating the rum. But I could see his face in the bar mirror. It was a deep-lined face under thin hair streaked with gray. A tired, loose-jowled face with failure written on it. In his young days he'd been a soldier without ever winning his stripes. Later he'd failed at mining and then at ranching. He'd tried running a saloon in Buffalo but couldn't make it go. As a last stand he'd set up shop on this barren riverbank, midway between the Badlands and the Big Horns.

But now his face had something else than failure on it. His eyes had a scared look. Seen in the mirror they weren't fixed on Doug and me but on five men at the rear. Five men who were killing a pint while they waited for supper.

My own gaze swung that way. So did Doug's.

They looked tough, but no tougher than you'd expect to find at a spot like this. Four of them were shaggy and past forty. The other was a dandified kid, clean-shaved and around twenty. All five wore belt guns and two of them had brought saddle guns in. They might be stock hands. They might be drifters or even outlaws. I noticed the young man had his left arm in a sling. He had black eyes and black hair with deep sideburns reaching almost to his jaw line. Spanish, maybe. Anyway he looked foreign. They were sizing us up, just as we were sizing them. Doug and I each wore a belt gun. I glanced at Suggsby's face in the mirror and the scared look was still there.

The Chinese cook came in with five bowls of soup. One of the five men had a bullish build and wore a red and white cowskin coat. "What about crackers, Funnyface?" he growled.

"Clackers cloming up," Charley promised, and backed into the kitchen.

Suggsby didn't bring us our drinks. We had to go to the bar for them. That put us face to face with him and I saw sweat-beads on the bristles of his chin. I got the idea he wanted to tell us something but was afraid to let loose. His eyes sneaked past us to the soup eaters and one of them snapped him an order. "What about some light, Buddy?"

Day was fading outside as Suggsby lighted a

lamp on the backbar. Then he stood on a chair to light one which hung from a rafter. Doug and I took our rum toddies to the stove. We were a long way from dry yet. But mainly we left the bar so our backs wouldn't be to the other customers. I figured it was their first stop here. Calling the cook Funnyface and the storeman Buddy meant they didn't know the real names.

The cook came in with a heavy tray. He put five tin plates on the back table. Each plate had crackers and what looked like half-burned beans and slivers of sow belly. "Cloffee, yes?"

The big man in the cowskin coat nodded. "And get a move on. We're pulling out soon as our broncs finish the bale of mildewed weeds you sold us for hay."

As the cook backed away Doug McLaren called after him. "Two more orders of the same, Charley. And pie if you've got it. We've been living outa cans ever since we left Sundance."

The five toughies seemed to relax a little— as though relieved to learn we'd come from the east. It gave me the idea that they themselves had come from some other direction. Doug held a match to his cigaret and over cupped hands gave me a nod of warning. Not that I needed it. It was even money that those fellows were on the wrong side of the law and had just ridden fast from the wrong kind of a job.

Rain, which had been thumping the roof,

stopped suddenly. Then, from the stillness, we heard the bray of a mule. Not from the corral out back but from across the trail where the covered wagon outfit was camping.

Doug and I put on our boots and sat down at the front table. This put the barrel stove between us and the five toughies. One of them was a beanpole with a bullet head and I heard the others call him Jody. They all looked like sheriff bait except the young fellow with his arm in a sling.

So far Suggsby hadn't spoken a word to us. I got the idea he'd been warned to keep his mouth shut.

To draw him out I said: "She's been rarin'. Powder River, I mean."

"Some." Suggsby mopped his bar and didn't look my way.

"I bet most of it," Doug offered, "came down Crazy Woman."

"Likely," the storeman agreed. The Crazy Woman came in about twelve miles above here. Its steep watershed in the Big Horns was famous for making flash floods.

"What about putting us up overnight?"

We knew the storeman had cots upstairs. Before answering he shot an uneasy glance toward the rear table. "I guess so." He mumbled it like a man scared out of his skin he'd say the wrong thing.

Charley brought our supper in—soup and burned beans. The sow belly was gone, he said.

Then someone came in at the front door and every head in the room turned that way. It was a young girl, small-built and yellow-haired, and she was fresh and pretty as a rain-washed daisy. She had on a slicker three sizes too big. It hung open in front and we could see she wore Levis and gum boots. I figured she belonged to the stranded wagon outfit. Likely she'd been waiting for the rain to stop before crossing to the store.

"Do you have any fresh milk?" She spoke to Suggsby after a quick, curious glance at the rest of us.

"No," Suggsby said.

A man's felt hat was on the girl's head. Under the brim of it we could see sun-tanned cheeks and clear blue eyes. I'd just decided they were uncommonly intelligent eyes with plenty of good breeding back of them, when a man at the rear got up and sauntered toward the front. He was the young fellow with a bandage-slung arm and deep, black sideburns. His dark, foreign-looking face and his flat-crowned, braided hat had given me the idea he was Spanish. But he smiled and spoke to the girl without any accent. "Haven't you heard? Cows in the cow country don't give milk."

He said it with such impersonal good humour that she couldn't take any offense. As she smiled back at him I changed my mind about him being Spanish. More likely he was from the deep

15

south—maybe Florida or Louisiana. He strolled to the cigar counter, opened it, took out a cheroot and tossed a dime on the bar. "Rain let up yet?" he asked, glancing toward the girl. When she didn't answer he went to the front door and stood looking out, as though interested only in the weather.

"You have baking powder, I suppose," the girl said to Suggsby. "And a pound of shortening, please. And some tea . . ." She consulted a list and read off other items.

Suggsby crossed to the grocery side of the room. There he filled her order. Canned tomatoes made it bulky and when Suggsby put it in a sack it must have weighed close to ten pounds. The girl paid for it, picked up the sack and started out.

"Sort of heavy for a girl. Better let me tote it across the road for you." Again the voice was polite and impersonal. The young fellow was still in the doorway where he'd pretended to look out at the weather. The girl would need to brush by him to leave the store. I saw Doug stiffen a little as he caught the drift of it.

But the girl didn't need any help. Her "No thank you" was prompt and final. It was plain she knew just how to handle any stranger who might try to pick her up in a wayside store. Then she looked at the kid's crippled arm and relaxed. "It's nice of you to offer," she said, smiling up at him. "But I can manage all right."

He shrugged slightly, his own smile faintly rueful as he stepped aside to let her pass out. "Watch your step," he warned, "or you'll fall in a puddle."

Then she was gone and I saw Doug loosen up again. It wasn't more than a furlong to the girl's camp and the oversize slicker meant she had men folk there.

A chuckle came from the back table. "Losin' yer touch, ain'tcha, Bruno? I can remember when you usta knock 'em dead."

The jeer was from Jody. But the big shaggy man in a cow-skin coat wasn't amused. "We got no time for foolin'. Let's eat and get outa here."

Bruno rejoined them but didn't sit down. His free hand lighted the cheroot just as the cook came in with coffee.

"None for me," Bruno said. "So I might as well step out to the corral and see if the hosses have cleaned up that hay yet." He took his raincoat from a peg and went into the kitchen. We heard him go out the back door.

The four others fell to eating and I wondered which way they were headed. If they were on the level why would they pull out at all, on jaded horses through the mud and dark?

The cook brought us coffee and promised pie later. By then I noticed a suspicious look narrowing Doug's sky-blue eyes. With the stove screening him he leaned toward me. "Takin' him a long time, that fella," he whispered.

I caught what he meant and nodded. Maybe Bruno hadn't given up. Maybe he'd faked a trip to the corral so he could circle the store and stroll over to the covered wagon camp. He'd be glib enough to rig up some plausible excuse. Maybe he figured he'd really made a conquest and all he needed was to follow through.

A cackle from the back table meant the same idea had struck Jody. "Never passes up a chance, that kid don't. When they're young and goodlookin' he just can't stay away."

But the cowskin-coated man didn't like it. "Look, Dakota," he said. "If he ain't back in twenty minutes you fog over there and get him."

I saw red creep up Doug's neck. He went to the bar and spoke to Suggsby. "How long have those folks been camping over there?"

"Since yesterday," the storeman said.

"Which way are they headed?"

"Sheridan."

"How many in the party?"

"Five. The girl and her old man and three brothers."

"Oh!" Doug relaxed and came back to his chair. I grinned at him and said, "So it's none of our business!" He nodded and looked a little sheepish. Since the girl had four menfolks in camp, we'd been wasting our worry.

Yet another ten minutes ticked away and Bruno didn't come back. Jody reached for his rifle and slicker. "We can't ride till we saddle up," he said. "I'll go saddle the broncs and if he ain't here by then, I'll go fetch him myself. Let's have a lantern, Buddy."

"A lantern? Sure." Suggsby brought one from a cabinet and lighted it.

Jody took it and his spurs clinked as he went out through the kitchen. The others poured themselves more coffee. Doug's knitted brows and narrow, knowing gaze at them told me his thought. I was riding the same idea myself. If these men were outlaws on the run they were smart not to leave Suggsby alone with us until all the horses were saddled. By letting one man saddle up, the rest could keep an eye on Suggsby and us till the last minute.

But the last minute never came. For Jody came hopping back in with bad news. "He ditched us! He's gone! So's every horse in the corral. The son-of-a . . . !"

Roars from the others drowned him out. They were all on their feet and the air was blue. Then, with Cowskin-Coat a jump in the lead, they stampeded out through the kitchen.

Doug and I weren't far behind. For it meant we'd lost our own mounts too. By emptying the corral Bruno had made sure he wouldn't be chased. "It figures," Doug said.

19

"What figures?" We catapulted out into the backyard and there the dark and the puddles slowed us up.

"He only faked a play for the girl," Doug reasoned. "It was just an excuse to get out. When she turned him down, he pretended to have a look to see if the horses had finished feeding. He knew they'd think he was out chasing the girl. 'Stead of that he was making off with the loot."

There was only one hole in it. "What loot? Come again, Doug." For if they were running with loot they wouldn't leave it in their saddle-bags unguarded.

Doug couldn't explain it. And when we got to the corral he didn't need to. The gate was open and every horse was gone, including our own and the pack mules. But the saddles were still under the shelter shed. Jody had the lantern and its light showed us the four stranded toughies in a huddle.

One of them stooped to pick up something. It looked like a white cloth tied in a long, loose loop. Doug squeezed my arm and we froze there. "It's the sling, Harry. He threw it away."

A storm of plain and fancy cussing kept them from hearing us. Out of it came a bitter lament from Jody. "And it was *him* talked us into that busted arm idea! They won't search a guy, he claimed, if his arm's in a sling!"

We knew then that there'd been no lame arm. And that whatever of value these men had made off with had been concealed, at the suggestion of Bruno the Kid, not in pockets or saddlebags which might be searched, but in the cast and sling of what looked like a broken arm.

CHAPTER II

FOR A WHILE they were too mad to be scared. But they'd begin to get scared when they took time to think a little. Any man on foot at a place like Powder River Crossing isn't going to feel very good about it. Especially if he's on the wrong side of the law and has to keep moving.

While they stood there in the corral cussing Bruno, Doug and I hurried back to Suggsby's bar. Suggsby looked like a man sitting on dynamite. "Talk fast!" Doug shot at him. "What do you know about 'em?"

The storeman passed a hand over the pale, flabby flesh of his face and cocked a fearful ear toward the back. "Can they hear me?" he whispered.

"Not from the corral. Talk fast before they get back."

He leaned across the bar, his voice hoarse and jittery. "Dale Hasker rid by here yesterday."

We knew Hasker. He was a Johnson County deputy sheriff and lived at Buffalo. "What did he want?"

"He ast if I'd seen five men headin' south from

23

Montana. A wire to Fort McKinney said five masked men held up an N.P. train west of Miles City. They took eight thousand dollars and lit out south."

"Which way did Hasker go?"

"He hit for the Circle Cross to ask there. Said he might be back this way."

"These five men got here just a little before we did?"

" 'Bout half an hour before you." Suggsby kept his scared eyes toward the rear. "I was afraid they'd figger you for deputies and start shootin'. Or maybe Hasker'd pop in again. I didn't want 'em to cut loose, right in my bar."

Doug's look at him had more contempt than pity. "All right. Pretend you don't suspect a thing. They can't track Bruno in the dark so they're stalled here till daylight. Then they'll make a grab at the nearest horses. How many've you got, Suggsby?"

"Five. A four-horse freight team and a pony."

"Where are they now?"

"Ed Wimple took 'em to the railhead for a load of store and bar stock. Ain't due back for three days yet."

Wimple was Suggsby's roustabout hand. He'd taken the riding pony along so that he could let the harness stock graze loose at night and have a mount to round them up with every morning.

"What horse stock have they got over there?"

The impatient jerk of Doug's head was toward the covered wagon camp across the road.

"A riding pony for each of the kids," Suggsby said, "and another for the girl. The old man drives the wagon mules."

"Kids? You said she had three brothers."

"Just kids. The oldest is maybe fourteen and the youngest's around ten. They . . ." He broke off as we heard boots thumping through the kitchen.

Doug and I moved to the stove as the four outlaws tramped back in. All four had hip guns and two of them had rifles. They looked mad enough to cut loose if we even batted an eye.

Tying into them wouldn't get us anywhere. They had us outnumbered. Anyway we were only guessing that they were train robbers. So Doug just put on a dry grin and said to them: "Looks like we're in the same boat you are. Afoot in the tall sage. Got any idea which way he went?"

The man in the cowskin coat snapped back: "What do you think I am? A bat? How can I see tracks in the dark?"

"And even when daylight comes," I put in, "we won't be much better off. Him on a horse and us afoot. Look, Doug. The quicker we hit for the Circle Cross the quicker we'll get mounted."

Doug took the cue and nodded. It was twelve muddy miles to the Circle Cross on Spotted Horse Creek. "That's further 'n I've walked in a coon's age," he groused. "But what else can we do? Suggsby, take care of our saddles and packs. We'll pick 'em up day after tomorrow. Let's go, Harry."

I paid Suggsby what we owed him. Then we walked right through those four toughies half expecting they'd start gunning us. But they didn't. When we got to the corral we left our saddles right where they lay but took the carbines out of the scabbards.

Then we circled the store and headed for a grove of cottonwoods up the riverbank. The thing we had to do was so plain that neither of us even mentioned it.

The weathered gray of a wagon top showed up in the dark. Beyond it we saw a bed of coals and a lantern. A dog barked. Then a man's voice challenged, "Who's there?"

"Friends," Doug called back. "Something happened at the store and you oughta know about it."

As we rounded the wagon I wasn't surprised to see they weren't taking us for granted. It was a wild country and immigrants couldn't be sure who they'd run into. This man had a short, graying mustache and a craggy face. He stood solid on his feet with a shotgun in the crook of his arm, his steady, hazel eyes searching us out. A boy at his elbow had a .22 rabbit gun. The girl was at a camp table further back. Except for her braided yellow hair I'd have taken her for a boy, and a small boy at that. Without the oversize slicker she looked tiny and slim in the gloom there. She was at a pan of supper dishes and had a still smaller boy drying them for her. I guess Doug and I looked plenty tough to them, popping out of the dark with rifles and hip guns. A terrier growled and the girl said, "Quiet, Rowdy." She didn't sound the least bit scared. Beyond her a third boy was peering from an olive drab army tent. "Is there trouble?" the man questioned cautiously.

"Yes, but none of our making, neighbor." Doug leaned his rifle against the wagon and unbuckled his belt. He hung the belt and holster on the endgate and I did the same with mine. Then Doug laughed and he had the kind of laugh people trust. When he stepped into the firelight I saw the girl's face change. Suspicion faded and she smiled. It was plain she remembered seeing him at the store and he hadn't made too bad an impression. "Won't you sit down?" she invited.

We sat on a log and I let Doug tell what they needed to know. The man listened gravely and once the oldest boy broke in excitedly. "Train robbers! Golly!" The youngest one came from the tent with big, staring eyes and the girl slipped an arm around him. "Come daylight," Doug finished, "they're likely to raid your horses."

I could hear the horses champing in the dark. They'd been grazing in hobbles all day and had been brought in to pickets at nightfall.

The girl smiled at her own expense. "And he was such a nice looking young man!"

The father questioned, "They'll want our ponies to chase him?"

"Partly for that," I said. "But mainly to get far away and fast."

"They'll make a try at tracking Bruno," Doug guessed, "soon as it's daylight. Which they can't do on foot. So I look for them to pay a call over here at the first crack of dawn."

"We'll be ready for them," the immigrant vowed grimly. "And thanks, boys. I'm Bruce Gordon and this is my girl Carrie."

"Meet another Scottie, then," I grinned. "He's Doug McLaren. My name's Harry Riley. We delivered some stock to Sundance and are heading back home to Sheridan."

The Gordons too were heading for Sheridan. "We figure to take up some land over that way," the man said.

We lost no time making plans to defend the camp. The wagon team and riding ponies were brought in closer, where we could see them even in the dark. The boys, protesting bitterly, were made to go to bed in the tent. The girl's bed was in the covered wagon.

"I'll be too excited to sleep," Carrie Gordon said, and her small, flushed face proved it. "What about *your* horses? Won't you try to get them back?"

"One thing at a time," Doug grinned. "First job's to see they don't grab yours."

She said goodnight and climbed out of sight into the wagon. Her father set a coffee pot on the coals and we three men picked spots well apart from each other. Those fellows might sneak up in the night, figuring to catch the camp asleep. "The dog'll warn us," Gordon said.

Nobody slept that night, not even the boys in the tent. It seemed like one of them wanted a drink every ten minutes. They made a hundred excuses to come out and ask questions. "Are you a cowboy?" the smallest one asked me. "I am now," I told him. "In my young days I was a soldier." Along about the third cup of coffee the girl's voice spoke from the wagon. How long would it take, she asked, to drive to Sheridan?

"It's a two-day wagon drive," Doug called back to her, "if you don't run into any high water."

"How big is Sheridan, Mr. McLaren?"

"Let's see!" Doug used his fingers to count on. "Four general stores, two hotels, two drugstores, one bank, eight restaurants and boarding houses, six saloons, two livery barns and three smithies, one barber, one millinery shop and . . ."

"Oh!" Carrie broke in with a laugh. "Then women live there too!"

"Enough for a dance once a month," Doug said. "There's a big one coming up in honor of Governor Tom Moonlight. He's making a horse-

and-buggy tour of the territory. There'll be a banquet and speech-making and after that they'll dance all night."

He told her a good deal about Sheridan as she asked bright, eager questions. Then her father broke in on it. "That's enough, Carrie. You go to sleep."

Just at daybreak I caught myself nodding. Then Bruce Gordon made a breakfast fire and its crackling aroused me. There was enough light to see the outline of Suggsby's store about two hundred yards away.

Silence from the tent meant the boys had finally fallen asleep. As we heard the girl stirring Gordon called to her. "Stay right where you are a while longer, Carrie." His speech had a faint Scotch burr in it.

Doug moved forward to peer from our screen of cottonwoods. "Here they come!" he announced brusquely.

The four toughies had crossed the road and were heading this way. They wore holster guns but carried no rifles. I guess they left their rifles in the store so they wouldn't look too warlike. They didn't know Doug and I were here. And by getting face-to-face with Gordon they could bat him down with a six-gun. "Keep back of a tree," Doug whispered, "till they tip their hand." He picked a cottonwood and I got back of another.

Bruce Gordon sat on the wagon tongue with the shotgun across his knees. The four men were nearly to us when the terrier yapped at them. It stopped them for a moment; then they came right on.

"Mornin', neighbor." It was the big, cowskin-coated man who hailed Gordon. He tried to look hearty but didn't do a very good job of it. Then sight of Gordon's shotgun halted them about ten yards away.

From there the big man spoke his piece glibly. "Our broncs got loose last night. We need some saddle ponies so we can round 'em up."

"What about loanin' us yourn?" This in a wheedling tone from Jody. "We'd only need 'em about half an hour."

It wouldn't have convinced Gordon even if we hadn't warned him. *One* wrangle pony would have been enough. Gordon gave them a level stare and shook his head. "We're pulling out right away ourselves," he said.

Jody and the big man exchanged signals and I was afraid they'd cut loose on Gordon. Instead they began spreading out so that his shotgun couldn't cover but one man. So Doug and I stepped out with our rifles. "Reach!" Doug yelled.

The surprise of it made them look silly. The man they called Dakota was the only one who didn't put up his hands. Then he yowled as Doug pulled a trigger and whistled a bullet past his ear.

"Let this be a lesson," Doug chided. "Never try to steal horses before breakfast."

"Better light out," I warned them, "before this pard of mine gets mad. He's a bearcat when you make him fight on an empty stomach."

They turned and legged it for Suggsby's. Doug fired once more just to spatter mud on their heels. The minute they dived through the store door I was sorry we'd let them go. Now they had rifles and shelter to shoot from.

But so did we. The cottonwoods had big thick boles. Carrie jumped from the wagon and the boys tumbled out of the tent. "The nerve of them!" the girl exclaimed. "Trying to take our horses! Do you think they'll come back?"

"No tellin'," Doug said. Then unconsciously he took command, as he had a way of doing in a crisis. "You folks better break camp right away. Make tracks for Sheridan. Harry and I'll cover you while you're crossin' the river."

No one argued with him. We brought the mules up and slapped on the harness. Gordon traced them to the wagon while I saddled the ponies. Doug helped the boys strike the tent. Carrie made coffee and fried bacon while we loaded the wagon.

The sun was topping the badlands to the east of us when the outfit was ready to move. Bruce Gordon was on the wagon seat and the rest of them were asaddle. "Drive straight down that cut in the bank," Doug advised. "The bank'll screen you from the store."

Gordon looked dubiously across the wide, flood-cut river bed. "It's a long piece over there. Reckon we can make it?"

"You can," Doug promised, "if you follow the trail ruts. Most of the way you'll be on sand that's nearly dry now. You'll hit two or three channels but no water more 'n a foot deep. Better get going."

"Why can't you come with us?" Carrie worried. Astride a stock saddle in tight Levis she looked as boyish as her brothers.

Doug shook his head. "You won't get across at all unless we keep those birds cooped up till you're out of range."

Gordon drove down a steep cut to the river bed. Doug and I got behind trees at the edge of the grove. From here we could pick off anyone who tried coming out of the store.

We heard the wagon creak out over the river sand but for a while the high bank kept us from seeing it. Men in the store wouldn't be able to see it either. A window went up and Jody leaned out of it. He had a rifle and was looking toward the river. Just to pin him down Doug fired into the sash over his head.

The man jumped back and didn't show there again. And the next time I twisted to look out over the river I could see the wagon. But it was out of range now. The girl and her brothers were riding ahead to feel out the soft spots. They splashed through the main channel and the wagon followed.

We saw them climb up the far bank onto a sagebrush prairie. The girl turned to wave her hat. Her hair made a tiny dot of gold in the distance. Then they moved on toward the snowy skyline of the Big Horns and the sage swallowed them.

"Where do we go from here, Doug?"

"We better keep 'em pinned down a while longer," he advised. "Then we can hit for the Circle Cross."

"On what?"

"On shank's mares. What else've we got?" He gave me an impudent grin, knowing I'd as leave be hung up by the thumbs as to travel twelve miles afoot.

As for the four outlaws, they at least had food and shelter and all the liquor they could drink. They could stick around till another immigrant came along. Then they could hold the man up and steal four of his horses.

But fate gave us a reshuffle. Doug let out a whoop and pointed southeast. And there we saw riding stock. I counted eight head. It was still a mile away and coming single file at a slow walk. Loose stock, unsaddled and undriven. "That's Bessie in the lead!" Doug chortled. "Bless her heart!"

One of our pack mules was a jinney we called Bessie. And the whole thing was plain as Wyoming daylight. Bruno had driven the stock ahead of him to keep from being chased. But it would slow him down, so he wouldn't drive it more than ten miles or so. Then he'd pick out the best of seven horses and leave the rest right there.

The best would be Doug McLaren's long-limbed sorrel. And as the file of animals came nearer I could see the sorrel was the only one missing. Bessie was leading the others straight back to Suggsby's corral.

"She'll do it every time," Doug crowed. "Turn her loose and she heads right for the spot where she was last grained."

I was glad we'd fed oats last night. Bessie figured there'd be more of it for her this morning. Back she came with the broncs trailing her. In that way broncs are a little like sheep—they'll follow a leader.

I heard a kitchen door slam. Then Suggsby stuck his scared face out of the store's front door and beckoned us. We cocked our carbines and ran toward him. He hardly needed to tell us his customers had seen the saddle stock coming and were waiting in the corral to grab it.

We went in at the front and out through the kitchen. Three of them were out of sight under the corral shelter shed. But Jody was at this end watching for us and he opened up. A slug breathed on me and smashed glass out of a kitchen window. Then Jody doubled up at Doug's first shot. We ran right on over him and pulled up at the shed corner.

There only an inch of pine board screened us from three riflemen. Their rifles cracked and a splinter hit my leg. A step further would put us right in their sights.

"I better go in from the other end," Doug said.

The shed was forty yards long and he raced down the back side of it. When I heard him shoot from the other end, I dived around my end and made a belly landing. Two of them had whirled to face Doug and the one looking my way shot too high. I dropped him before he could shoot again. Beyond him was gunsmoke and through it I saw the backs of two men. Doug, carbine stock at his cheek, was walking straight at them. I saw his hat bounce and red splotch his face. He kept coming, shooting. One of the men went to his hands and knees. The other ran toward the corral gate, then stumbled with a bullet in his leg and went sliding down the mud.

Doug got to him and took his rifle. Then we dragged him back to the shelter and tallied up. Three of them had bullet trouble but would live. Only Jody was dead. Doug rolled a cigaret and passed me the makings. After that we just stood there and watched the saddle stock, minus Doug's sorrel, come walking in through the gate.

CHAPTER III

WE TOSSED a saddle on one of them and sent Chinese Charley jogging toward the Circle Cross. Doug and I were catching up on sleep when he got back with Deputy Dale Hasker and two ranch hands. They brought along a buckboard and an extra horse.

We'd tied up the three wounded men and laid a tarp over Jody. Hasker took a fast look, then woke us up. "Seems like you been busy, cowboys." A sardonic smile creased his plump, stubbled face.

"You got a line on them?" Doug asked. He poured water into a china basin and doused his head. We were in the cot room over Suggsby's bar.

"There's circulars out on three of 'em," Hasker told us. "A bank killing at Rawlins. Only one I can't place is the beefy guy in the cowskin coat." His eyes narrowed. "Seems to me I've seen that coat before. Only someone else was wearing it."

Doug looked up, nodding with a half-sure agreement. "It hit me the same way, Hasker, the minute I saw it. A coat made from the hide of a red-and-white spotted cow with the hair side turned out. I saw it in Sheridan one time. Coupla years ago when I first landed there."

"What about Bruno?" I asked, and described him.

"Can't place that kid," Hasker said.

We pulled on our boots and went down to question the prisoners. One of them, who'd been circularized as Ab Riddle, had a bullet between the ribs and was in no shape to talk. He was white as the sheet Suggsby used to stop the flow of his blood. Another of them, known to Hasker as Dakota Smith, had been shot through the upper leg. He was able to talk but wouldn't. He and Riddle and the dead Jody were the killers wanted at Rawlins. The cowskin-coated man was barely scratched. He gave his name as Frank Gomer and said he was a trader up on the Crow reservation.

Hasker fixed a cold stare on him. "What do you trade 'em? Whisky?"

"You can't hang that one on me," Gomer shot back. "Or anything else. I'm legal." And actually we hadn't a thing on him, yet, except that he'd been caught with Riddle, Jody and Smith.

"Where did you meet up with 'em?"

"Up the range a piece. We just happened to be riding the same way."

"Where were you Monday night at ten o'clock?" Hasker asked, naming the hour of the Northern Pacific holdup near Miles City.

Gomer had a fast answer. "At a bar in Sheridan. The Ace of Diamonds. Ask Martie LaSalle."

"We will," the deputy promised. He turned to Suggsby, Charley, Doug and me. "Write down just what happened here and sign it. Then two of you better come along to testify at a coroner's inquest."

I thought he'd take Doug and me, but Doug talked him out of it. "Look, Hasker. Someone's got to take a shot at tracking Bruno. It's my bronc he got away with. So let Harry and me take out after him."

"Him and eight thousand in cash loot," I put in.

The deputy himself couldn't go because he had a dead man and three prisoners on his hands. In the end he decided to have Suggsby and Charley lock up the store and go along with him to Buffalo. They set out, one of the Circle Cross men driving the buckboard and the other guarding the prisoners. Their route would take them by the Ucross on Clear Creek and from there up Clear Creek to the county seat.

They left four head of stock in the corral—my own horse, the extra Circle Cross horse and our two pack mules. When these finished feeding Doug and I rode out through the gate, leading the mules. Speed didn't matter much because Bruno was too far ahead to be caught while travelling. But maybe we could track him to whatever town or ranch or camp he'd pick for a hideout.

The sign led southeast and for a few miles even a drug clerk could have followed it. That far we were back-tracking the eight animals Bruno had turned loose. We found the place where he'd changed from his own horse to Doug's sorrel. The sod was plenty soft from yesterday's rain.

Now it was a little past noon and the sun was summer bright. "Bruno," Doug guessed, "is heading for the Black Hills." But a little further on he changed his mind. The sign began curving to the right and was soon pointing southwest. By sundown it had led us back to Powder River right where the Crazy Woman came in.

Here Bruno had crossed to the west bank and we followed his sign across the wide, treacherous bed of sand and muddy water. The mule Bessie bogged at the channel. It took two ropes and half an hour to drag her out.

So we only had a little twilight left before dark caught us. The sorrel's sign was now leading up the west bank of Crazy Woman. And while this stream was down to its normal, sluggish flow, it was plain that a wall of flood water had rampaged by here only a few days ago. The high banks were slimy and sticky debris clung to the sagebrush. Doug whistled softly. "Gee! She must've been deep enough to float a barn!"

Dark forced us to pick a dry knoll and make camp for the night. We were only about fifteen miles east of Buffalo and I wondered why Bruno would risk passing so close to the county seat. "He'd need to," Doug reasoned, "if he aims to cross the Big Horns at Powder River Pass."

At daybreak we broke camp and moved on along the sign. It kept on up the west bank of Crazy Woman and in a little while disappeared into the tracks of loose range horses. Most of them were unshod breeding mares but a few were shod ponies turned loose after the spring roundup.

We followed a dozen sets of shod prints but in each case came to a free grazing pony which wasn't a sorrel. "Looks like Bruno ditched us," Doug said.

We were still on the west bank of Crazy Woman and what looked like a painted board caught my eye. It was plastered against a sage bush with flood-washed mud clinging to it.

We rode to it and saw that it was an end-gate. "An end-gate off a spring wagon, Harry." Doug looked up the river bed and saw something else. "And there's a wheel! Somebody had hard luck."

We went out there and found the wheel of a spring wagon with half a broken axle. Beyond we came to a wagon seat and a double-tree. Keeping on we ran into the three-wheeled wreck of what had been a two-horse spring wagon.

"Some poor devil was crossing above here,"

Doug concluded, "when a cloudburst flood whanged into him."

"Wonder if the guy got out, Doug!" A fifteen foot wall of water, boiling down a channel like the Crazy Woman, could sweep a team away like a shaving.

Maybe the team had gotten out because we'd seen no dead horses. The driver himself might jump and let the flood beach him at the first bend in the bank.

We followed on up the river looking for sign of him. But all we found was a small, brassbound trunk. It was half buried in silt and we had to dig before we got a rope around it. Then we dragged it to a high dry bank.

There was no name or initial on it. But it was sure to be part of the spring wagon's cargo. "See 'f it's locked," Doug suggested.

It wasn't. Yet strong brass clamps had kept the torrent from bursting it open. I looked doubtfully at Doug and he nodded. "Sure. We better look inside and see who it belongs to. Then we'll know where to take it."

I pried the clamps back and raised the lid. Then we stood batting our eyes. We weren't used to gear like this. Woman gear! Silks and laces. Petticoats and long stockings! Doug gaped a minute and then looked off downstream. The woman herself might have been washed far below here; right now she might lie buried under tons of mud and sand. What about the man who'd been driving her? She'd hardly be travelling alone, this far off the regular trails.

"Kinda young lookin', this stuff!" Doug muttered. Enough water had seeped into the trunk to give a soggy, bedraggled look to the clothing there. Doug took a pink underthing gingerly between two fingers and hung it on a sage bush to dry. "There's bound to be something," he argued, "to let us know who she is."

And since it needed to have an airing in the sun, we took the clothing out piece by piece and draped it on the sage. Piece by piece we looked for a name but didn't find any. "She's just a kid, Harry. Look!" Doug held up a pair of dancing pumps small enough for a child.

We couldn't find any identification till we got to the bottom. And there lay a leather-bound book frayed at the edges. "There'll be a name in it, likely." Doug opened to a flyleaf and nodded soberly. "Yeh, here it is. The name's Prather."

Here was a family Bible with birth, death and marriage recorded by date. There were four entries.

John Prather, born May 10 1840
John Prather & Susan Roth, married
    May 4, 1866, Toledo, O.
Mary Prather, born Nov. 25, 1867

Susan Roth Prather, died Feb. 16, 1881,
Toledo, O.

"Makes her about twenty years old," Doug said. "Mary Prather."

"This is her stuff," I said. Neither of us knew anyone named Prather.

"We can ask at the Ucross, Harry." The Ucross was right on our way to Sheridan. It was a big outfit. The winter had hit it pretty hard but it still had half a dozen riders. If the Prathers had escaped with their lives maybe the Ucross had picked them up.

I brought up the mules and changed the pack hitch on Bessie. When the girl's clothes were dry Doug put everything back in the trunk and balanced it across the pack. I threw a hitch and we were ready to go.

"What's that name again?" I asked, as we took off through the sage, a little west of north.

"Prather. Mary Prather." Doug twisted toward me with a puzzled look. "There's one thing I can't figure, Harry."

When I asked what he meant he seemed not to hear me and I didn't press the point.

It was sundown when we hit the Ucross. Its buildings and hay-topped sheds made brown lumps against the green of the Clear Creek Willows. The bad winter had killed more than half of its cattle but this outfit had eastern capital

44

back of it. And so stuff to restock it was already on its way up the Bozeman.

Gus Canby was in the corral taming a colt. "Rest of the outfit," he told us, "took off a hun'erd miles or so down the trail."

"What for?"

"To meet a new herd comin' up from Texas. What the heck you got on that mule?"

"A lady's trunk," Doug explained. "She got caught in high water. You got any idea who . . . ?"

"Sure I have," Gus broke in, grinning. "It was Jim Hutton and his daughter. They came in here like drowned rabbits, a few nights back, ridin' bareback on a spring wagon team. Their outfit went down the Crazy Woman. So I loaned 'em some dry pants and a buggy and they driv on to Sheridan."

Jim Hutton! Early this spring he'd bought a ranch up the Big Goose, west of Sheridan. Doug and I knew and liked him. But we'd never heard about him having a family.

"Is the girl's name Mary?" I asked.

"Nope," Gus said. "It's Joan. Joan Hutton. And if you guys are smart you'll get acquainted with her right quick. She's purty as a . . ."

"What was Jim Hutton," Doug broke in, "doing down this way?"

Gus perched himself on the corral fence and rolled a smoke. "She came out from the east and

45

Jim had to fetch her from the railroad. Met her at Douglas with a spring wagon."

Douglas was on the Bozeman Trail about a five day buckboard drive south of Sheridan. Meeting the girl's train there and returning by the same route, Hutton would cross the Crazy Woman thirty miles above where we'd found the wreck. Which was a lot too far to make sense.

But Gus explained it. "When he got to where the trail crosses Crazy Woman, Jim left it and drove downriver to show her the homestead where he got his start back in '81. Sentiment, maybe. Or maybe the gal wanted to see the place because he'd written her about it so much. So they were a long piece off the trail when the flood smacked 'em."

"What I can't understand," I puzzled, "is why . . ."

But again Doug broke in and this time he frowned a warning. "So Jim Hutton's luck played out on him! Eh, Gus?"

"This time it did," Gus agreed. "But he had enough luck before that to last a lifetime. Jim's the only cowman I know who didn't lose his shirt in them blizzards."

The reason was that Jim Hutton had sold out for cash late in the fall. He'd banked the money and waited till spring before buying a new place on the Goose. So he'd had no cattle to die in the hard winter. Lucky Jim! folks were calling him.

"Right now he's got new stuff comin' up the trail," Gus reminded us, "to make a fresh start with."

Again I opened my mouth and this time Doug stopped me with a kick on the shin. When we'd unpacked, and Doug had pasted court plaster over a bullet nick on his face, we picked ourselves bunks in the bunkhouse.

"The name in the family record," I said, "is Prather."

"Which they don't want folks to know, I guess," Doug said.

I blinked at him. "What gave you an idea like that?"

"Some of those duds had labels on 'em, one time. Store labels. But the labels were cut out. She don't want folks to know they came from Toledo, Ohio."

"But why, Doug? I always figured Hutton for a square shooter."

"He could have had trouble," Doug argued. "Bad trouble he doesn't want followin' him to Wyoming. So when he changes his name to Hutton, the girl has to change her name too. In which case we don't want to go blabbing."

"We sure don't," I agreed. "Come to think of it, we didn't have any business lookin' in that trunk."

CHAPTER IV

GUS CANBY didn't need to be told about the shooting fracas at Suggsby's. Hasker had passed by with his prisoners on a short cut to Buffalo.

"What do you figger they'll do with them birds?" Gus pondered during supper.

"They'll bury Jody," Doug promised him, "and send two of 'em to be hanged at Rawlins. What they do with Gomer depends on Martie LaSalle."

"You mean that Frenchie who runs the Ace of Diamonds in Sheridan?"

"Yeh, he's Gomer's alibi for a Montana train job." We let it go at that and went to bed.

Gus fed us a sunup breakfast and we took off on a beeline for Sheridan. "I've been studyin' about that cowskin coat," Doug said as we jogged along. "Hasker said it looked familiar and I got the same idea myself."

"I got a funny feeling too," I said. "Not about the coat but about Bruno."

"You mean you saw him before one time?"

"Maybe. Or maybe he just reminds me of someone. It's so dim I can't toss a loop on it, Doug."

The mule I was leading shied as we passed the

49

bleached bones of a steer. I looked back to make sure the trunk was riding all right. In the next hour we passed a dozen more sets of ribs. This was near the head of Dutch Creek where winter losses had been especially heavy. A deserted cabin brought grim memories. In March its owner had been found frozen stiff, as dead as the cows in his pasture.

We topped a rise and angled down toward Prairie Dog Creek. A line of willows there had a flat-roofed shack by it and no sign of life. It was the Job Potter claim and Job had been blizzarded out, in January. He'd staggered into Sheridan on frozen feet to buy a stage ticket east. "I'm done with Wyoming!" he'd sworn.

"But it looks like he came back," Doug said.

"Why?"

"Last time I passed here the door was boarded up."

No boards were across the door now. It was time to water the stock, anyway, so we reined left to stop at the Potter place. Maybe Job had come back for another go at it, or maybe a squatter had moved in.

"Funny there's no wagon in sight," Doug puzzled. "Or gear of some kind." There wasn't even an axe at the woodpile. The windows of the shack, I noticed, were still boarded.

We came to the creek willows, which were thick and high, and suddenly we heard the neigh of a horse. A horse tied out of sight in the brush!

Doug looked warily at the cabin. "Sounds like an old friend, Harry. Or am I dreaming?"

We pushed into the willows and there was Doug's sorrel—the one Bruno had gotten away on. A saddle lay on the ground by him. "Did he treat you all right?" Doug gave the horse an affectionate slap. "Looks like you been bog-riding."

Dry mud was caked on the sorrel's forelegs and on the skirts of the saddle. I remembered one of our mules had gone in belly-deep, crossing Powder River. Bruno had made the same crossing.

But why would he double back this way?

"He fooled us by heading south," Doug concluded, "till he lost his sign in those loose horses. Then he took off northwest for Sheridan."

It made sense if Bruno had friends in Sheridan who could hide him or stake him to a fresh mount.

"He wouldn't dare ride into town by daylight," Doug reasoned. "Not with eight thousand in cash loot and on a sorrel everybody knows is mine. So he's stopping here till dark. All he had to do was pull boards off the door."

The cabin's front side had a boarded window. But cracks would be wide enough to let Bruno look out at us over the sights of a rifle. So we hid our stock in the willows and circled on foot toward a blind wall of the house. Maybe Bruno was asleep after his long, forced ride. And maybe he wasn't. "He's tricky," Doug warned. "He sure fooled us at Suggsby's."

We got to the blind wall and cocked our ears. I couldn't hear a thing. Doug drew his six-gun and slipped around to the front side. "Cover me, Harry." I kept right back of him and put my eye to a crack of the boarded window. It was too dark inside for me to see anything. So I pried off the board and rubbed dust from the pane.

I still couldn't see anything so Doug went to the door and pushed it open. Enough daylight went in to let me see through the pane. The place looked empty. "I don't smell any smoke," Doug said, meaning that if Bruno was inside he'd be shooting at us by this time.

When Doug stepped in with a cocked gun I was at his heels. We relaxed when we saw there was only one room. Burlap hanging over a corner made a triangular closet. Job Potter had left a stove and a cot and a chair. There didn't seem to be any place a man could hide except behind that burlap curtain.

So Doug and I were both covering it when a rifle barrel hit the back of my head. I went down in a cloud of bouncing stars.

In a minute I came out of it with hot needles jabbing my brain. Then I saw Bruno. He was poking the muzzle of his rifle into the small of

Doug's back. Doug had dropped his forty-five and his hands were up. Bruno put out a Spanish-spurred boot and kicked the gun across the room. He'd already done the same with mine.

I was too dizzy to figure out right then that he'd worked the old door trick on us. When I'd peeked through the window he was stooping under it. Then as Doug pushed the door open he'd flattened against the wall back of it. Naturally the burlap curtain had drawn our eyes, giving him a chance to step out and crack down on me. And Doug, facing the other way, was covered before he could whip around.

"It's your drop, Bruno." Doug said it like he was madder at himself than at Bruno. "What are you going to do with it?"

"I'll give you one guess," Bruno said. His voice was pleasant but his black-eyed stare wasn't. I was sprawled on my back and the idea hit me I might grab his ankle and tip him off balance. But when I wriggled an inch his way he said quickly, "I wouldn't try that, Shorty." I saw him thumb back the rifle's hammer.

One little squeeze would send a bullet through Doug. So all I could do was lie there and hate him. I'm five feet seven and I never did like people who call me Shorty. Especially if they're dark, handsome guys with parlor manners around women and barroom manners around men.

This one backed off about three steps with the

rifle still aimed at Doug's middle. That way he could cover us both and be further out of my reach. "You can turn around now, Scotty."

"Reckon you think we're not very smart," Doug grimaced as he turned around.

"I've seen smarter." The voice was still pleasant but the stare had a killing in it. "Right now you better fill me in, Scotty. What happened after I left Suggsby's?"

"There was a gunfight," Doug told him, "and those playmates you ran out on got the short end."

"How short?"

"Jody's dead. Other three are in jail at Buffalo. What else do you want to know, Bruno?"

"Only one thing, Scotty. How could you follow me this far? I thought I covered my sign."

"You did," Doug admitted. "Only time you slipped up was when you pulled the boards off Job Potter's door. Your next mistake will be when you pull that trigger."

Bruno shrugged. A devil's smile lit his deep-sideburned face. "It'll be a mistake if I don't," he said.

The look in his eyes told me he'd made up his mind, that he meant to kill us before we were ten watch-ticks older. "And that's the kind of a mistake I don't make, Scotty."

By his way of thinking he was right. If he left us alive, even if he took our guns and horses, we could have the whole county looking for him by morning. And he didn't dare let himself be caught with that train money on him.

It gave me a chill at the pit of my spine. But if Doug felt that way he didn't show it. Instead he began grinning like the end man in a minstrel show. "Okay," he said, staring into the muzzle of Bruno's rifle, "go ahead and shoot. But before you do, think back to that bog hole your horse went belly deep in, crossing Powder River. It sure fouled up that saddle of yours. I noticed it just now out in the willows."

Some mysterious hint of a warning stayed Bruno's trigger squeeze. "Yes?" he prompted curiously. "So what?"

"So your saddle's muddied clear up over the stirrups—and halfway up the scabbard. That scabbard's open at the bottom, I noticed. So when the sorrel floundered in the bog, the bottom ten inches of the scabbard punched into silt. There was a rifle in the scabbard, stock up and muzzle down. The same rifle you're pointing at my stomach."

All at once it hit me. From where I lay the rifle barrel looked clean enough. The scabbard leather would protect the outside of it, no matter how deep it punched into mud. But if the scabbard had an open bottom, the end ten inches of the barrel would fill up with silt.

Doug McLaren, looking straight at the muzzle,

was the only one of us who could see its bore. He could be bluffing. Or he could be telling the truth.

He grinned at Bruno. "If you want to bet your life against mine, go ahead and shoot."

Doubt or alarm shadowed Bruno's face. If the barrel end had filled with mushy silt yesterday, by now the mud would be caked hard. Like cement. In that case a shot would be more dangerous to Bruno than to Doug. It might even burst the barrel in Bruno's face.

"I keep my guns cleaned," Bruno said. But his uneasiness told me that in this case he hadn't. No doubt his holster gun was clean. But the rifle would stay in its saddle scabbard until the man arrived here. Riding hard day and night would leave him no time to clean guns.

"Cut loose," Doug dared him, "if you want to risk it."

He must have guessed what Bruno would do. And Bruno did it. He took one hand off the rifle to draw a forty-five from his holster.

It takes a wink longer to do that than it takes to squeeze the trigger of an already aimed weapon. That wink was all Doug hoped for and it was all he got. He dived head-on at Bruno just as I rolled that way myself. A gun roared—not the rifle but a half-drawn forty-five. A boot kicked my head and my snatch at an ankle missed.

Then someone fell hard across me. It was Bruno

with the wind knocked out of him. I looked up and saw Doug standing over us. He was clubbing Bruno's rifle and I saw caked mud clogging its bore. "Let's wrap him up, Harry," Doug said, "and hit for town."

Before starting out we lost a couple of hours hunting for eight thousand dollars. Bruno was supposed to have made off with it. But it wasn't on him; nor could we find it in or near the shack.

When we set out for Sheridan, Doug was on his own sorrel. Bruno, his hands knotted to the saddle horn, was on the Circle Cross horse. I came along behind leading the mules.

It was only five miles from Prairie Dog Creek to Sheridan. So at a little after sundown we hit the end of Brundage Street and forded the Little Goose there. Half a block short of Main Street we came to Dillon's Livery barn and went in to off-saddle.

No one was there except the night man who'd just come on duty. His eyes bugged when he saw our hand-tied prisoner. I kept watch on Bruno while Doug got the packs and saddles off. He tied his yellow slicker back of the cantle and racked the saddles. We turned the stock loose in the barn corral.

"What yuh doin' with that trunk?" the barnman asked.

"We'll store it in the barn office," Doug

told him, "while we hunt up the law. Don't let anybody monkey with it."

We put the little trunk under the office desk and Doug took a grip on Bruno's arm. "Come on, Pretty Boy. Let's see who's home at the jail."

The nearest courthouse was at Buffalo, thirty-eight miles south. But the county kept a deputy here in Sheridan and the town had a small, rock jail fronting an alley back of Mills' drugstore.

We hustled Bruno half a block west to Main. Right away I noticed the town was fuller than usual. People were milling up and down the high, board walks and every rack had teams. The Star Saloon, on this corner, sounded like it had a full house.

A Patrick Brothers puncher bumped into us. Doug hailed him. "Hi, Bud. Something special goin' on?"

"Not today but tomorrow," Bud said. "The governor's due in from Cheyenne. So the town's loaded and waitin'."

"Seen Roy Malcolm around?" I asked.

Bud shook his head. Malcolm was the deputy sheriff assigned to this end of the county. "But you'll likely find Mark Walsh at the jail," Bud said, eyeing Bruno's roped hands. "Whose calves has this gent been brandin'?"

"He never bothers with calves," Doug grinned. "Don't usually fool with anything smaller than an N.P. mail train. Let's go, Bruno."

We crossed to the Mills drugstore corner with Bud gaping after us. And if I knew Bud, it wouldn't take long for the story to spread.

We kept on west along Brundage to the next alley. A few steps north up this alley brought us to the jail. It was dark and empty but the door stood open. Constable Mark Walsh hardly ever had an overnight prisoner. Generally he turned them over to Malcolm who'd hustle them down to the county jail at Buffalo.

We went in and lighted an oil lamp. At the back the place had a small cell with a barred window. The cell was locked so we couldn't put Bruno into it. He hadn't said a word since leaving Prairie Dog Creek but his sly look might mean he'd figured a way to get even with us. Doug waited there with him while I went back to Main Street looking for Walsh or Malcolm.

I scouted the west sidewalk a block south to the Bank of Sheridan. There I crossed Loucks Street to the Smith drugstore and ran into Tom Cotton. Cotton was editor of the *Sheridan Weekly Post*. "I'm looking for Roy Malcolm," I said, and told him why.

He already knew about the N.P. holdup where five men had gotten away with eight thousand dollars. "So you caught one of them!" It meant a big story for him and he hurried off toward the jail.

I kept on along the walk, still looking for

Deputy Malcolm. In the middle of the block I came to Leaverton's store. The dance floor above it, which we called The Pleasant Hour Hall, was being decorated for tomorrow night. I could hear a lot of chatter up there. A girl ran up the steps with a bolt of colored bunting. Then I saw Cal Clanton lean out an upper window and begin pulling on a rope. The other end of the rope was tied to the roof of Hickey and Weaver's livery stable across the street. When Clanton pulled the rope tight and level with his window I saw a big banner in the middle of it, right over the street. It said

WELCOME, GOVERNOR MOONLIGHT

When anything social was going on Cal Clanton was likely to be chairman of the committee. He owned a ranch up the Goose, but most of the time you'd find him right here in town. He saw me and waved a hand. "Got your tickets yet, Riley?"

"Not yet," I said, and was hurrying on when something about his face made me stop and look again. He was still leaning out the window tying his rope. And that long, good-looking, dark-skinned face reminded me of someone. It was a deep South face, lean through the cheeks with a narrow nose and heavy, straight eyebrows. His black hair was parted far down on one side and had sideburns reaching to the jaw lines. He looked about thirty-five and he stood a good six feet in his boots.

"How much are they?" I asked, meaning dance tickets.

"Two bucks a couple," he said, and all at once I knew who he reminded me of. Bruno the Kid! Bruno lacked three inches of his height and was ten or fifteen years younger. But they looked enough alike to be cousins. Cal Clanton, I'd heard, had come originally from New Orleans. Some said he'd been a river boat gambler. I remembered my first hunch about Bruno—that he looked Spanish, or foreign.

I moved on past the Loucks furniture store and came to Henry Held's blacksmith shop on the next corner. There I crossed Works Street to the Windsor Hotel and it looked full to the rafters. It was the same at the Sheridan House on the opposite corner. There'd be no chance to get a room at either place.

But what bothered me was Cal Clanton. I remembered Doug's feeling about Gomer's cowskin coat—he'd seen it before somewhere. And now I knew *where*. Two years ago Cal Clanton had stepped off a stage from Cheyenne wearing a fancy cowskin coat with the red-and-white hair side out. After a month or so he'd quit wearing it.

If it was the coat Gomer was wearing now, it made two links between Cal Clanton and the crew we'd run into at Suggsby's. Gomer's coat and Bruno's face!

Bruno who'd doubled back toward Sheridan, like he might have a connection who could hide or remount him!

I went into the Windsor lobby but neither Walsh or Malcolm was there. A name in the desk register caught my eye. "James Hutton and Daughter, H Bar ranch." The date was three days ago and they'd stayed only one night.

"They just stopped long enough," the clerk told me, "to buy Miss Hutton a new outfit. Seems her stuff got washed down a creek."

Across at the Sheridan House I found a man who'd just seen Roy Malcolm. "He was in Conrad's about twenty minutes ago."

J. H. Conrad's big store was diagonally across from the bank. "Roy just left," I was told there. "He heard talk about a train robber at the jail and went to check on it."

At least twenty curious people were at the jail when I got back there. Most of them were looking in from the dark alley. Inside I found Doug and Constable Walsh and Deputy Malcolm and Editor Tom Cotton all confronting Bruno. Bruno had the same sly, get-even-with-you look sloping from his eyes. Put fifteen years on him, and three inches more height, and he'd come pretty close to passing for Cal Clanton.

Roy Malcolm was a gaunt Scot, rawboned

and red-haired, his skin the color of a half-ripe strawberry. "Begin at the beginning, lad," he said to Doug, "and tell it again."

Doug told it again, skipping the part about finding a girl's trunk.

Malcolm turned his slate eyes on Bruno. "And you, young man. Where did you hide the money?"

I expected a lie from Bruno. But not the one he let fly with. "I didn't hide it, sheriff," he said. "It was in my pockets when these two cowboys grabbed me. Last I saw of it, they were stuffing it in their jeans. If they haven't ditched it somewhere you'll find it on them right now."

CHAPTER V

I SAW red creep up Doug's neck. Mark Walsh grinned at him and said lightly, "Just to prove he's a liar, Doug." He patted Doug's pockets and then mine. Neither he nor Malcolm believed for a minute that we'd stolen Bruno's loot.

Malcolm kept working on Bruno. "So you admit making off with eight thousand dollars?"

"It was ten thousand," Bruno corrected. "Money I won in a dice game at Miles City."

Malcolm cocked a bristly red eyebrow. "Yes? Then what was the idea of hiding it in an arm sling?"

"To fool people who might want to take it away from me," Bruno explained glibly. "People like Jody and Dakota Smith."

"Is that why you left them and made off with the horses?"

"Sure, that's why. I turned the horses loose, didn't I? All but one. The one I kept belongs in Sheridan and I was heading this way with it, wasn't I?"

Malcolm didn't believe him and neither did Walsh or Cotton. But there was nothing to

65

disprove his story except my word and Doug McLaren's. And by accusing us of taking the money from him Bruno had partly discredited us as witnesses. A buzz from the alley told me the loafers there had heard everything. "Somebody's lyin', Monk," a voice cackled. "Either him or them two cowpokes."

But the people who counted, Walsh, Malcolm and Cotton, didn't doubt us at all. Malcolm was still working on Bruno when Doug and I went out to look for a room.

The two hotels were full, so we tried the boarding houses. We finally found a room a block east of Main on Grinnell Street. After a quick wash there we went back to Dillon's livery to get our bags.

The night man wasn't there. Later we learned he'd stepped across the alley to the Star Bar for a drink. A lighted lantern stood on a feed box and we took it to the saddle room where we'd left our packs. The idea was to unroll a pack and take out what we'd need here in town.

But somebody was ahead of us and had opened up everything. Both bedrolls were spread out on the floor and someone had gone through them. Looking for what? What else but Bruno's money?

We hurried to the barn office. And there it was—the Hutton girl's trunk! It had been treated just like our bedrolls. It was open. Silks and fluffs had been snatched out and scattered all over the floor. Nothing seemed to be missing. The sneak had been interested only in finding money which we'd never had at all.

It made us fighting mad. "You notice who was out there, Harry?" Doug asked, and he meant the score of curious loafers in the dark alley back of the jail. They'd heard Bruno claim we'd taken the money from him. If true, we'd hidden it somewhere. So someone had slipped off to search our trail packs—and a trunk we'd brought in with us.

He'd searched clear to the bottom—for even the family Bible had been taken out and tossed aside. Doug put it back in the trunk. "I'd like to get my hands on him, Harry." He didn't say anything more, just began repacking the trunk carefully and gently. While he was at it I went back to the saddle room, got what we needed and rerolled the packs there.

Doug heaved the little brassbound trunk to his shoulder. Then we walked two blocks north to the rooming house on Grinnell. We put the trunk in our room. "Let's go look up that night man," Doug said.

We found Dillon's night hostler at the Star Bar. I was afraid Doug would take him apart but he didn't. The man was watery-eyed from too many whiskies. "Nobody was around when I left," he wheezed. "I only meant to be gone a minute."

From there we went to the jail. Bruno was

in the cell. Everyone else had gone except Constable Walsh, who was locking up for the night. "Remember who was in the alley?" Doug asked him.

"Some of them," Walsh said, "but not all. It was dark out there." The ones he named were above suspicion. Others might be drifters whose names we didn't know. Sheridan was full of range tramps.

"One of them," I said, "slipped over to Dillon's barn and went through our duffel. Just on the chance we'd stashed the money there."

Mark Walsh shrugged tired, stooped shoulders. He was elderly and lame, unarmed except for a short billy-stick. No one had ever seen him with a gun. "Did the guy take anything?" he asked.

"No," I said. "I guess all he wanted was the money."

"In that case there ain't nothin' to cry about," Walsh said. "Reckon I'll hit the hay, boys." He limped off up the alley.

Doug and I took the opposite direction. As we hit Main Street a name came back to me. A name spoken by a voice from the dark. "Somebody's lyin', Monk. Either him or them two cowpokes."

"Monk Kincaid, on a bet!" I exclaimed.

We knew Kincaid by sight. He was lookout down at the Ace of Diamonds. People said he'd had a place of his own up at Bozeman, Montana. Since then he'd worked for other men, all up and down the trail from Fort Laramie to Virginia City, as lookout, bouncer, dealer or decoy. "Let's work him over," Doug said. We turned north along Main.

The north end was the sporting end of Sheridan. Of the town's six saloons, only the Ace of Diamonds had everything a man needed to make him wish he'd never gone there. Dice and faro and Monte and female entertainers and overpriced bad liquor. Just gaudy enough to make the transient trade flock there. Local men generally patronized the five quieter and more respectable spots, further south along Main.

A thought hit Doug. "That cowskin-coated guy's alibi! Remember?"

"Sure," I said. "Claimed he was at Martie LaSalle's bar the night of the train holdup. But that's not half. His cowhide coat looks like one Cal Clanton wore when he hit town two years ago."

The point didn't impress Doug. "Maybe it's not the same coat. Or maybe Clanton got tired of it and threw it away."

"But it's the same face!" I argued. "I mean Clanton's and Bruno's. Think a minute."

Doug had stopped to light a cigaret and over his cupped hands his eyes slitted. "Damn! You're right, Harry. Bruno looks enough like him to be a kid brother!"

"And him herdin' with a guy who sports

one of Cal's castoff coats! Top of all that, they say Martie LaSalle himself is a New Orleans Frenchman. Try tyin' it together, Doug."

We crossed a narrow street called Smith Alley and the only thing beyond that was the Ace of Diamonds. It was a big, two-story frame lighted above and below, noisy with bar sounds and with a full hitch-rack in front.

Inside we found a few men at a long, rosewood bar and twice as many clustered around game tables. On a platform at the deep end a girl was twanging a guitar and singing *La Paloma*. In her flared skirt and red sash and with a Spanish comb in her high, dark hair she wasn't bad looking. Anyway she was a cut above a couple of younger girls perched on stools at the bar. One of these deserted her bearded bull-whacker the minute she saw Doug McLaren. She caught Doug's arm and tried to coax him to the bar. "I've just signed the pledge," Doug said, and shook her off. He couldn't stand the smell of cheap perfume or the touch of a cheap woman. This one drooped her lips and went pouting back to her bull-whacker.

Kincaid wasn't around. But we saw Martie LaSalle dealing stud. Three men were with him. Two of them wore forty-five guns and brassy belts. There was a good deal of brass in sight, counting cartridges and the bar rail and three big hanging lamps. A pair of gilt-framed portraits on a wall showed General Sheridan, for whom the town was named, and President Cleveland. It was Martie's idea of making the place look respectable. But he didn't fool any of us who lived here. The Ace was a clip joint, above and below stairs.

We went right to Martie's table. His lean arms had the sleeves rolled above the elbows and there was a green celluloid shade over his eyes. His hair had a middle part and was roached in front. But it was a thin mustache and spiked beard which made him look French.

"Where's Monk Kincaid?" Doug asked.

LaSalle kept on dealing. He didn't even look up. "It's Monk's night off," he said.

"Know where he is?"

Martie shook his head. "Cards?" He dealt a card face up to the man at his left and another to himself.

"Who's in there?" Doug nodded toward a closed door at the rear. We knew it gave to a private room reserved for high play.

"Nobody." Martie pushed out a blue chip. "Your bet, Shonts."

"You know a man named Frank Gomer? Big guy who wears a cowskin coat."

This time Martie LaSalle looked up. His eyes looked thoughtful. "Gomer? Never heard the name before. But I remember a big man in a cowhide coat. He was in here one night, not long ago."

71

"What night?"

LaSalle rubbed a thumb along his mustache line and took a pose of puzzling. "It was the night the stage from Buffalo was seven hours late. That's why he was stuck here. He was waiting for it."

The night of the late stage from Buffalo was the night of the train holdup in Montana. Martie was confirming Gomer's alibi.

"Thanks," Doug said. "If you see Monk Kincaid, tell him we're lookin' for him."

We turned and went out to the front walk. But no further. For one of a dozen saddle horses at the rack caught my eye. It was a broad-chested bay with a wide-treed, ivory-horned saddle. The bay had a c in a C brand and I knew it was Cal Clanton's.

When I drew Doug's attention to it his eyes lifted toward lighted upper windows. But I shook my head. "He wouldn't be up there. Not Clanton. One thing you can say for him, he's choosy about his women."

But this was his horse. And the only place he could be was the private card room off the bar. "He's sitting in at a big game," I guessed.

This time it was Doug who shook his head. "Chips rattle in a game. And you hear bets. That room was quiet like a mouse. Let's take a look."

We went back in, moving fast, and were past LaSalle's table before he could stop us. This time we heard low talk from the card room but it broke off as we got closer.

Doug opened the door and we stepped inside.

"Howdy," Doug said, closing the door behind us. No game was going on. Two men sat in arm chairs, each with a highball in hand. One was Monk Kincaid; the other was Cal Clanton.

Monk wore a gun but if Clanton had one it was out of sight. He kept his seat while Monk jumped to his feet. Monk had a guilty look but Clanton only smiled and waved a friendly hand. "Hi, Riley. Hello there, McLaren." We'd often ridden by his little ranch up the Goose.

"Did Kincaid tell you about it?" Doug asked him.

"Tell me about what?"

"About us bringing in a boy named Bruno. He's up at the jail."

"Kincaid didn't tell me about it," Clanton said easily. "But I heard about it on the street. By the way, can I sell you some tickets for tomorrow night?" He brought a sheaf of them from his vest.

"Not just now," I said, and turned to Kincaid. "You were in the alley when we shook Bruno down. Notice who else was there?"

"Lots of people were there," Monk offered cagily. "Why?"

"One of them sneaked over to Dillon's barn and went through our duffle. Did you notice who slipped away?"

73

Kincaid gave us his best poker stare and then shook his head. I knew we'd get nothing out of him. But Doug made one more try. "We asked LaSalle if you were in here, Monk, and he said no. He claimed nobody was in here."

Clanton answered for him. "If you *must* know, McLaren, we told LaSalle we didn't want to be disturbed. He'd do the same for you."

"He backed up Gomer's alibi," Doug offered flatly.

"Who's Gomer?"

"Man in a cowskin coat," Doug said. "He helped Bruno stick up a train. Snappy looking kid, that Bruno."

It seemed to miss Clanton by a mile. You'd have sworn he'd never heard of Bruno. When he spoke it was to Kincaid. "Let me know if you change your mind. And it's twice what the land's worth. Right now I've got a committee meeting up at the hotel." He stood up, looked at his watch, then turned to us. "You boys going my way?"

We followed him into the barroom and he offered to buy us a drink. As we ordered I noticed that LaSalle's stud game had broken up. LaSalle sat alone and was laying out solitaire. Then I spotted two of the men he'd been playing with—the two who were gunslung. One stood at the deep end of the bar near the door we'd just come out of. The other sat about ten feet away and in a position to cover that same door. I got the idea

74

they'd expected trouble in the card room. Trouble between us and Kincaid; or maybe between us and Clanton.

And why would Clanton huddle with a sharper like Kincaid? Clanton held his drink to the light and grimaced. "I offered him fifteen an acre but he wouldn't take it."

"For what?"

"For a dry forty he happens to own adjoining my place. I need it to square out my pasture."

All just as innocent as dew on a cottage lawn!

We went out to the hitchrack where Clanton swung aboard his bay. "So long. Don't stay up too late, boys." With a mock salute he loped off up Main toward the Windsor Hotel.

Doug's smile was half sheepish. "For a minute it looked kinda funny, Harry. But he explained it all right. Guess he's on the level."

"About as level," I said, "as Bruno's rifle was when it was aiming at your stomach."

"Don't be so suspicious," Doug grinned. "Kincaid *does* own a forty up the Goose. He won it in a poker game one time."

"Which still doesn't explain," I argued, "why Clanton looks like Bruno's uncle. Or why he goes into a pussyfooting huddle with Kincaid right after somebody frisks our baggage for Bruno's loot. Let's amble up to the Windsor and see if he really is at a meeting. Kinda late for a committee meeting, I'd think."

We headed south up Main, which was a good deal darker now. Only the saloons and hotels were lighted. Three blocks brought us to Works Street and there we saw Clanton's bay at the Windsor rack. A hotel boy mounted it and rode off to stable it for the night.

Clanton wasn't in the lobby. We went in and Doug spoke to the desk clerk. "Who's on the committee for tomorrow?"

"If you mean the reception committee appointed to meet Governor Moonlight," the clerk said, "it's made up of Mr. Loucks, Mr. Perkins, Mr. Cotton and Mr. Whitney." He'd named the town's founder, its postmaster, its editor and its banker. As an afterthought he added: "But if you mean the dance committee, Mr. Clanton's chairman of that. He's in the parlor writing a letter."

"Thanks." We looked into the small, formal parlor and saw Clanton. He was at a writing table with his back to us.

Doug nudged me and we went out to the walk. We stood in the dark there looking in through the lobby window. Presently Clanton came out of the parlor with a sealed letter. He bought a stamp at the desk, then dropped the letter in a box marked "Outgoing Mail." "Call me at seven," Clanton said, taking his room key from the clerk. He went upstairs to bed.

"Committee meeting my eye!" Doug said.

Suspicions stung us like nettles. "Here's where we rob the U S mail, Harry."

We went back into the lobby and did it. While I drew the clerk's attention another way, Doug picked up the top letter from a pile in the outgoing mail box. He slipped it under his coat and we didn't open it till we got to our room on Grinnell Street.

The letter was addressed to Max Jackman at Cleveland, Ohio, and said:

Keep this confidential, Max. I want you to do a check-up for me. Find out if a John Prather of Toledo is wanted by the law. He's 47 years old and has a daughter Mary who's 20. Play this close to your vest, Max, and let me know quick.

Cal Clanton.

CHAPTER VI

WE SAT UP half the night figuring it out. And only one way of figuring made sense. Jim Hutton was a neighbor of Clanton's. The two ranches lay end-to-end along the Big Goose above Beckton. So Clanton naturally knew about Hutton losing his spring wagon in a flood on the way back from the railhead with his daughter. The whole town would hear about that as soon as the Huttons showed up in a borrowed Ucross buggy and began shopping for new clothes.

So three days later when Doug and I trail in with a lady's trunk, the dumbest man on Main Street would know whose it was. Likely a dozen people had seen us lead those pack mules, with a trunk on one of them, into Dillon's barn.

"So when Bruno claimed we'd grabbed ten thousand dollars off him," Doug reasoned, "Kincaid went on a prowl through our packs."

"He went through the bedrolls first," I said, "then dumped everything out of the trunk. And bumped into a family Bible which he didn't want. But he saw a name in it and the name wasn't Hutton. It was Prather. Maybe there was a way to make it pay off. So Kincaid went into a huddle with Clanton."

It looked like a shakedown. By cashing in last fall Hutton hadn't been hurt by the hard winter. He was a lot better off than most cowmen. Now he had a new ranch and a new herd on the way up the Bozeman, all paid for. If he had a hidden past, he'd make prime bait for blackmail!

"One thing's sure," Doug said. "Max Jackman'll never get this letter." He held a match to the letter and watched it burn.

"Burning that one letter," I said, "won't do any good. Clanton can write another. Maybe to someone else in Ohio. He knows Hutton hit this range in '81. He can have someone look through news files of a Toledo paper for that year."

We went to bed but didn't get much sleep. I liked Jim Hutton and it was hard to figure him for a runaway criminal. Yet why had he changed his name? Why had he lived among us six years without mentioning a daughter back east? A girl who changed her own name from Mary to Joan when she joined her father out west!

How ripe were they for blackmail? Cal Clanton had lost plenty of cows last winter. If he demanded Hutton's as the price of silence, what then? It looked like a showdown was shaping up—with Clanton and Kincaid holding the cards.

Between hot cakes and coffee next morning, Doug had an idea. "Look, Harry. We made that horse delivery for the Open 8 and they don't need us any more. But Jim Hutton does. I understand the only help he's got out there is an Indian kid he brought along from his old place on Crazy Woman. And when that new herd of his shows up from Texas he can use two riders about our size."

"We got to take the trunk out there," I agreed. "So while we're at it we can hit him for a job."

"Wonder what that gal of his looks like!"

"One way you could find out," I said, "would be to date her for the dance tonight."

"If she goes dancing," Doug brooded, "she'll need that trunkful of gear. So let's get started."

"We better let Walsh know where he can find us," I said. "They might want us as witnesses against Bruno."

Mark Walsh was a widower living alone. His cottage gate was off its hinges and the yard was full of weeds. "Door's ajar," Doug said, "so he must be at home."

When no one answered our knock, Doug pushed the door wide open. Just inside of it the old constable lay sprawled on his parlor floor. We thought he was dead until Doug chafed his wrists and caught a faint heartbeat. He was in night shirt and slippers and there was a lump on his head. It looked like he'd answered a knock, during the night, and had been batted down by a gun barrel.

I brought cold water from the kitchen while Doug checked to see if the jail keys were missing from his pants. They were. So I made a fast sprint up to Doctor Kueny's house on Loucks Street. I told him about Walsh and then doubled back to the jail. The jail door was open. So was the cell. The constable's keys were in the lock and Bruno was gone.

That spoiled our plan for an early start to the Hutton place. First we had to hunt up Deputy Malcolm. Malcolm had forty questions. We had to go clear back to Powder River Crossing and bring him up to date.

One thing we skipped. We couldn't tell him about Cal Clanton mailing a letter to Ohio because it would be giving away Jim Hutton's real name. All we said about Kincaid was that he'd been in the alley crowd last night.

Malcolm gave a dour nod. "Aye. Looks like you lads were right about Bruno having friends in Sheridan."

We were back in Mark Walsh's front yard when Kueny came out with a report. "He'll pull through all right. No fracture. But he'll be laid up a few weeks. I'll send someone to look after him."

"Did he see who hit him?" I asked.

"There were two of them, he says. One chunky and the other skinny. Their hat brims were pulled low and it was too dark to make out anything else."

I remembered the two gunnies in Martie

LaSalle's stud game. One chunky and the other thin. But it didn't prove a thing. You can't convict a man just because he's chunky or thin.

The morning was half gone before Malcolm got through with us. Then we hustled down to Dillon's barn and began saddling up for the ride to Hutton's. "We'll need only one mule," Doug said. He wrapped a tarp around the little trunk and made ready to pack it on Bessie.

Then a livery rig pulled in from Buffalo and its driver hailed us. "Hello there, Doug McLaren. Hi, Riley. You're just the boys I want to see."

"If it ain't the laughing Irishman!" I said. "How goes it, Mike?" A lot of people called Mike Fallon that. He was the county attorney's star deputy and they made him do most of the leg work up north here. And in spite his being young and brash and sometimes maybe a little too gay, we knew him as a pretty fair country lawyer.

"Full docket," he said, tossing his reins to the barnman. "Mostly gunplay cases. What I need's a little fun. Know anybody I can date for the dance tonight? But first I got to find out if we have a case against your man Gomer."

"He's not *our* man," I said. "We made a present of him to Dale Hasker."

"Two of those jiggers Hasker brought in," Fallon told us, "are on their way to Rawlins. The only one left on our hands is Gomer, so I came up to check his alibi."

"We already checked it," I said, "and it stands up."

"The heck it does! That knocks the train-robbing case into spilled milk." Then Mike's homely, freckled face brightened. "But we can still charge him with trying to raid horse stock from a camper. What was that camper's name?"

"Bruce Gordon," I said. "He was on his way to Sheridan to take up land around here."

"Where could I find him?"

The barnman answered for us. "You mean that covered wagon outfit with a yeller-haired gal and three young boys? They picked up a bag o' barley here and asked where they could camp near town. I told 'em there's a nice spot just the other side of the Loucks Street bridge."

Mike Fallon wanted us to go there with him. So he rented a saddle horse and the three of us rode up Main. Ahead of us, stretched from a window over Leaverton's to the roof of Weaver's barn, was a canvas banner with letters two feet high. WELCOME, GOVERNOR MOONLIGHT. A noisy crowd filled the walks and wagons were rolling in from every corner of the range. "There'll be a big time tonight," Doug predicted.

"The governor made a speech at Buffalo night before last," Fallon said. "He's been doin' it all over the territory. Speeches and banquets and fandangos at every stop. I don't see how an old Indian fighter like Tom Moonlight stands it."

"What's he doing it for?" Doug asked.

"He wants to see how beat up we are, after last winter."

Half a mile west on Loucks Street took us to the Big Goose bridge. Just beyond it we saw a cottonwood grove and the white top of a camp wagon. It was Bruce Gordon's outfit and it had company. Saddle broncs were tied to the cottonwoods and half a dozen punchers were hanging around. I saw Slim Dixon of the Wrench outfit and a couple of Flying E boys. And there was Fatty Dunton at the woodpile chopping wood. Fatty rode for the PK on Soldier Creek and some called him the laziest man on the range.

"Flies around honey!" Fallon chuckled as his eyes fell on Carrie Gordon. "Not that I blame them any!" Carrie had on a starched gingham dress and an apron that matched her hair. That pretty little face of hers had an excited look and I guess there's nothing else does so much for a girl as being appreciated by six men all at the same time. Every one of them, I figured, was trying to date her for the governor's ball tonight.

As we dismounted Doug looked at me with a grin. "Wonder who got here first, Harry." This was a land where single men outnumbered single women ten to one. As an escort for tonight Carrie Gordon could pretty near have her pick of the range. The two-day rest had brought color and sparkle to her. Right now she was training it on

85

Slim Dixon. "We're going to look at that place on Soldier Creek you told us is for lease, Mr. Dixon. Thank you so much. Mr. Dunton brought us some venison and it will be done any minute now. You'll stay, won't you?"

Of course Slim would stay. Wild horses couldn't drag him away.

"And so will we," Doug said, breaking it up. At the same minute the three Gordon boys came charging toward us. "Look, Dad! Sis! Here's the cowboys who chased away those horse thieves!"

Carrie held out her hands to Doug and me. "Our rescuers!" she exclaimed happily. "And just in time for dinner. But for them," she explained to the others, "we'd still be stranded on Powder River."

A Flying E man came up on our flank, gaping enviously. "The way I heard it, it was a gal's trunk they rescued. But chances are they made it all up."

"Meet our friend Mike Fallon," I said. "He's a lawyer from Buffalo."

Carrie gave Mike a dimpled smile. I thought he'd give off with some Irish blarney; and when he didn't, but just stood there looking at her like something terribly important had happened, I began to suspect the honey had collected one more fly. I'd heard about men tumbling hard and quick for a pretty face. This girl had a good deal more than that, but Fallon couldn't very well know it yet. All he could see now was that she was nice to look at, and warm and friendly, and tremendously excited about this raw new country where men wore guns and made love on sight; and that she probably was farmbred and as homespun as her father. To bring Mike out of his spell I said, "He wants to ask your pa some questions, Carrie."

To scatter us and get us out of the way Carrie put us to work. "Mr. Dixon, you make the coffee and Mr. Dunton, you lard the frying pans. And you Flying E men take over Dad's job so he can talk to Mr. Fallon."

After we'd exchanged greetings with Bruce Gordon Mike's first question was, "Just what did the Gomer gang do and say, that morning on Powder River?"

Gordon gave him a prompt answer. "They needed horses so they tried to steal ours."

"I haven't the least doubt they meant to steal your stock," Mike said. He was all lawyer again. "But what were their exact words?"

When Gordon repeated them they sounded flatly innocent. "Our broncs got away last night. We need some wrangle ponies to round 'em up. What about loaning us yourn?"

"That all they said?"

Doug and I and Gordon exchanged blank looks, nodding. Gomer's gang had been armed, they looked mean, and they'd no doubt intended to take the horses by force. But mean looks and suspected intentions couldn't convict them. Nothing could be established in court except a request to borrow ponies for an hour.

"Case dismissed!" Fallon concluded wryly. "There's nothing we can do except turn Gomer loose."

"What about the gunfight in the corral?" I asked.

"The man who opened fire was Jody. And Jody's dead. Gomer claims he had no connection with Jody and the others. Just happened to meet up with them on the range. We haven't an ounce of evidence to prove anything else."

We told about catching Bruno and about his escape from jail.

Then Slim yelled come-and-get-it and for the next hour we feasted on venison, picnic-style under the cottonwoods. All through it, I noticed, Mike Fallon managed to keep pretty close to Carrie Gordon. I could see something was on his mind, and it wasn't Gomer or Bruno.

I found out right after we finished eating when Carrie asked which was the highest peak in the Big Horn range that raised up right west of us. And Mike beat everybody else to the answer. "Cloud Peak," he said. "Come along and I'll show it to you."

That way he coaxed her into a short walk with him to the edge of the grove, to an open spot from which the whole skyline could be seen. I grinned as I saw him pointing southwest toward Cloud Peak. The PKs and FEs looked a little sullen about it and I couldn't help kidding them a little. "You guys are too slow to catch cold."

Then I remembered I'd forgotten to loosen the cinch of my saddle. So I sauntered over to my horse and it put me close enough to catch a word or two from Carrie Gordon. "Why thank you, Mr. Fallon. But I've already promised someone else."

Half an hour later we were saying goodbye and curiosity got the best of me. I just couldn't help wanting to know whether the PK or the Wrench or the FE had dated Carrie for the governor's ball.

So I wrangled her off to one side. "Look, Carrie. I'm old enough to be out of the running myself. But if it's any of my business, who's squiring you tonight?"

She gave me a teasing smile. "It *isn't* any of your business, Mr. Riley. But there's really no secret about it. His name is Clanton. Mr. Calvin Clanton."

CHAPTER VII

THE SUN was two hours past noon when we rode back to Main Street. "Just to make it official," Fallon said, "I'd better check Gomer's alibi myself."

So we took him to the Ace of Diamonds. The place looked dead, with not a single horse at the rack. As we tied ours there I noticed a Crow half-breed squatting with his back to the wall, eyeing us with a lazy insolence. The upstairs windows were down and not a whisper came from the barroom. "Just like a morgue," I said.

"Nobody wants to miss anything," Doug said. "They're all up at the south end waiting for the governor. He'll pull in from the south and stop at the Windsor till the speechmaking's over."

When we pushed through the half-doors the only man in the barroom was Martie himself. He stood back of the bar, elbows on it, reading this week's issue of the *Sheridan Post*.

He looked up. "Don't tell me I've got customers! What will it be, gents? Even my bartender went up to see the parade come in. Is it here yet?"

"Not yet," Fallon said shortly. He showed his credentials and asked the same questions we'd asked last night. And got the same answers. A big man in a cowskin coat, Martie swore, had sat six hours in this barroom waiting for a late stage from Buffalo. It was the night of the Montana train robbery. "The stage kept getting later and later," Martie remembered, "until finally he said to hell with it."

"How did he leave town?"

"I didn't ask him."

Fallon gave an incredulous shrug. "But I guess that gives him a clear bill. Let's go, boys."

Doug McLaren shot a question. "Where's Monk Kincaid?"

LaSalle used both hands to roach back his center-parted hair. "How would I know? Up at the other end of town, I suppose, along with everyone else."

"Who were those two gunnies last night? The ones you played stud with."

"They didn't say."

Doug kept at him. "They're about the size of two guys who slugged Walsh and let Bruno out of jail. When was the last time you saw them?"

"They left right after you did." A flush climbed Martie's spike-bearded face. "You wouldn't call me a liar, would you?"

"I sure would," Doug said. "Remember last night when you said Kincaid wasn't here?" An afterthought veered his eyes toward the door of a card room at the back. "Wonder if it's the same way now!"

His spurs clinked as he moved that way and a quick change came over LaSalle's face. I knew he was covering up something, just like last night. So Fallon and I followed Doug to the card room door and got there just as he pushed it open.

A thin man and a chunky man sat at a table. One of them had bloodshot eyes and needed a shave. Both of them had guns in open holsters and they were the stud players we'd seen last night. Evidently Fallon knew them because when they saw him they stood up and backed away from the table looking just scared enough to be dangerous. The skinny one crooked his arm, half a mind to go for his gun.

"Help yourself," Doug said, and they knew what he meant. Mike Fallon wasn't armed, so we were two to two against them.

The crook in the man's arm straightened as his red-streaked eyes flicked from Mike to Doug. "Names are Shonts and Tuttle," Mike told us. "I prosecuted them one time on a stage hold-up charge."

"We was acquitted, wasn't we?" the chunky man mouthed sullenly.

There were three chairs at the table with a half-finished drink in front of each. Also there was an open window giving to the alley. "Who was it ducked out?" Doug asked.

"Nobody."

It was the only answer we could get. But we heard a horse down the alley jump into a gallop from a standing start. The third man was making off.

So Doug and I sprinted for our own mounts at the front. We could hear the man pounding away north toward the screen of the Goose Creek brush. He might be Kincaid; he might be Bruno; or he might be Clanton! We were in a sweat to be after him.

But two things held us up. Someone had tied our bridle reins in hard knots at the hitchrack. It took a minute to untie them. Then, as we stepped to the saddles, the saddles rolled. I landed on my back in the dust. I heard Doug swear at his cinch as he tightened it. Mine was the same way. Somebody—maybe the Crow halfbreed who'd been loafing on the walk—had let our cinches out four notches.

When we finally got to and through the creek cottonwoods it was too late. Our man was out of sight. By now he could have made the hard-trod stage trail where a hundred other hoofprints would swallow his own.

We turned back to the Ace and picked up Fallon. "I got nowhere with LaSalle," he said. "Swears there were only two men in that card room. Claims he has a perfect right to protect the privacy of customers. Nothing we can hold him for."

We rode to Mark Walsh's cottage to see how he was getting along. Deputy Malcolm was there and we brought him up to date. By then it was too late for a ride to the Hutton place.

"Let's go fancy up, Harry," Doug said, "and join the crowd upstreet."

We slicked back our hair and put on our best shirts. Then we stopped at Mac's barbershop to get our boots shined. When we came out the crowd was packing Main Street a block each way from the Windsor Hotel. Hardly any of them had ever seen a real live governor before. Not only everyone in Sheridan was on hand, but Big Horn City and Dayton had crowded in on us. It looked like not a single rancher in all north Wyoming had stayed at home.

Flags fluttered from roof tops and store windows. At the bank corner a man was selling colored balloons to kids. It was like county fair day at Big Horn City.

Right in front of the Windsor they'd built a speaker's platform. The speaking would have to be done outside because no building in town was big enough to hold the crowd. Doug and I found places in front of the Sheridan House, right across from the Windsor, and stood leaning against the porch rail. The porch back of us was full of ranch folks, mostly women, and some of their kids had climbed the railing to see over the crowd.

Every few minutes there was a false alarm. "Here they come!" But it would only be another ranch rig rolling in. From sagebrush and pine they kept coming. Women in silk and women in homespun wool. Duded-up cowboys in tall, creamy hats fresh out of the stores; others who were powdered with alkali or plastered with last week's mud. I saw faces that hadn't worn a smile since the winter blizzards, all shiny and happy now. A Cheyenne chief stalked by in full-feathered head-dress. On the opposite walk I saw a sullen Sioux warrior with folded arms and bitter black eyes, staring hate at this mob of whites who'd stolen his hunting ground. Nelson Story rode by on a fancy, trick-gaited thoroughbred. "It won't be long now!" someone yelled. "They crossed Massacre Hill more 'n an hour ago."

Massacre Hill was sixteen miles south of Sheridan and it was there, twenty-one years ago, that Red Cloud's Sioux had butchered the Fetterman command—killed and scalped them to the last bluecoat. When I mentioned it Doug murmured, "That was the year I was born."

I looked along the street for Cal Clanton but didn't see him. When a celebration was on tap he was usually right in the middle of it. Everybody else was on hand. Bob Otis passed by and I hadn't seen him since he'd quit riding for Ollie Hanna, a year ago. Then I noticed Carrie Gordon. "Look who's with her, Doug!" I said. Doug followed my eyes and gave a low whistle. "He sure works fast, that Irishman!" Carrie was with Mike Fallon and they were standing in a livery rig parked in front of the Held smithy. Doug called to her but couldn't get her attention. We saw Mike take off his five-gallon hat and put it on her head. It went clear over her ears and Mike laughed like a schoolboy as he took it back. Then he held it like a parasol to keep the sun off her face.

"Here they come!" Excitement stirred along the walks and this time it wasn't a false alarm. The two-horse rig which rolled into Main from the south had a mounted escort. Yells went up. "Hi, Tom." "Howdy, Governor." "The town's yourn, General."

To some of the old-timers Moonlight was General rather than Governor. They knew him as a veteran campaigner from the Sioux wars. Right now he looked every inch of it as he waved his center-creased cavalryman's hat at the crowd.

George Beck of Beckton was driving. The mounted escort was made up of our local reception committee—Banker Whitney, Postmaster Perkins, Editor Cotton and the town's founder, J. D. Loucks. Beck pulled up at the Windsor walk and the governor stepped down. His face had tired, gray lines but there was no droop in him. He was a rawboned Scotchman, six feet in his boots, and looked just as fit as when I'd served under him twenty-two years ago at Fort Laramie. While the cheers lasted he kept standing there, straight as a cadet, waving his hat.

The committee led him inside and the street quieted. "All tuckered out like he is," Doug said, "it's not right for him to have to make a speech."

"Betcha he makes it short, Doug."

And I was right. For when Tom Moonlight came out to the sidewalk platform he said what he had to say in two minutes. It wasn't the kind of talk you'd expect from an old soldier.

He spoke of the bleached bones of winter-killed cattle he'd passed, coming up the Bozeman. He spoke of a graveyard of hopes left in the wake of man-killing, brute-killing blizzards. No raid by the Sioux or the Cheyenne, he said, had ever left such a toll of the tortured and the dead. Never before, he said, had the Forbidden Valley looked so forbidding!

"But it's nothing that Wyoming sunshine can't cure. It's nothing that Wyoming courage can't lick. Our cattle died, yes, but we've sent for more. I passed thousands of them moving this way up the trail; already they're spreading out dewlap-deep in the strong lush grass of our pastures. Gone is the 'winter of our discontent,' and it's summer again in Wyoming."

Tom Moonlight waved to the crowd, slapped the campaign hat back on his head and stepped down. Cheers came from the street and a cowboy emptied his six-gun into the air. They were still yelling when the governor went back into the hotel.

Then I heard a girl's voice on the porch behind me. "You say most of the big cattlemen dislike him, Dad. But why?"

A man's voice answered: "Because of his policy of encouraging new settlers, Joan. 'Land for the landless,' he said when he took over, 'instead of more land for the landed.'"

My head whipped around and so did Doug's. Right across the porch rail we saw Jim Hutton. The girl with him was tall and dark and looked city-bred. A shovel bonnet shaded her face, which struck me as pale and delicate and what you'd call intellectual, under a high white forehead and brown eyes. She had Jim Hutton's narrow nose and straight, sensitive mouth, and a kind of stateliness about her matched Jim's lean, clean-limbed height. She wasn't what you'd call pretty like Carrie Gordon. Doug found his tongue quicker than I did. "Hello, Mr. Hutton," he said. "We were just about to take a ride out your way."

"Come out any time you like," Hutton said. His face had hard knocks on it. Life hadn't been easy for him, getting his start down on the Crazy Woman. But now, in his snug new layout up the

Goose, he was in a more sheltered spot. "Meet my daughter, boys. Joan, this is Harry Riley and Doug McLaren."

Before I could even say howdy Doug was telling her about the trunk. "We fished it out of a creek." Then, so she wouldn't know we'd opened the trunk he added quickly, "It's bound to be yours because the Ucross said you got swamped on Crazy Woman."

"We fetched it to town," I put in.

Delighted surprise on the girl's face changed to anxiety. "But isn't it all battered to pieces?"

"It's in pretty fair shape," Doug assured her. "Have you folks got rooms somewhere?"

"Right here at the Sheridan House," Hutton said.

"I can bring it right here if you want," Doug offered.

"Of course I want it," Joan said. "But you mustn't go to so much trouble . . ."

"No trouble at all. Just you wait while I fetch it." Before anyone could stop him, Doug darted off down the crowded walk.

I climbed over the railing to join the Huttons on the porch. "How do you like New Caledonia, Miss?" I asked.

"I suppose you mean Wyoming," Joan said. "It's wonderful. But why do you call it New Caledonia?"

"Because in the early days that's what they

100

called Wyoming. The first settlers were mostly Scotch. Lot of 'em still here too. Tom Moonlight himself's one of 'em. So's that cowboy who just left us—Doug McLaren."

"How long have *you* been here, Mr. Riley?" Joan asked.

"Nobody's been here long," I evaded, "except the Indians. That governor you just heard, he's been here longer than most."

"Ranching?"

"No. Soldiering. He was colonel of the 11th Cavalry back in '65 and had the job of protectin' the Overland Trail. He had to scatter his troops out thin, just a few at each stage station clear across Wyoming, and it was a dull day when the Sioux didn't make a play for his scalp."

Jim Hutton eyed me speculatively. "Didn't I hear somewhere, Riley, that you were in that command yourself?"

"I was only a buck private," I grinned, "and they didn't know I was just eighteen years old."

Hutton smiled. "Old enough to keep your scalp on, I notice. They tell me you were at Fort Laramie the day Colonel Moonlight captured those two bad Sioux chiefs. Tell her about it, Riley."

We were marking time, anyway, till Doug got back with the trunk. The girl seemed interested so I told about the band of bad Sioux led by Two Bear and Black Foot. "They raided a stage station and scalped a dozen whites including Joe Eubanks the stage keeper. Then they kidnapped Eubanks' wife and her little girl. Held 'em captive fourteen months. How they kept alive that long nobody knows. When Colonel Moonlight rescued 'em they were skin-and-bones, half naked and with torture bruises from head to foot."

Joan shuddered. "What a horrible thing! Did they recover?"

"Yes, but those two Sioux chiefs didn't." It wasn't a pretty story and I wanted to leave it right there. But Jim Hutton nodded me on. "She might as well know what kind of a wild and woolly country she's come to, Riley. So tell her the rest."

"Colonel Moonlight's superior officer was General Connor at Julesburg. He wired Moonlight, 'Where are those villains now?' Moonlight wired back, 'In chains.' The general wired back, 'Hang them in chains.' After thinking it over an hour or so he sent another wire, 'I was a little hasty; bring the wretches to Julesburg and we'll give them a trial.' And Tom Moonlight wired back, 'I obeyed your first order before I got your second.'"

The girl's sensitive face winced. "But that was wrong! Everyone has a right to a trial, no matter how terrible his crime."

"That's what the newspapers back East said. They made a scandal of it. The army was no better than a lynch mob, they said, treating the poor Indians that way. Tons of tears were shed. After that, whenever the Sioux massacred a wagon train, people back East said it wouldn't have happened if the army hadn't been so cruel. The very next year Captain Fetterman and his entire command were wiped out only sixteen miles from where we stand right now."

"I read about it in a history book," Joan remembered. "Wasn't it near Fort Phil Kearny?"

"That's right. Everybody in the fort would have been killed, too, if a blizzard hadn't saved them."

The dark brown eyes under the shovel bonnet looked at me curiously. "How could a blizzard save anybody?"

"After scalping Fetterman and his eighty men," I explained, "four thousand blood-thirsty Sioux surrounded the fort. The fort was undermanned and didn't have a chance. But with night came hail and wind—so fierce that even the Sioux couldn't face it. The snow piled as deep as the stockade fence and the garrison had to shovel like mad or else the Indians would have walked right over it on snow. Everybody got his fingers and feet frozen and the officers' wives were put in the powder magazine and told to blow themselves up when the Indians came."

"And then what happened?" Joan asked breathlessly.

"The Sioux decided to wait till the blizzard was over. And while they waited, a man named

Portugee Phillips slipped out of the fort on a thoroughbred horse and rode two hundred and forty miles to Fort Laramie. He told 'em about the Kearny garrison and Laramie sent help in time to save it."

Joan looked at me and asked suddenly, "Why did Governor Moonlight call this the Forbidden Valley?"

"A year or so after the Fetterman massacre," I told her, "the government made a treaty with the Sioux. Under it we agreed to abandon all three forts along the Bozeman Trail and to forbid all white travel along it and to forbid all settlement by whites on the whole Powder River watershed. For ten years that treaty was in force and for that long all the land between the Big Horns and the Badlands was a Forbidden Valley."

An odd reaction came to Joan Hutton. She exchanged quick looks with her father. When she turned back to me her voice seemed nervous and annoyed. "I don't like that name! Forbidden Valley! It has a sinister sound. I'd rather think of it as a haven—a refuge where everyone's welcome."

"Well, that's what it is now," I said.

"There comes your friend," Jim Hutton broke in. Doug McLaren was striding up the walk with a little brassbound trunk on his shoulder. He'd come four blocks with it, carrying it as lightly as a leg of mutton.

"How can I thank you?" Joan exclaimed as he joined us. "It looks as good as new."

"We swabbed the mud off it," Doug said. "Can I pack it upstairs for you?"

"I'll show you the way." The girl went inside and Doug followed. I heard his spurs clank on the bare board stairs.

It left me alone with Hutton for a minute and I made the most of it. "We understand you've got some stockers on the way here. If you need anyone to look after 'em, Doug and I happen to be out of a job right now."

"You're hired." Hutton held out a hearty hand. "Move in tomorrow if you like."

CHAPTER VIII

I CROSSED to the Windsor hoping maybe I could get close enough to the general to pay my respects.

The lobby was full to bursting, everyone trying to get tickets for a banquet due to start in a little while. I looked into the dining room and saw a horseshoe-shaped table with places set for a hundred people. A committee of ladies was putting flowers on it.

The governor, they said, was up in his room resting. I went upstairs and one look was enough. A herd of important citizens was milling around outside Tom Moonlight's door. Voices told me the room was full. Some wanted political jobs. Some wanted an anti-sheep law passed. Others wanted to know when Wyoming would get statehood. Most of them wanted to know about the chances of getting Johnson County split in two, with Sheridan the county seat of our half.

What with a banquet coming up, and then a grand ball, the governor wouldn't get much rest tonight.

I was backing toward the stairs when I saw

Monk Kincaid. He'd darted up from the lobby and was catfooting toward the opposite end of the hall. I saw him tap on a door and go in. Then I remembered Cal Clanton had a room here.

So I slipped down that way myself and stood just outside the door. Kincaid's voice came to me in an undertone. "He's still in town, Cal."

The answer came irritably from Clanton. "Is he crazy! Tell him to get out and stay out."

"I did. But he says he won't go till he gets even."

"All he'll get," Clanton predicted, "is a rope around his neck."

"I told him that. But he won't listen."

"*Make* him listen. Slap his ears back and take away his gun. Then put him on a fast horse and start him running."

A dry chuckle came from Kincaid. "He's got a fast horse and he's already had to use it. But he doubled back to town . . . Which reminds me, Cal. Did you get that letter off?"

"Two of them," Clanton said. "Just in case one of 'em doesn't pull an answer."

Nothing more was said. And I got out of the way in time to keep Monk from bumping into me. He went down to the street and took off toward the north end. After I'd followed him a block he looked over his shoulder and saw me. Right away he crossed to Enoch's pool hall and pretended to watch a game there. He'd be too smart to lead me to Bruno.

And there was no use looking for Bruno at the Ace. Not after his narrow shave this afternoon, when he'd given us the slip out an alley window. It was bound to be Bruno, after what I'd heard Kincaid say to Clanton. Bruno who'd doubled back to town. Bruno who wouldn't leave till he got even!

Even with who? Did he mean Doug McLaren? It was Doug who'd bested him at Job Potter's place.

Twilight was getting deep but Main Street was as full as ever. It was a crowd of men now; all the women had gone to get fixed up for the grand ball. About half the men were range riders and most of the younger ones wore belt guns. Among them I saw Doug McLaren with his hat cocked at an angle and a grin on his face.

I joined him in front of the IXL Restaurant. "Hutton hired us," I said.

His grin widened. "Sure. Joan just told me."

"Joan! You're workin' kinda fast, seems to me."

"I had to—so I could date her for the fandango."

We had supper at the IXL and I told him about Kincaid's call on Clanton.

"Which means," he concluded soberly, "that we wasted our time when we tore up that letter. Because he wrote two of 'em, you say."

"Take about eight days, I figure, to get an answer from Ohio."

Doug checked me on that. A letter to the east would go by stage to Custer Station on the Northern Pacific. A thirty hour trip. A train trip to Ohio would be about three days. The same for an answering letter would make a minimum of eight or nine days.

"Meantime," I warned, "get ready to duck a bullet. Bruno's gunning for you. It might even happen tonight."

Doug shrugged impatiently. "To hell with Bruno! It's Clanton I'm worried about. Clanton and his letters to Ohio. Looks like he's out to get somethin' on Jim Hutton."

"That's a sweet layout Jim's got up the Goose," I brooded. "With a drive of bally heifers on the way to stock it, all paid for. Clanton's place adjoins it and it would make a nice pot—if he could rake it in."

"It's all our fault," Doug brooded, "for leaving that unlocked trunk in a livery barn." He was as sure as I was that Kincaid had searched the trunk merely on the chance that we'd hidden Bruno's loot in it. Instead he'd stumbled on a family record indicating that for reasons unknown John Prather of Ohio had become Jim Hutton of Wyoming.

If the reasons had enough teeth, and Clanton learned the facts, he could dictate any terms he liked. Hutton's land, cattle, honor, maybe even his life, would be in Clanton's power.

And there wasn't a thing we could do about it. Tipping the law would spoil Clanton's game—but it would also expose Hutton. Beginning right now Hutton was our boss. Our job was not to get him into trouble but to get him out of it.

The frustration on Doug's face made me follow his eyes to the door. Two men coming in were Mike Fallon and Roy Malcolm. They were the law in Sheridan and we didn't dare tell them about Hutton.

But when they joined us I *did* tell them about Kincaid's pussyfooting call on Clanton. "They didn't mention any name," I admitted, "but it's a cinch they meant Bruno."

"If you look at 'em close," Doug put in, "Clanton favors Bruno a little. Enough for 'em to be brothers or cousins."

Fallon rubbed his chin thoughtfully. "That slap-his-ears-back talk sounds kind of like it. Like a man with a renegade kid brother in his hair. I'll give odds Bruno's the one who slipped out a window on us."

"Not so fast, lads," Malcolm objected. "Cal Clanton's a leading citizen. I've nae heard an ill word against him." He hadn't noticed any resemblance between Bruno and Clanton. He'd only seen Bruno once and then only in the dimly lighted jail last night. And as a canny, conservative Scot, he'd be slow to condemn a leading citizen.

"Just the same we'd better pick Bruno up," Mike Fallon insisted, "before he starts 'getting even.' "

"Aye, and I'm with you on that," Malcolm agreed. The gaunt deputy stood up and took a hitch at his gunbelt. "You lads want to come along?"

"I want to but I can't," Doug said. "I'm dated for the fandango."

I started to say I'd go with them, then changed my mind. "Count me out this time," I said.

After they'd gone Doug gave me a puzzled look. "They're wasting their time," I said. "They won't find Bruno at the Ace. More likely he's hiding in a barn loft, or in willows along the creek."

A customer stopped by our table and spoke to Doug. "I found that slicker you lost," he said. "I hung it up in the store and you can stop in for it some time." We recognized him as a clerk at Eads' Harness Shop at the corner of Main Street and Smith Alley. "A yellow slicker with your name on a tag under the collar."

"Where'd you find it?" Doug asked.

"Right on the sidewalk in front of the shop," the clerk said, "early this morning when I opened up for the day."

"Thanks. I'll pick it up tomorrow."

The Eads' man went on out and Doug's eyes narrowed. "Wonder how it got there!" he puzzled. "When we saddled up this morning I noticed it wasn't tied back of the cantle. I was about to ask the barnman if he'd seen it when Mike Fallon drove in from Buffalo. It made me forget all about the slicker till right now."

"Looks like somebody swiped it," I said, "and then threw it away on a Main Street sidewalk."

It was dark when we left the restaurant, but lights from the saloons made the walks bright enough to see faces. A few doors south, over Leaverton's, we could hear the fiddlers tuning up. The drugstores and hotels and eating places were lighted too. But it wouldn't make a very good hunting light for Bruno. He'd need to shoot from a distance if he made his try here on Main Street. And something told me he would. He was a rifleman, rather than a hip-gunner, and he might snipe from a roof or an upper window. He was delaying his flight for one purpose only—to get even. The delay was risky. So it stood to reason he'd want to get it over with and be gone.

Doug and I walked north to Grinnell and there we turned east to our rooming house. The cinder walk along Grinnell was pitch dark. If Bruno wanted close shooting, here was his chance. He probably knew we had a room on this street.

But there wasn't any danger as long as Doug

and I were both armed and together. That's why I'd passed up the chance to go along with Malcolm and Fallon. I remembered a notice posted at the foot of the steps leading up to Pleasant Hour Hall. A notice giving rules for the dance tonight and signed by the committee chairman, Cal Clanton. No one wearing a gun would be permitted on the floor.

Doug would have to leave his gun at home. So would I unless I stayed on the street. And with Bruno out to get even it didn't seem like a good idea for both Doug and me to be caught gun-less.

Up in our room Doug scrubbed his nails and sleeked back his hair. All I did was lounge on the bed. "I'm goin' to skip it, Doug. Kind of feel stiff in the knees and anyway I haven't got a date."

He brushed his coat and made neat dents in the crown of his hat. He'd already hung his gunbelt on a bedpost. "Too early to go to bed," I said. "So I might as well walk up the street with you and watch the gals go by."

Even then he didn't suspect I'd appointed myself his bodyguard for the evening. He'd pin my ears back if I suggested he wasn't able to take care of himself. Doug was a little sensitive that way.

At Main Street we took the east walk because the Sheridan House was on that side. Doug was picking up Joan Hutton there. At the Brundage Street corner a couple of OZ punchers had a pet cub bear on a chain. Loafers in front of the Star Bar were feeding the cub peanuts. We crossed Brundage and bumped into Roy Malcolm. "We searched LaSalle's place," he told us. "No sign of Bruno, upstairs or down."

"Where's Mike?" I asked.

"Fixing himself up for the dancing," Malcolm told us, and passed on.

At Loucks Street, Doug and I crossed to the Conrad store. It was the biggest store in the county, with warehouses back of it, and with branches at Buffalo and Fort McKinney. No week passed without a freight outfit trailing down from the Northern Pacific with stock goods for Conrad's shelves. There was a bench on the walk in front of the store, where stage passengers sometimes waited. The express office was in Conrad's and so the daily stage both ways always stopped in front. Just now a hooded and veiled woman was sitting on the bench.

She was alone, which was odd because unescorted women generally kept off of Main Street after dark.

The upper windows over Leaverton's, across the street, were open and lighted. Hanging lanterns lighted the carriage block in front, brightening the walk there. Couples were already arriving. Doug lengthened his stride and I had to stretch mine to keep up. He gave me a funny look, so I stopped just short of Works Street. "Don't step on her toes, fella," I said. "Remember, she's the boss's daughter."

He grinned and moved jauntily on across Works to the Sheridan House. When he disappeared inside I crossed diagonally to the Windsor walk and joined Chuck Saterlee of the Flying E there. He looked at my holstered gun. "Better ditch it, Harry," he advised. "They're barred from the floor."

I told him I wasn't going anywhere. Just then the banquet inside broke up and the banqueters began coming out in couples. Postmaster Perkins came out with Clara Cotton, the newspaper man's sister. "They're gettin' married in the fall," Chuck whispered, nudging me. Then came Jim Leaverton and Carrie Briskin, daughter of the general in command at Fort McKinney. Regina Gambs, the new teacher just arrived from Iowa, came out with some dude I didn't know. Then came Kate Ivy from Big Horn City with one of the Sackett boys. After that most of them were married couples. "They tried to make Governor Moonlight lead the grand march," Chuck told me, "but he begged off; said his marchin' days are over."

I kept an eye on the Sheridan House, across Main. Doug and his girl hadn't come out yet. Works Street was dark in both directions, so it wouldn't be too hard for Bruno to get within rifle shot of this lighted corner.

Then it occurred to me I hadn't seen Cal Clanton. Evidently he'd passed up the banquet. But he had a date with Carrie Gordon so he'd be showing up with her pretty soon.

When all the banquet couples had come out of the Windsor, the men without ladies began drifting out in twos and threes. Last of all came the guest of honor, Tom Moonlight, flanked by Loucks and Whitney. "I'm no hand for night life, gentlemen," the governor was saying. "So I'll just put in a token appearance and then go to bed."

He got to the sidewalk and saw me standing there. Right away his face lighted up. "Aren't you Harry Riley? But of course you are!" He held out a firm warm hand.

I didn't mean to snap to attention but maybe I did. At Fort Laramie I'd been his personal orderly and had brought his mount to the headquarters hitchrack every morning. "Thanks, General," I said, proud enough to burst the buttons off my vest.

He looked at my bowed legs and smiled. "I see you're still straddling leather, Riley. What kind of a saddle do you ride these days?"

"A stock saddle, sir. Took me a long time to get used to one."

"I still use a McClellan." Then he added sadly:

"Not that I get many chances. Most of the time I ride a swivel chair. Drop in on me, won't you, any time you're down at Cheyenne."

He clapped me on the shoulder, then went on with Loucks and Whitney. I saw them disappear up steps leading to the hall over Leaverton's. "At ease, soldier," Chuck said with a teasing laugh.

I was still at attention and didn't know it. Before I could relax a shot off in the night made me jump. It was only a cowboy loping up Main, shooting the sky to blow off steam. He wheeled out of sight around Conrad's corner, a block north. At the same moment I noticed again the bench in front of Conrad's, with a veiled woman sitting alone on it.

But suppose it wasn't a woman! Suppose it was Bruno with a woman's veil and hood and cloak! Bruno sitting right across from the lighted entrance of a dance hall where Doug McLaren was due any minute! The idea sent me hopping that way. Chuck Saterlee yelled after me: "There ain't any bugles blowin', cowboy. I said *At Ease, not Double Time!*"

CHAPTER IX

BY THEN I was across the street and legging it to the next corner north. When I got there I slowed down and felt sheepish. Because it really was a woman. I saw her slim, gloved hands and small, high-heeled shoes and they certainly weren't Bruno's.

Just the same she could look across the street and right into the open, upper windows of Pleasant Hour Hall. The place was full and noisy now, with the orchestra tuning up for the grand march. People nearest the windows were easy to see from here. If I was Bruno with a rifle, I could pick off almost anyone I wanted.

But the woman on the bench wasn't Bruno and she didn't have a rifle. I stopped back of her and rolled a cigaret. She turned to look at me and I saw who she was. She was the Spanish dancer from the Ace of Diamonds. Last night I'd seen her twanging a guitar there. The veil and hood would hide her face in profile; you had to be close and directly in front to tell who she was.

She turned her back on me. Maybe she thought

I wanted to pick her up, and was being coy about it. Or she might be here as a lookout for Bruno!

To find out I sat down by her on the bench. "Where's Bruno?" I asked.

"Bruno? The name is strange to me, señor." Her tone was strained and cautious but not hostile. All I could see was her hooded profile as she looked across at the lighted dance hall.

Late-comers were turning up the steps over there. Two of them were Doug and Joan. Doug had a firm, proud hold of her arm, and she was using both hands to keep her skirt clear of the dusty walk. A tall, slender girl coming well above Doug's shoulder. He said something to her and her laugh floated gaily across to us. I had a feeling they'd make the handsomest couple at the ball.

But the woman on the bench showed no interest in them. Nor in any of the couples turning up the steps. Watching them might make her a little bitter, perhaps. For she herself was barred from places like that. Sheridan had its hard-drawn caste line and saloon women must never cross it. Nor did they ever try. It was a code they accepted, a price they paid whenever they danced or sang or entertained in a barroom. Men who met them there were called respectable, but women who would even speak to them weren't.

Suddenly this one went tense. Two tumultuous, passionate words escaped her. *"Sin verguenza!"*

120

She was staring at an open rig which had just pulled up in front of Leaverton's.

"Here we are, Beautiful!" The buoyant, possessive laugh was Cal Clanton's as he handed Carrie Gordon to the sidewalk. Then he tossed the reins to a boy. "Take it to Dillon's barn, boy." The entrance lights gave me a good look at his face and I thought I saw a pinkish line across his left cheek, like he'd cut himself while shaving. Carrie took his arm and they went up the steps to the hall.

"Who's without shame?" I asked. "You mean Cal Clanton?"

The woman on the bench turned toward me and for a moment her mask slipped. What I mistook for a jealous fury flamed her face. "I will make him sorry!" She bit her lip to keep from saying more.

"Did he run out on you?"

Tears flooded her eyes, melting her fury and leaving her only a thing to be pitied. "I would rather be alone, señor." The dignity of her answer dropped a curtain between us.

So I left the bench and walked south past the Hickey and Weaver barn to the hotel corner. When I turned to look north again, the bench was empty.

Shameless was her word for Clanton! She'd been in his life, some way, and it was a fair guess that he'd pushed her out of it.

Right now I pushed her out of mine and concentrated on Bruno. His best chance for a shot at Doug, I decided, would be after the party broke up around two in the morning.

So I crossed to the Windsor lobby and made myself comfortable. To kill time I picked up the latest issue of the *Sheridan Post* and skimmed through it.

It was dated July 7th, 1887, and the front page told about Queen Victoria's Jubilee in London. It said she'd reigned fifty years.

The next page had cattle tallies from spring roundups all over Wyoming. It was like an obituary and sort of gave me the shivers. It said Alex Swan had gone into bankruptcy. Last fall Alex had tallied thirty thousand head. But this spring his count was less than ten thousand—not enough to meet his liabilities. Here it was, all down in black and white. Figures for Moreton Frewen's Powder River Cattle Company were nearly as bad.

This cow page was too depressing so I turned to a local gossip column headed BREVITIES. It had a sub-heading which Tom Cotton used in every issue:

"A chiel's amang you takin' notes,
And faith, he'll prent it."

The column said Henry Coffeen of Big Horn City gave a Fourth of July oration. It said two thousand heifers were trailing up from Texas to stock Jim Hutton's new place up the Big Goose. It said the stage time from Sheridan to Douglas had been cut to forty-five hours. And Cal Clanton of the c in a C, I learned, had killed a grizzly with one shot from his rifle, at a range of three hundred yards.

I couldn't quite swallow that last. Generally it takes more than one shot for a grizzly. But it made me stop reading and start thinking. If Cal Clanton was a rifle-shooting liar, so was another rifle-shooting liar named Bruno. Bruno who looked like Clanton. Bruno who wasn't leaving town till he got even!

How far would he go to get even? What risks would he take? He'd taken a big one already. For it was to get even with us that he'd admitted having a fat wad of money. Just to put us under suspicion he'd been willing to tighten the case against himself.

What else did I know about him? I'd run into him only three times: at the Powder River store; at the Job Potter cabin; and at the Sheridan jail.

At Suggsby's he'd acted like a show-off—a bold, tricky show-off with eight thousand dollars hidden in his arm sling, and playing to a gallery of a girl, a bartender, two strange cowboys and four partners he was about to doublecross. I got the idea he liked to dramatize himself, shock people with his boldness and startle them with his tricks.

What would a man like that do tonight? It was pretty apt to be something sensational; like walking into a crowded ballroom with a gun in his hand, a ballroom where guns weren't allowed, and cutting loose at Doug McLaren! Right in front of the whole town, including a visiting governor. Bruno might even get away with it, him being the only man with a gun.

The idea sent me scurrying back to the bench at Conrad's corner. From there I could look at the open, upper windows across the street and see waltzing couples glide by. Everything seemed normal. Bill McClinton, the head musician, was giving out with "Over the Waves." I saw Dave Dunnick of the Murphy outfit swing by with Minnie Whittington. Then Hardin Campbell and his wife. Then I had a glimpse of Doug and Joan.

I relaxed and rolled a cigaret. Maybe I was just an old woman, fretting about Bruno. Pretty soon I saw three men come down from the hall and turn south up the sidewalk. One of them was the governor. The pair with him were George Beck and a man named Miller from Cheyenne. They went into the Windsor and would likely go straight to bed.

Other men came down, generally in pairs hunting for the nearest bar. Through a dull hour or so I watched them come and go.

Twice I saw Cal Clanton dance by with Carrie Gordon. And twice I saw Mike Fallon dancing with Carrie. Everybody seemed to be having a good time.

It was close to midnight when Shag Shannon came along and sat down by me. Shag drove a bull team for Charlie Rounds and was usually on the road between here and Custer Station. On his off days he hung around Martie LaSalle's place and I wondered how much he knew about the crew there.

"Who's that Spanish singer," I asked him, "down at the Ace?"

He rolled his cud to the other cheek and spat in the street. His eyes veered slyly my way. "You ain't tumblin' fer her, are yuh, Harry?"

"I'm just curious, Shag. She was sitting on this bench a while ago looking across at the party. I kinda got the idea she was mad at somebody over there."

"Her name's Rosa," Shag said. "Who did she look like she was mad at?"

"Cal Clanton pulled up in a rig about that time. Ever see him hanging around her?"

"Nope. Never did."

"Ever notice Clanton at the bar there? Or bucking the games?"

Shannon thought it over. "Once or twice, maybe," he said. "Which don't mean anything much. I guess about every gent in town goes down there once in a while—in the dark of the moon."

"Where did Rosa come from?"

"Dunno. Always struck me as bein' straight, Rosa did. I saw a guy make a pass at her one time and she told him off. Told him she's a married woman and her only job there's to sing."

"Married to who?"

"She didn't say. But they's a good streak in Rosa, all right. Once they was a sixteen-year-old country gal got tired of the sagebrush and ran away to the bright lights of Sheridan. She found 'em at the Ace—but Rosa got her out of there right fast. Used her own money to rent a rig and drove the kid back to her ma and pa."

After Shag moved on it gave me something to think about. I couldn't imagine Rosa being married to Clanton. Yet she'd called him *sin verguenza* when she saw him out with another girl. Maybe she hated him for some wrong he'd done her husband. "I will make him sorry!" she'd said.

Not being used to late hours it was no great wonder I fell asleep, right there on the bench. From then on till two o'clock Bruno could have walked up those steps with a shotgun without me seeing him.

The sound of livery rigs stopping in front of Leaverton's woke me up. Couples were coming down from the hall and the street was full of gay chatter. My watch said ten after two.

126

Doug McLaren and Joan Hutton were on the walk over there, saying good night to people. I didn't see Mike Fallon. But I saw Cal Clanton hand Carrie Gordon into a rig and drive off toward her wagon camp on the creek. Then Doug and Joan started walking south toward the Sheridan House.

I kept opposite them, on my side of the street where it was too dark for them to see me. They crossed Works to the Windsor corner and then crossed Main to the Sheridan House. I kept in the shadows of Weaver's barn so Doug wouldn't catch me playing bodyguard.

The Sheridan House had a kerosene lamp burning on the porch. Doug and the girl stopped under it to say good night. I could see them plain as day; they looked happy as jaybirds, both of them.

He held the lobby door open for her but that's as far as he went. When she left him he turned and started down the porch steps. Then his arms flung out and he pitched forward on the walk. It seemed to happen even before I heard the shot—a rifle shot. The shot came from the darkness of Works Street, about half a block west of Main. Then came another one and I saw its flash at the deep corner of Held's smithy.

Before its echo died I was running that way, pumping bullets from my forty-five. Wasting them into the dark. A fine bodyguard I was! I was even madder at myself than at Bruno. He must have been waiting there half the night, while I dozed on the stage bench in front of Conrad's. Waiting with a fast horse tied back of Held's smithy—because now I heard him pounding away on it. He was angling across the wagon lot behind the Loucks and Becker store. By the time I rounded the back of Held's shop the night had swallowed him. And me on foot with an empty six-gun! All I'd ever seen was the flash of his rifle. It was a clean getaway even if we picked him up later. Because in court I couldn't swear it was Bruno.

CHAPTER X

WHEN I got back to Doug a dozen people were huddled around him. One of them was Joan Hutton. She was kneeling by him on the sidewalk, her face deathly pale. The hotel clerk had come running out and there were three or four couples on their way home from the dance.

One of the women took Joan's arm and coaxed her aside. A clerk from Mills' drugstore took her place and after a quick look he told us Doug wasn't dead. "Get a cot," he said. The hotel clerk brought a folding army cot. The hit seemed to be in Doug's left shoulder, dangerously close to his neck. His coat sleeve was bloody. We used the cot for a stretcher and carried him inside.

Joan was right with us as we took him to a little sample room back of the lobby. The hotel cook came in with a kettle of hot water and I scooted the porter off for Doctor Kueny. Then Doug opened his eyes and gave us a pale smile. "Was it Bruno?" he asked faintly.

"It wasn't Sitting Bull," I said. The drug clerk took over till Kueny could arrive. Joan told him

129

she'd had training as a nurse. So he let her help him slip off Doug's coat and shirt.

"You didn't see the guy?" I asked Doug, and he shook his head. His eyes fixed on Joan as she tore a sheet into strips. She had them ready by the time the drug clerk had washed the wound. They were putting a bandage around the shoulder when Roy Malcolm came in. He started asking questions and I cut in impatiently. "Bruno did it! Let's after him."

"Did you see the man?" Malcolm asked.

"How could I see in the dark?" I exploded. "But it was Bruno all right."

A couple of Flying E boys offered to vacate their room so that Doug could have a bed. We'd no more than moved him there when Doctor Kueny showed up. He cleared the room and went to work. The noise aroused Jim Hutton and he came out to find Joan and me in the hall. It was almost daylight and I remembered we were due to go to work for him in the morning.

"Looks like you'll have to get someone else," I said, and told him why.

But he shook his head. "I'm no fair weather boss, Riley. If a man of mine gets pitched from a horse, or stops a bullet, it's all in a day's work."

He sent Joan to bed and pretty soon Kueny came out with a report. It was a clean wound and there'd be no complications. "Give him ten days," he said, "and that boy'll be as good as new."

It made me feel a lot better. When Hutton and I went down to the kitchen for coffee, light was beginning to show outside. "How long before the trail herd gets here?" I asked.

"I got word today," he told me, "that it's at Pumpkin Buttes." Those buttes were a little more than a hundred miles down the Bozeman.

"Will they deliver the stuff at the ranch, or here at Sheridan?"

"At the ranch. We don't even have to brand. I had my H Bar put on in Texas, so they could use it for a trail brand. Two thousand head of two-coming-three-year-old heifers."

I did a little figuring. Driving cattle from Pumpkin Buttes to the upper Big Goose would take close to ten days.

After making sure Doug wouldn't need me I went down to the Grinnell Street room for a few hours sleep. It would take ten days for Doug to get well, and about the same time for the cattle to arrive. That far everything was fine. But a third deadline, ten days away, spoiled my sleep. It would take about that long, maybe a little less, for Clanton to get an answer from Ohio.

In the middle of the morning I checked out and moved up to the Sheridan House. Doug was asleep and looked like he was doing all right. I went downstairs and found the Hutton buckboard tied in front with the little brassbound trunk in it.

Deputy Malcolm crossed from the Windsor and hailed me.

"Has the governor pulled out yet?" I asked him.

"Aye. He went over to Mr. Loucks' house for an early breakfast and his party left from there."

Jim Hutton and his daughter came down with their bags. The girl looked anxiously at Malcolm but he shook his head. "No, lass. We haven't caught the man yet. We don't even know who did it."

He showed us a bullet hole in the porch post where the man's second shot had struck. Then he showed us two empty rifle shells he'd picked up on Works Street, half a block west of here. They were centerfire 44-40's.

Hutton handed Joan to the buckboard seat, climbed aboard himself and took the reins. "Come out to the ranch, Riley," he said, "soon as you're not needed in town."

Joan gave me a smile. "And thanks again for saving my trunk."

A tall dark man came out of the Windsor and crossed to join us. He was Cal Clanton and again I noticed what looked like a tiny razor cut on his cheek. It began at a corner of his mouth and disappeared into the deep, shaggy sideburn at his left temple. "Morning, neighbors." He looked at Joan and added lightly: "Understand you ran into some gunplay last night, Miss Hutton. That's what you've got to expect when you go out with one of these feuding cowboys."

He was trying to make her think some cowboy with an old range grudge had fired the shots. He tipped his hat to the back of his head and the cowlick of his curly black hair, over the straight, heavy eyebrows, made him look more than ever like Bruno. "Speaking of feuds," I said, "looks like you've been in one yourself."

His hand went to the scratched cheek and his laugh had a hint of nerves in it. "I'll have to be more careful," he said, "next time I ride through a brier patch."

But it didn't look like a thorn scratch. It hadn't been there evening before last. All day yesterday he'd stayed in town. So if he'd ridden through briers he'd done so late night before last, after I'd seen him at the Ace of Diamonds.

"We'll be looking for you, Riley," Hutton said. He flapped the reins and his team trotted off down Main. I saw him turn west on Loucks Street, to take the Beckton road.

Then Malcolm went up to see if Doug was awake yet. It left me standing at the hitchrack with Clanton.

"Looks like Monk was right," I said, wondering if I could bait him into admitting something.

He studied me for a moment, his eyes narrowed and half contemptuous. But his tone had caution. "Right about what, Riley?"

133

"About Bruno."

"Bruno? Who's Bruno?" The caution doubled and the contempt disappeared.

"He's the boy you and Monk were talking about just before suppertime last night. Remember? Monk told you Bruno wouldn't leave town till he got even."

It was the same as telling him I'd listened at the door. Clanton wasn't wearing a gun this morning, and I was. So I didn't think he'd come at me. But he did—and his punch was quick like the strike of a snake. So quick I didn't see it coming. All his weight was in it and he had thirty pounds on me; he was taller by five inches and had a longer reach. The punch clipped the point of my chin and knocked me ten feet.

The next I knew Roy Malcolm was helping me up. "What happened, man?" I'd been out maybe half a minute.

I looked around and didn't see Clanton. "He socked me," I said.

"What for?"

He got me on the porch and when my head cleared a little I told him about it. "I just wanted to get a rise out of him," I said, rubbing my chin. "And I sure did."

Roy Malcolm had a hard-headed Scotch stubbornness which still made him cling to a respectful opinion of any highly popular citizen like Clanton. To him it was a natural burst of temper

134

directed at a self-confessed eavesdropper. We were arguing about it when Mike Fallon joined us.

Mike made me repeat the exact words used by Kincaid and Clanton. "Clanton," I said, "told Kincaid to put a fast horse under Bruno and get him out of town."

"Did they mention Bruno's name?"

I admitted they hadn't. "But who the heck else could they mean?"

Mike shook his head. He was on my side but he had a lawyer's mind. "It's not court evidence, Harry. You can't convict a pronoun. Besides they'll deny the whole conversation and have two words to your one."

The worst of it was that I didn't dare tell them about Clanton sending letters to Ohio. If I did they'd run it down because they were both conscientious lawmen. And that would mean trouble for my new boss Jim Hutton.

When my chin quit aching I went down to Dillon's barn. I knew Clanton kept his horse there. "Where's Zeke?" I asked. Zeke was the night man and not on duty now.

They told me he had a room on Gould Street so I went there and woke him up. "Look, Zeke. Did Cal Clanton take a ride late night before last?"

"If he did," Zeke said, "it wasn't on his own horse."

"Are you sure?"

135

"Dead sure. The hotel boy brought his bay to the barn about ten o'clock. Nobody called for it after that. It stayed right in its stall till morning."

"Thanks, Zeke."

I was sure now that Clanton had lied about the scratch on his face.

"Someone else come in though," Zeke offered with an odd chuckle, "and wanted to take a moonlight ride. She rented a saddle horse and was gone with it two-three hours."

"She? You mean some woman came in?"

"Yeh, Rosa LeFevre. Her that sings at the Ace of Diamonds. All by herself, too. Didn't know her at first, in her Levis and boots."

That was about the last thing I'd expected. "You're sure it wasn't *last* night?" I prompted.

"It was night before last—a few hours after somebody went through your duffel. Three dollars is what we charge for a saddle horse and she paid cash in advance."

"You say she brought the horse back in two-three hours?"

"About that. He was saddle-sweated some. I noticed she had a package when she come back. About the size of a shoe-box. She walked out with it and that's the last I seen of her."

I walked back to Main Street, my mind chewing on it. So her name was LeFevre! It sounded French. Martie LaSalle was supposed to be a New Orleans Frenchman. Cal Clanton, too, had come from down that way. And I remembered my first impression of Bruno.

And now Rosa LeFevre! A married woman, according to Shag Shannon.

A bee began buzzing under my hat. What about the eight thousand dollars Bruno had hidden somewhere near Job Potter's cabin? Doug and I had failed to find it there. Nor had Deputy Malcolm been able to uncover it the next day. But at night Rosa had taken a ride and come back with a package! It was only five miles to Prairie Dog Creek.

Rosa couldn't have found the money in the dark—unless Bruno had told her right where to look. Would he do that?

He would, I figured, if she was his sweetheart or his wife. Night before last he was in jail. But Rosa could go there around midnight and talk to him through the barred window of his cell. If he trusted her he'd tell her where the money was and that she'd better pick it up before morning. Because when daylight came the law would be there looking for it. So she'd rented a horse. Two or three hours would be about right for a round trip to the Potter cabin.

Then I remembered Cal Clanton's scratched face. A scratch that got there some time late night before last. I remembered Rosa on the bench last night, her eyes shooting hate at Clanton. "*Sin verguenza!*" she'd called him.

There was no brush between here and Prairie Dog Creek which could scratch his face. Yesterday he'd kept out of circulation. Everybody else had watched the governor arrive and make a speech. But not Clanton. And he'd passed up the banquet. Why? Was it because of his scratched face?

Then why hadn't he also skipped the dance? I could think of two reasons. First, he had a date with Carrie Gordon; second, he was chairman of the committee. So there'd been no ducking the dance.

It wasn't likely Rosa would tell me anything but I had to try anyway. So I walked down the east side of Main to the narrow cross street called Smith Alley. Eads' Harness Shop was on the corner there and it reminded me of Doug's slicker. I went in and a clerk gave it to me. It was a yellow slicker with Doug's name under the collar. They'd found it on the front sidewalk early yesterday morning.

I rolled a cigaret and tried to tie the slicker in with Rosa. Rosa, on her way home from Dillon's barn with a package, would have to pass three saloons—the Star, the Arctic and the Little Gem. If her package had big money she'd want to hide it. So before leaving the barn maybe she'd picked a slicker off Doug's saddle and used it to cover her package while she walked along with it. After she got by the three saloons she'd drop the slicker and go on to the Ace of Diamonds.

It was as good a guess as I could make, right then.

So I angled across to LaSalle's place. The games didn't open till afternoon and only a few people were in sight. Martie himself was at the bar splitting a bottle of beer with one of his dealers. Benny the piano thumper was practising a number. On a stool at the deep end of the bar was Rosa. She was late-breakfasting on a sandwich and a mixed drink.

I took the next stool and tried to be friendly. "Mornin', Rosa. Seen anything more of that *Sin Verguenza*?"

She recognized me as the man who'd sat by her on the bench. "No, señor." Trouble rode her face and she hadn't taken time to make herself up this morning. In noon daylight she wasn't pretty.

"Why," I coaxed, "do you call him shameless?"

While she hunted for an answer I noticed three things. There was a black-and-blue bruise at her throat which I hadn't been able to see on the dark bench. The hand which held her glass had long, sharp fingernails. And her gaze fixed with a startled stare on the yellow slicker I carried.

"I have no wish to speak of it, señor. So if you will excuse me . . ." Leaving her drink and sandwich on the bar she crossed to the stairs and went up to her room.

Did that bruise at her throat and the scratch on Clanton's face mean she'd had a fight with him? Had he tossed a slicker over her head so she couldn't see who was snatching her package? In the struggle she might scratch him without knowing who he was—until a night later when she saw him arrive at a dance with a scratched face!

If I was right, she'd waited on the bench not to see what lady Clanton might bring to the party but merely to look at his left cheek. One look and she'd know he was the package-snatcher. "I will make him sorry!" she'd said. And I hoped she would.

CHAPTER XI

WHEN I got back to the Sheridan House Doug was taking nourishment. Pain at his bandaged shoulder made his left arm no good but he could feed himself with his right. The waitresss who'd brought the tray had propped him up in bed.

He grinned. "I hear you got poked one. Right on the button."

"It was a one-punch fight," I admitted, then told him about Rosa's midnight ride and sketched my theory.

Doug gave a low whistle. "Looks like a lot of double-crossing's going on. If you're right, Bruno didn't expect to be broken out of jail later that night. So the only way he could save the money was to send Rosa for it."

"Which he'd do," I agreed, "if she's either his best girl or his wife."

Doug looked for holes in it and couldn't find any. We agreed that Clanton, knowing Rosa's close relation with Bruno, might expect her to call at the jail window. In which case he might follow her from there to the barn in time to see her ride off on a rented horse.

"Why didn't he chase her?" Doug wondered.

"If he chased her in the dark she'd hear his hoofbeats. So he just stayed in town and waited for her to come back."

"Meantime," Doug reasoned, "he snitched the slicker off my saddle so she'd think I was the one who looped it over her head. But when she got untangled, she just dropped it and went on home."

"All of which needs a lot of provin'," I said.

"The way I figure it," Doug concluded, "they sprung Bruno out of jail just to get rid of him. Say he's a kid brother gone outlaw. Kind of embarrassin' for a respectable gent like Clanton to have people peeking through the jail bars at his own spit image. So he wants Bruno to ride far and fast."

"That's exactly what he told Kincaid," I remembered.

"Another thing, Harry. It plugs up a hole in Bruno's motive. I mean him sticking in town to get even with me. Why just me? We were both in on his capture. See what I mean?"

"Not quite," I said. So while I rolled a smoke for him Doug explained. "Where would Bruno go when they let him out of jail? Straight as a shot to Rosa. He'd sent her for the money, so he'd stop by her room to pick it up."

At four in the morning, I agreed, it would be easy for him to slip up back steps to her room over the Ace. "Sure, Doug. He'd want to pick up the money."

"Which she didn't have, Harry. She'd tell him about some guy snatching it away from her at Eads' corner. She didn't know who the guy was, but he'd looped a slicker over her head and neck. And she could show Bruno a bruise to prove it. So what would Bruno do then? He'd hike to Eads' corner for a look at the slicker. It was still on the walk where she'd dropped it. A yellow slicker with my name on it—the same one he'd seen me wearing at the Powder River store."

That did it. A cloudy motive suddenly became airtight. No wonder Bruno had hung around to get even! It wasn't because Doug had bested him at the Potter cabin, but because he thought Doug was the slicker-winder who waylaid Rosa.

Which was exactly what Clanton would want him to think.

Someone knocked and when I opened the door there stood Bruce and Carrie Gordon. "Can the patient have visitors?" Carrie asked, looking past me at the bed.

"Come on in, folks," Doug grinned. "I'm not near as bad off as I look."

"We hear you got shot up," Gordon said as they came in.

"By the Powder River bad man," Carrie added with a lilt of excitement. While I rounded up a couple of chairs she pressed eagerly for details.

"You were on your way home from the dance, weren't you? With that stunning brunette? Wasn't she frightened to death?"

"She didn't even bat an eye," Doug said. "What about you? Have a good time at the fandango?"

"A perfectly marvelous time. Everybody did, don't you think? Even the governor."

"I know one guy that did," Doug said slyly. "A young lawyer chap from Buffalo named Fallon. Every time I looked he was takin' turn about with Clanton. Not that I blame him any."

A chuckle came from Bruce Gordon. "Tell them how you met Clanton, Carrie."

"Yeh, I been kind of curious about that," Doug put in. "Because you only hit town a day before the party."

"That's right," Gordon said. "We pulled in only the day before and went into the Windsor Hotel for lunch."

"And in the lobby there," Carrie laughed, "I insulted a perfect stranger. He was reading a paper and all I could see was the top half of his face. 'You?' I gasped, backing away in terror. 'Dad, call the sheriff quick.' Then the man stood up and I saw my mistake. He was taller and older and much better looking than the Powder River bad man. I was mortified. All I could do was apologize."

"By the time she got through apologizing," Gordon chuckled, "Clanton had invited us to take

144

lunch with him. And by the time we got through eating, he'd signed her up for a dance."

With bright spots in her cheeks, Carrie quickly changed the subject. "We've filed on land, did you hear? And leased a farm right next to it."

"Whereabouts?" I asked.

"I've leased the Ruggles farm on Soldier Creek," Gordon told us, and am filing a quarter section homestead adjoining it. We can live in the Ruggles house while we build on the homestead."

Doug nodded. We knew about poor Jeff Ruggles. He'd been blizzarded out last winter and had moved back east. His two hundred and forty acres on Soldier Creek, just above the PK ranch, had been offered for lease. "It's just over the hill," I said, "from the Hutton ranch where Doug and I'll be working."

"Where are the boys?" Doug asked.

"They're watching a big cattle drive go through," Gordon said. "Come on, Carrie. We'd better round 'em up and get started for Soldier Creek."

"We're moving out there today. Both of you come to see us." Carrie gave a smiling goodbye and followed her father downstairs.

A distant lowing reached us from a herd moving north. It was avoiding Main Street and keeping to the east outskirts along the Little Goose. "The Wrench outfit," Doug said, "is expecting a big bunch from Texas."

"Guess I'll go have a look, Doug, and see what shape they're in."

The grass they'd trailed over was the same Jim Hutton's bunch was now feeding on. So naturally I was interested. Down on the street I met Roy Malcolm. We walked a block east to Gould Street and were in time to see the tail end of the drive go by. The stuff looked in fair flesh and I figured the Hutton cattle, eight or nine days back of them, would be about the same.

"The Wrench," Malcolm told me, "is accepting delivery right here in town. Just across the Goose Creek bridge on North Main. Which I dinna like too much."

"Why?"

"We've had trouble before, when a Texas drive ends here and they pay off the trail hands in Sheridan. There's like to be a few lads who spend their money too fast."

Less than an hour later I found out he was right. A bewhiskered trail boss came up Main Street looking for the law. He ran into Malcolm and me in Mills' drugstore and his eyes picked up the badge on Malcolm's vest. "You the sheriff?"

"Aye, as near as they've got to one around here."

The trail boss led us aside. "This is the end of the line," he said. "So I've just paid 'em off. Fourteen trail hands and a cook. Only two of 'em, though, could give you trouble."

"Couple of hell-raisers?" I asked.

"Not when they're broke and sober. But right now they got time on their hands and a pocketful o' money. Names are Sweetwater Burns and Red Fitch."

Malcolm wrote down the names. "How bad are they?"

The trail boss grinned. "After two drinks they get playful. After four they want to fight. After six they want to shoot badges off of sheriffs' vests."

The deputy smiled. "Aye. So after five nips the lads had better be locked up. Mind pointing them out?"

We went up the street looking for Burns and Fitch. The two rowdies weren't in the Star Bar or the Arctic or the Little Gem. Nor at the Ace of Diamonds which was the first bar they'd come to after being paid off on North Main.

A customer heard us inquire of LaSalle's bartender and he followed us out to the walk. "Is one of 'em a redhead wearin' crossed belts?"

"That's Fitch," the trail boss said. "The other's a towheaded Swede."

"Two punchers like that came in about twenty minutes ago. They asked for a couple of fellas named Shonts and Tuttle. The barkeep said he hadn't seen 'em today. So the punchers went out."

"You mean they didn't even buy a drink?"

"Nary a drop. I seen 'em climb their broncs and ride off thataway." Our informant thumbed east along Smith Alley.

That could be a shortcut toward the back end of Dillon's barn. "Howcome they'd know their way around?" I asked as we took the same direction. "And how could they know Shonts and Tuttle?"

"This is their second trip up the Bozeman," the trail boss explained. "Last summer they helped deliver a herd to the OZ on Tongue River. Chances are they were paid off right here in Sheridan. In that case they'd hang around a few days before starting back to Texas."

In stalls at Dillon's barn we found two Texas horses which had just been left there. "Yeh, a whitey and a redhead," the day man said. "They took off toward Main Street a few minutes ago."

We started at the most southerly saloon on Main, which was the Sheridan Bar next to the Loucks store.

"Yeh, they were here," the barkeeper said. "Ast fer a coupla guys named Shonts and Tuttle. I told 'em they were at the wrong end of the street."

"How many drinks did they have?"

"Not a one, Roy. Maybe they're Republicans and don't like my decorations." A portrait of Grover Cleveland was over the bar.

"They can't be Republicans," I said, "because they're from Texas."

In the next block north we asked at the Cowboy

Bar. Again we learned that our trailsmen had inquired for Shonts and Tuttle and had left without spending a cent. It was the same at Zan's Place next door.

"It ain't like 'em," the trail boss worried. "They got a two-month thirst."

"Maybe they signed the pledge," I grinned.

We crossed Brundage and for the second time made the three saloons between there and Smith Alley. In each case the Texans had been about twenty minutes ahead of us. Always they asked for Shonts and Tuttle, then left without taking on any liquor.

We began to sense what it meant. "They're manhunting," I said. "They figure on a showdown with those birds and so they're keepin' sober."

As we left the Little Gem the trail boss ran into a group of his own men. "Were any of you boys," he asked them, "on the same drive with Sweetwater and Red last summer?"

None of them had been on that drive. But one man had heard talk of it. "Red's tongue got to waggin' the other night," he said. "About what happened when him and Sweetwater got paid off in Sheridan."

"Yeh? What happened?"

"Coupla sharps got 'em in a stud game, slipped knockouts in their likker and then rolled 'em. When they came to they was skinned clean."

"Did Red mention any names?"

"Nope. Just said they were a coupla sharps at Sheridan."

"Did it happen at the Ace of Diamonds?"

The cowboy thought a moment. "Nope, it happened in a hotel room. The Inter-Ocean, I believe he said."

The trail boss looked puzzled till I explained. "M. C. Harris took over the Inter-Ocean a few months back. He remodeled it and changed its name to the Windsor."

The trail boss had duties at his camp. After he left us, Malcolm and I walked up Main to the Windsor. There we asked to see the registry books inherited from the Inter-Ocean. Mr. Harris himself brought them and we found a year-old registration made by Ike Shonts and G. G. Tuttle. On the same day a pair of Texas trailsmen named Burns and Fitch had taken a room here.

There was no record of a complaint made by Burns and Fitch. "But lads like that," Malcolm said, "are like to mend their own fences. They hardly ever go crybabying to the law."

"They've had a year to think it over," I said. "The longer they thought the madder they got. Betcha that's why they signed on for another Bozeman drive this year."

"They'll cut loose on sight," Malcolm foresaw, "unless I lock them up."

"How can you lock 'em up?" I argued. "They haven't made any threats. They haven't even had a drink. It's no crime to walk in and out of bars askin' for Shonts and Tuttle."

"What's this about Shonts and Tuttle?" Dave Dunnick of the Flying E had come up behind us.

"If you see them," Malcolm said dourly, "tell them to get out of town for a day or two. There's trouble stalking them."

"They're already out of town," Dave told us. "They just passed me, riding fast, as I came in from Big Horn City."

Malcolm relaxed and we rolled cigarets. "It figures," I said. "They heard about those gunnies lookin' for 'em, so they lit out. They can lay low at Big Horn till it's safe to come back."

We went down to the IXL for pie and coffee. Before we finished a couple of Wrench riders popped in. "It's shaping up, Roy," one of them said. "Looks like a showdown."

"Where?"

"At Big Horn. Red and Sweetwater just saddled up. They heard bar talk about Shonts and Tuttle hidin' out at the Big Horn hotel."

Malcolm got grimly to his feet. "I'd better take a ride over there. You lads want to come along?"

I hurried to Dillon's barn and got my horse. Then the four of us took off up the Little Goose. It was only eight miles to Big Horn City and we made it in forty minutes. The town was older than Sheridan and until lately had been some bigger.

Now Sheridan was on its way up and this place was on its way down.

The town looked lazy-peaceful as we rode in—Malcolm, myself and the two Wrench men. The Big Horn Mountains made a steep, piney backdrop and you couldn't find a prettier place in Wyoming. Bard's Hotel was a two-story frame on the main corner. Right across from it was Skinner's store with an eight-mule freight wagon in front. The Custis saloon, diagonally across from the hotel, had a few hipshot ponies at the rack. The fourth corner had the big Coffeen store which wouldn't be there much longer. Coffeen planned on moving it to Sheridan.

We went into the hotel for a look at the book. Shonts and Tuttle had taken a room but they weren't in it just now. Charlie Bard said two strangers had come in asking for them.

I looked both ways along the street but didn't see any Texas horses. Pool balls clicked in Frenchie's Place and a clean, sweet smell came from the Little Goose meadows. We inquired at Skinner's store and then tried Custis' saloon. An Open 8 hand said he'd seen Shonts and Tuttle. Before I could ask where, we heard shooting. It came from up by the stage station at the west end of the street.

Roy Malcolm ran that way with me and the Wrench boys pounding after him. One of the Wrenches tripped on his bat-winged chaps. As we passed Skinner's warehouse the shooting opened up again. It came from both sides of the street. There was a blacksmith shop right between Odd Fellows' Hall and the stage station. Two guns were spouting lead from it. Then smoke puffed from the Little Goose Bar right across the street. "Hold your fire!" Malcolm yelled, "in the name of the law!"

He was wasting his breath. No one could stop those Texans after they'd nursed their grudge a whole year. They charged out of the smithy and ran straight toward the Little Goose Bar. One got as far as the middle of the street and a bullet dropped him there. The other kept on toward the saloon door, tripping his trigger at every step.

His face had blood on it and he stumbled to his knees at the sidewalk. Another bullet doubled him up there—he went down hugging his stomach and his gun went sliding along the boards. "Hold it!" Malcolm shouted again, getting there three jumps too late.

The twin half-doors of the Little Goose pushed open and Ike Shonts walked out. Chalk wasn't any whiter than his face but he hadn't been hit. He held his powder-hot gun by the barrel and handed it butt-first to Malcolm.

"We tried to keep outa their way, sheriff," he said.

Nor could anyone deny it. Tuttle and Shonts had made themselves scarce, slipping quietly out of Sheridan to avoid being caught up with. "Aye, they forced it on you," Malcolm admitted gravely.

Just inside the twin doors lay G. G. Tuttle. He'd been hit twice and was dead. So was a Swede with pale hair who'd dropped in the street. Red Fitch, jackknifed on the walk, still had life in him. "It won't be long, though," a Wrench man announced after a look. "He took one right through the stomach."

By then the whole town was bearing down on us. People from Skinner's store and Sackett's barn—the stage station crew and everyone from Bard's hotel. Frightened women looked at us from the back street cabins. Big Horn City had known other gunfights but never one like this.

"One up and three down!" a stage hand summarized grimly.

Malcolm asked me to make sure Tuttle was past help. So while he wrote down the names of witnesses I went into the Little Goose for a closer look at Tuttle. He was dead, all right. I wondered just how close he'd been tied up with LaSalle and Clanton and Bruno. Was he anything more than a card-sharp gunman?

Maybe something on him would give me a lead. I went through his pants pockets and found money, keys and a pair of dice. A vest pocket had two mashed cigars. Over the vest was a chamois jacket and in its inner pocket I found a letter. The postmark showed it had been mailed two weeks ago at Miles City, Montana. The envelope was addressed to George Tuttle, Sheridan, Wyoming.

That would be only a few days before the N.P. train robbery near Miles City. So I took out the enclosure and read it. It was signed "F.G." and I remembered Frank Gomer, the man in the cow-skin coat who'd traded bullets with us on Powder River.

"Okay George," the letter said, "I'll try to make Bruno stay away from the Ace. But he's a cocky little devil and bull-headed no end. He thinks he can walk in and out any time he wants just because his wife works there and his brother owns the joint. I'll see what I can do. Meantime keep your fingers crossed.   F.G."

CHAPTER XII

WHEN the *Sheridan Post* came out on Thursday, it printed that letter.

Doug read it sitting up in bed. "Proves we were right," he chuckled. "I mean about Bruno and Cal being blood kin. Kind of pulls the mask off that guy."

But it didn't. Cal Clanton kept his mask of respectability in the eyes of Sheridan. He kept on riding around like a gentleman rancher and society-man-about-town. He could still make dates with nice, innocent girls like Carrie Gordon.

Because whatever disgrace there was in being brother to an outlaw and owner of a vice joint, Martie LaSalle took it.

"That's right," Martie admitted to Malcolm. "Bruno's my kid brother. He's a bit wild maybe but I've done my best to tame him down. No, sheriff, I've no idea where he is right now. Nor Rosa either. She slipped out last night and nobody's heard from her since."

Which left Clanton completely out of it. Out of it, that is, in the eyes of everyone except those of us who'd noticed a facial resemblance between him and Bruno. Of those few, only three on our side of the law had been impressed by it—Doug McLaren, myself and Carrie Gordon. Malcolm had seen Bruno only once, in twilight dimness at the jail.

"If they look alike," Malcolm argued, "it's maybe because they both got deep, black sideburns and part their hair the same way. Anyway, why would a high class stockman like Clanton want to own a honkytonk like the Ace?"

What stymied us was that we didn't dare tell Malcolm, or even Tom Cotton at the *Post*, about Clanton writing letters to Ohio. Not as long as there was a chance of getting Jim Hutton into trouble.

Doug beat the schedule getting well. He was a healthy young cuss and by Saturday he was sitting up. Sunday I took him for a walk over to Mark Walsh's cottage. Roy Malcolm was holding down a rocker by Mark's bed and he told us a coroner's jury had whitewashed Shonts. We'd expected that. Everyone knew that Shonts hadn't started shooting till he'd been chased and caught.

"Where's Mike Fallon?" Doug asked.

"He went back to Buffalo," Malcolm said. "Which reminds me, they had to turn Frank Gomer loose down there. His alibi's too good, they decided."

Monday, Doctor Kueny had a look at Doug's shoulder. "It's doing fine," he said. So Tuesday we saddled up for the ranch.

Everything we owned was on the pack mules as we led them out of Dillon's barn. Doug had a hawk feather in his hat. Being laid up a week hadn't set him back much. "Powder River, let 'er buck!" he yelled.

We stopped at Mills' drugstore for the Hutton mail. A tall man at the post office wicket had his back to us, asking if there was a letter for him. He was bareheaded and for a second I didn't know him.

Then he turned and we saw he was Cal Clanton. It was the first time we'd stood face to face since he'd clipped me on the chin. I didn't think he'd try it again here in the post office. Then I saw why he didn't look quite natural.

"I don't blame you, Clanton," I said, staring at his unhatted head.

His smile had ice on the edges and he tried to talk down at me. "You don't blame me for what, Shorty?"

"I don't blame you for shaving off those side-burns; and for parting your hair different; and for going bareheaded so people can see it. It makes you look a lot less like Bruno."

I thought I saw his punch coming and made ready to duck. Then maybe I could head-dive at his middle and butt him down. There was a letter in his hand. I wondered if it was postmarked Ohio.

All he did was push by me and leave the store.

The postal clerk gave us Hutton's mail. It was only a seed catalogue and a copy of *Frank Leslie's Weekly*. We went out with it and rode west along Loucks Street.

"He's Bruno's brother, all right," Doug said. And I agreed with him. I figured LaSalle was claiming kin with Bruno just to save Clanton's face. *Somebody* had to, after we'd published the Tuttle letter.

Our road followed the north bank of the Big Goose to Beckton. This was a crossroad ten miles west of Sheridan where George Beck had just about the sweetest little ranch layout I ever saw. He had meadows of alfalfa and timothy and a full-flowing ditch from the creek. His house was a two-story frame on a knoll with the Beckton post office in one of its outbuildings. We passed between it and the creek. The creek "had a timber bridge and a little the other side of it was a water-wheel mill three stories high. Right now it was idle because they didn't run it until after the grain harvest.

The main road left us here and turned north toward Dayton. Doug and I kept on up the Goose, along a farm trail which served the Clanton and Hutton ranches. Cottonwood and choke cherry grew thick along the creek. Looking through these, and across the creek, we could see a small country school. It was right below where Rapid Creek came in from the south.

"If I ever settle down, Doug, I'd sure like to do it right here."

"You couldn't beat it, Harry." Doug waved a hand toward the snowtops of the Big Horns. We were right under them now, their slopes purple-black with pine and fir. Here along the Goose were lush meadows sweeping in to haw thickets and wild fruit peeking out from the groves of fat-boled cottonwood. George Beck's ditch curved out from the creek with sweet clover rank along the ditch bank. Here and there a lateral sluiced clear mountain water down the meadow. "Yeh," I sighed, "when the time comes you can bury me right here, Doug."

Every cowboy in the world, I guess, dreams of a spot like Beckton.

Above the Beck land we came to a fenced meadow. The hay land there was native grass with a patch of alfalfa at a far corner. A brown dot in the alfalfa looked like a burro grazing belly-deep.

This was Cal Clanton's c in a C. His rock house lay close to the creek and about half a mile beyond a gate in the fence. It was a private gate and our upvalley trail didn't go through it. Instead it circled the fence and as we followed it we got no nearer the house.

"Wonder who's working for him now," Doug said.

"Nobody but Dumb George," I said. "He sold what cattle the winter didn't get and he hasn't restocked yet. Till he does he won't need anyone but George."

"I kind of feel sorry for George," Doug said.

"There he comes now." A monster of a man had just left the corral and was riding this way. His hugeness made me pity the horse under him. With what wits he had, he was childishly loyal to Cal Clanton.

Since he was coming toward us, we stopped just outside the fence and waited.

But he was only interested in the trespassing burro. Arriving at the burro, he scolded it and then began driving it toward the nearest fence, which happened to be in our direction.

"He's dumb, all right," Doug grinned. "There's no gate on this side. Why doesn't he drive it to a gate?"

What happened next should have been in a circus side show. At the fence George dismounted. He picked up the burro, which couldn't have weighed less than five hundred pounds, hoisted it over the top wire and dropped it on the outside. "Now don't you come back!" he scolded.

"Hi, George," Doug said. "I'd sure hate to be in a wrestling match with you."

The giant stood just across the wires looking

at us from glossy brown eyes much as an ox would look at a pair of jackrabbits. He seemed neither hostile nor friendly. "You all alone here, George?" I asked.

He nodded. "But soon I will have company," he said.

I wondered what company. Was Bruno planning to hide out here? What about the cowskin-coated man who'd just been freed at Buffalo? "You seen Bruno lately?" I asked.

The bovine eyes kept staring. And when the giant spoke he was like a backward schoolboy reciting a lesson by rote. "I do not know Bruno. I do not know Rosa. I do not know Shonts. And if two come by to ask questions, I am to knock their heads together."

He looked speculatively at the five-wire fence, as though wondering how best to get through it. He'd lifted a burro over it but he couldn't lift himself. It made a problem for him and Doug and I didn't wait to watch him solve it. We spurred on up the trail, leading our mules.

And Dumb George kept opposite us on the other side of the fence. The fence corner stopped him but we, being outside the meadow, kept right on. I looked over my shoulder and saw George staring with a baffled look at the five tight wires. "He can't quite make up his mind," I said, "whether to bust through and come after us."

Doug laughed. "Let this be a lesson, Harry. Next

time don't ask him any damnfool questions."

A mile more brought us to the lower gate of the H Bar, Jim Hutton's place. We crossed his small horse pasture to a second gate and beyond this, at the creek side of a narrow, clover meadow, we came to his building layout. The main cabin was solid logs and had a bunkhouse close by it. The corral was still nearer the creek with a stock shed along one side of it. A ditchful of water ran between a hillside and the house.

Chickens scratched in the shed yard and a calf bawled from the corral. At a pulley well a teenage Indian was drawing water.

We rode to the well trough and let our animals drink. "Hi, Johnny," Doug said. "Boss around?"

Johnny Beaver, a Hunkpapa Sioux who'd been raised in the household of a reservation missionary, had a gleaming, toothy grin and fair English. "They visit with neighbors," he told us, pointing north.

Soldier Creek lay that way, beyond a grassy ridge. Maybe the neighbors were the Gordons who'd moved onto the Ruggles farm over there. By crow-flight the distance would be less than three miles.

At the bunkshack we found a note Hutton had left for us.

> Make yourselves at home, boys. Joan and I will be back by sundown. Harry,

don't let Doug strain himself any. That drive will be showing up any day now. Meantime take it easy.

Jim Hutton.

We offsaddled and unpacked, picked our bunks and made coffee. I bullied Doug into taking a nap, then went out to help Johnny Beaver with the chores. The sun slipped down to balance gently on the Big Horns. Cool, friendly smells came from the pines there. "Johnny," I said, "we're sure lucky to be working at a spot like this."

"They are good to me," the boy said. His broad copper face, high-boned but never stolid like most Indians', again flashed a smile. "Here I like. But there I do not like." He pointed downcreek toward Clanton's c in a C.

"Why?" I prodded.

"Once I am chore-boy there. It is a year ago when I am only fourteen summers old."

"Yeh? And what happened?"

"There is a neighbor I like much. One time he comes by and stays all night. At supper he is happy. At breakfast he is sad. At supper he has a fine horse and saddle; at breakfast he is on foot. He walks away on his feet and I never see him again."

"Sounds like he got cleaned in a poker game. What was his name?"

"His name is Otis," the boy said.

I remembered Bob Otis, who'd left these parts a year ago stony broke. I hadn't seen him again till he turned up in the crowd in front of the Windsor Hotel during Governor Moonlight's speech.

In the bunkhouse Doug was awake and I checked with him. "Yeh," he said, "I spoke to Bob and he said he'd made a fresh start over at Lander. Rode over here on a stock trade of some kind."

"Did you see him at the dance?"

"No. He had a ticket to the banquet but he passed up the dance. I heard he pulled out early the next morning."

An odd fact struck me. Otis had attended the speech and banquet but not the dance. Clanton, on the contrary, had skipped the speech and banquet but had attended the dance. Why? To avoid coming face to face with Otis? Otis who'd spent the night at Clanton's ranch, a year ago, arriving happy and leaving sad, minus his horse and saddle!

Wheel sounds drew us outside. Joan Hutton waved to us from the seat of a buckboard. "I hope you're not too hungry. Because supper won't be ready for hours." She let Doug hand her down from the rig.

"Maybe I could help," he offered hopefully. And by the time I'd unhitched the team he'd promoted himself into the kitchen.

· · ·

Help at the Hutton place ate in the main house, family style, and this included the Indian chore-boy, Johnny Beaver. "They're grand people," Joan said during supper. She meant their new neighbors, the Gordons. This afternoon the girl and her father had driven over there to give them a clucking hen and a setting of eggs. "Carrie has done wonders with that old farm house. I don't see how she finds time."

"Why not?" Doug asked. "What else is she doing?"

Joan laughed. "For one thing, there's always a beau or two around expecting to be entertained and fed. Some PK men were over there today. But she's so sweet and lovely, who can blame them?"

"Top of all that," Bruce Gordon added, "she's brushing up for a teacher's examination. Has to pass it before she can get the Beckton school next fall. Superintendent Gridley loaned her last year's questions. They'll be different this year—but it gives her an idea what to expect."

"Tough, are they?" I asked.

"They're terrible!" Joan said, rolling her eyes. "Listen; I copied down a few of them and you can judge for yourself." She brought out a slip of paper and read us five of last year's questions.

Name the highest mountain in Africa and give its height.

Extract the square root of $998,001.

State the principal cause of the French and Indian War.

Describe the effect of alcohol on digestion.

At what rate percent will $640 gain $96 in 3 years, 9 months?

"The rest are just as bad!" The expression of horror on Joan's face made us all laugh, including Johnny Beaver.

"It's been my experience," Jim Hutton put in, "that the further you go back into the wilderness the more they expect you to know. Now where I came from, in . . ." He broke off into an awkward silence.

He'd almost made a slip and I saw Joan flash him a warning. They weren't telling where they came from. And now the fact that Hutton had almost done so brought a change over them. A minute ago they'd been easy, airy, jolly; now they became reserved, repressed, cautious. The shadow of something like fear came over the girl's dark, sensitive face.

It was like that moment on the hotel porch when I'd explained why all the Powder River range had once been a forbidden valley. Her quick reaction—"I don't like that name! It sounds sinister!"

Why? Was it because a dread hung over them? A dread that this snug home they'd found here might be snatched away—forbidden to them—if a secret of their past leaked out?

Naturally they couldn't guess that Doug and I already knew two things. Their name was Prather and they came from Ohio.

Later Doug McLaren talked without restraint about his own childhood on a Minnesota farm, telling how he'd come west with a bull team at the age of fifteen.

"What about Johnny Beaver?" I asked after the boy had gone to bed. "A year ago he was choring for Cal Clanton, wasn't he?"

Hutton nodded. "He didn't like it there, so he started out to join a lodge of his people in the Black Hills. It took him by my place on the Crazy Woman and I let him stay all night. In the morning he helped with the chores and I took a fancy to him. Offered him a job and he's been with me ever since." A gentle smile came over Hutton's face as he added, "Truth is I owe that kid more 'n I'll ever be able to pay back."

At my look of puzzlement Joan said, "Tell them, Dad."

"I had a big herd on the Crazy Woman and by rights the blizzards last winter should have wiped me out. But in the fall Johnny Beaver advised me to sell every hoof and horn. On a hunch I did. And the ranch too. Then Johnny told me about a place for sale here on the Big Goose, near where he'd worked for Clanton. With money in the bank I bought it, and in the spring sent to Texas for new stock."

I was still gaping. "But how could Johnny know we'd have a winter like that?"

"Maybe because he's an Indian," Jim said, "and closer to nature than we are. Anyway in the fall he called my attention to things white men were overlooking. He showed me where beaver had piled up abnormal quantities of saplings for winter food; he showed me that the bark of the younger cottonwoods was thicker and tougher than usual. Native birds were bunching earlier than usual. Wild animals were growing heavier coats of fur. Wild fowl began migrating south six weeks ahead of time. Nature knew! And so did Johnny Beaver. He told me and I believed him. So I sold everything and rode out the winter in town."

"So now you know all!" Joan said, trying to look gay again.

But we didn't, of course. We knew only about the last six years. Back of that lay a buried past, sealed and forbidden.

CHAPTER XIII

IN TWO MORE DAYS the trail herd arrived from Texas. Hutton held to the letter of his contract, which allowed us not to accept delivery until the stuff was tallied through our gate. Hutton and I sat our saddles to the left of the gate, counting as the heifers filed through. Joan, her cheeks flushed and excited, helped Doug tally from the right of the gate.

They were native white-faces, line-backed and curly-maned. The dewlaps hung low and creamy, and I didn't see a single humped back. They were trail thin, naturally, but foothills grass would soon take care of that. And they'd slipped in a few yearlings on us, although the contract called for two-coming-threes. But it wasn't enough to get mad about. The horns weren't old enough to be long or mossy. All in all the Texas seller had done right by us.

Every time I counted a hundred I made a mark in a book. What I liked most was that Hutton had paid a nickel a head to have his H Bar put on in Texas. The brands had scabbed over now, showing up big and brown on the left ribs. It

171

would help a lot when we turned them loose in the hills. We could tally for shortages a long way off.

Here at the receiving gate our tallies all came out different. Mine was three head over two thousand and Joan's was five head under. Jim receipted on the basis of the high tally and the delivery was complete.

Joan wore Levis today and they made her look like a gangling boy. "Come and get it!" she called out, and loped toward the house. The Texas trail crew streaked after her. Hutton had barbecued a lamb for them.

But Doug and I had to stay with the cows. That little horse pasture didn't have room for them. So we pushed them out the upcreek gate and let them drift on up the valley. The further we went the better the grass. "Look at 'em go for it!" Doug said.

"It's a heifer's heaven," I agreed. A grouse whirred from under my horse and made it shy. The valley pinched narrow from here on, cottonwood petering out and alder taking its place. There was gooseberry and wild cherry, and enough wildflowers to make a baby smile. "It's right pretty stuff!" Doug crooned, meaning the cattle.

"And is Jim proud of it!" I exclaimed.

"Joan too," Doug said.

"Let 'em drift, Doug." I looped a leg around

the saddle horn and rolled a smoke. The heifers drifted on ahead of us, feeding their way dewlap-deep through bluestem.

Then we got off, loosened our cinches and let the heifers find home sweet home. Their contented moos floated back to us as a paradise of pasture opened up. "They never had it so good!" Doug chuckled.

My thoughts strayed back to Johnny Beaver. To his prejudice against the Clanton place because a man had arrived there happy and left sad. When I mentioned it again Doug shrugged. "It's happened before, Harry. A guy bets his horse and saddle against a full house and gets called."

"Maybe it was that way," I brooded, "and maybe not. It's hard to figure Bob Otis being a poor loser like that." What had an Indian boy seen on Bob's face, when he left the next morning? Fear? Despair? "Maybe he made a mistake once," I said. "And Clanton knew about it. Clanton could say, 'Leave what you got right here, Otis, and start walking.' "

"Blackmail?" It was an ugly word and after speaking it Doug spat into the sand. "It's a long guess, Harry."

Maybe it was. But something else wasn't. On the ridge above us I saw a horseman. The horse was bay and the rider's profile stood clear against the sky. We were in the alder shadows and probably he didn't see us here. His gaze was fixed intently on cattle which now grazed slowly up the canyon.

Doug's eyes followed mine. "Clanton!" he muttered.

"It's a free range, Doug. He's got as much right here as we have."

"Darned neighborly of him," Doug said dryly. "Takin' an interest in our cows. Lend me the makings, Harry."

I tossed him my Durham sack and he rolled one. When I looked up again at the ridge top, Clanton was gone. No life was in sight up there except a buzzard circling high.

At the house we didn't mention seeing Clanton. Jim Hutton had a glow on his face and we didn't want to spoil it. And those gentle brown eyes of Joan hadn't been made for tears. Anyway we were only guessing. All we knew was that Clanton had written letters to Ohio.

"How do they like it?" Jim asked eagerly, meaning the cows.

"A heap better than Texas," I said.

"How far up do you think we'd better push them?"

"About where Walker Creek comes into the West Goose," Doug suggested.

"We could hold 'em right close there," I said, "if we salt the mouth of Walker."

Hutton nodded. "I'll drive in for a load of rock

salt tomorrow," he decided. Two thousand heifers would lick up plenty of it.

"That was the hungriest bunch of men I ever saw," Joan laughed. The trail crew, after dispatching the barbecued lamb, had gone loping off toward the fleshpots of Sheridan.

In the morning Hutton hitched up a spring wagon and got an early start for town. Doug and I took the opposite direction, catching up with the cattle a little way above where Red Canyon comes in. Some had drifted a piece up Cave Creek. We bunched them in the main valley and got their heads toward the mountains. They did the rest themselves. In early summer cattle just naturally drift toward high country. Unless you hold them with salt they'll go higher and higher till snow turns them downhill again.

A set of bleached bones by the creek made us remember last winter. "Won't happen again in a hundred years," I said.

We took the whole day getting the stuff a couple of miles on to the mouth of Walker. I'd brought along one block of salt, hung from my saddle horn. I dropped it at the creek fork. The fork had three prongs—East Goose, West Goose and Walker. Later we could put a hundred pounds of salt a half mile up each of the prongs.

Joan had supper ready when we got back to the ranch. "I wonder what's keeping Dad," she said.

Twilight deepened and Jim Hutton still hadn't

come back from town. "Lots of things could happen," Doug said when he saw Joan begin to worry. "Like one of those trail herders needing to be bailed out of jail."

"Sure," I chimed in. "Stop frettin', Joan. He'll stay in town all night, likely, and come out in the morning."

She put supper on and we called Johnny Beaver. "We have company today," Johnny beamed as he tucked a napkin in his neck. "I like."

"Carrie Gordon rode over," Joan explained. "I loaned her some beads and a pair of combs. She wants to look her best tonight."

"She's got a date with one of those PKs," I suggested.

Joan smiled mysteriously. "Guess again."

"Cal Clanton?"

"Not him. You're not even close."

After a few more guesses we gave up.

"He's a dashing young lawyer from Buffalo named Fallon," Joan said.

I whistled. It was a fifty mile ride from Buffalo to Soldier Creek.

"He's been very attentive," Joan confided.

"Gosh!" I said. "Why doesn't somebody tell me these things?"

"They wouldn't have to," Joan laughed, "if you'd read the *Sheridan Post*." She brought out the latest issue which had the Big Horn City gunfight spread all over the front page. I'd read that much but hadn't looked inside. Now I turned to the "Brevities" column and to Editor Cotton's pixie-like heading:

"A chiel's amang you, takin' notes,
And faith, he'll prent it."

The first item under it was:

Mike Fallon is again in town and stopping at the Windsor. Rumour has it that he thinks of resigning his county job in order to open a private law practise in Sheridan. Having kept our eyes open, we think we know why.

In the morning Doug took a ride to Wolf Creek to look at some young bulls for sale over there. Hutton wanted us to keep our eyes open for a good buy in bulls, as we'd need about forty for a herd of our size.

I rode alone to the forks and checked for springers. These Texas heifers weren't supposed to be bred and I hoped they weren't, because we didn't want any winter calves. But I counted about fifty that looked calvy. These we'd have to cut out and hold in the meadow for special feeding.

In early afternoon I rode back to the ranch expecting to find Jim there. But he wasn't. Joan met me at the corral. "What can be keeping him?" she worried.

My private idea was that he'd got wind of a good buy in bulls and had gone for a look at them. "If he don't show up by the time you can make me a cup of coffee, I'll ride to town and find out."

Just as she finished making the coffee Doug came back from Wolf Creek. "They're crumby," he said, meaning the bulls over there.

After coffee we saddled up for Sheridan but didn't get any farther than the gate. From there we saw Hutton coming, his team at a walk and his head bowed like an old man's. When he got to us, the look on his face made me sick. We could see he hadn't slept any. His skin was like wood ash and his eyes were bloodshot. I got down and opened the gate. "What's the matter, Jim?"

He drove through the gate like he didn't see us. At the shed he got out and walked slowly toward the house, like a man on his way to the gibbet. Johnny Beaver stood by the well, watching him. It made me think of Bob Otis who'd stayed all night at the c in a C a year ago. And Johnny's telling of it—"At supper he is happy; at breakfast he is sad."

It was like that with Hutton. He'd gone to town happy; he came home sad.

We saw Joan open the door for him. The bright welcome faded from her face when she saw the grayness of Hutton's. "Dad!" she cried. "Is something wrong? What happened?"

"Do I need to tell you?" His voice reached us, dead and hopeless. Joan drew him inside and we didn't hear any more.

Doug and I sat on a wagon tongue and stared at the house. "We got to do something!" Doug said it savagely, helplessly.

"Like what?" I flung back. "Like tossing a slug at Clanton?"

We both knew that wouldn't help the Huttons. It would only throw a spotlight on whatever they were hiding. So all we could do was sit there and feel sick. An hour dragged by and not a sound came from the house. Day faded and we weren't called to supper. Johnny Beaver came from the corral with a pail of milk and headed for the kitchen with it.

In a little while he came out and Doug asked him, "What's going on up there?"

"They are very sad," Johnny said.

CHAPTER XIV

AFTER DARK we went to the kitchen and found Joan setting out three plates. A pot of stew was on the stove. "Dad and I aren't hungry," she said. Her eyes showed she'd been crying. Then she went to her room and didn't come out again.

But at bedtime we saw Jim Hutton. It was bright moonlight and we saw him go to the well for a bucket of water. "Putting off a showdown won't help any," Doug said, and walked resolutely to the well.

"Mind if we have a palaver, boss?" he asked.

"About what?" The full pail was in Hutton's hand and he moved a step toward the house with it.

"About Clanton." I could see Doug meant to show every card we had so I joined them at the well.

"Clanton?" Hutton looked genuinely puzzled.

"Sure. You saw him in town, didn't you?"

"No." The word was prompt and convincing. "I haven't seen Clanton. Not in town or anywhere else."

"Okay. Then maybe you saw Martie LaSalle.

Look, boss. If they're putting a bite on you, please let us in on it. We want to help."

It was my turn. "You don't need to be afraid of us, Jim. We already know more than you think."

He turned a gray, hopeless face toward me. His streaked eyes had a question but fear muzzled it.

"We know Clanton wrote letters to Ohio, Jim, about a John Prather of Toledo. Fact is we got our hands on his first letter and tore it up. But he wrote another one."

The sigh Hutton let out almost had relief in it. Like the thing had been penned up inside of him so long he was all but glad to have it burst out. Before he could answer me, Doug asked bluntly, "How much did they nick you for, Mr. Hutton?"

"A hundred heifers," he said. He set the pail on the well coping and sat down, his shoulders hunched wearily.

"You gave them a bill-of-sale?"

"What else could I do?" He held his head between both hands like needles were stabbing there. "They've got the goods on me and they're cracking a whip."

"They?"

"Three of them. LaSalle, Kincaid and Shonts."

"Not Clanton or Bruno?"

"No. Only those three. They called me John Prather and said a murder warrant's waiting for me in Ohio. As though I didn't know! I've been hiding from it six years."

"Joan knows about it?"

He nodded bitterly. "She knows I'll be hanged if they find me. They'll find me if I say no to LaSalle."

"LaSalle," I told him, "is only the front man for Clanton." Then I told him about how we'd emptied the trunk on the bank of Crazy Woman so we could hang things on the sage to dry; and about our noticing names in a family Bible. "Later Kincaid searched the same trunk looking for Bruno's loot and stumbled on those same names. He took them to Clanton and Clanton wrote to Ohio."

Little by little we pried the truth of his trouble out of Hutton. He told us that seven years ago he'd owned a livery business at Toledo. "A customer rented a rig and brought it back with the horse winded, whip-cut and cruelly abused. It made me so mad I used the same buggy whip on the customer. Right in front of the stable hands. He dropped dead while I was doing it—how could I know he had a weak heart? They called it manslaughter and gave me two years at hard labor."

I'd expected something worse than that.

When I said so he nodded. "There is. Mary—I call her Joan now—was thirteen then. Since her mother's death a sister of mine had helped me raise her. Before the trial came up I put my property in my sister's name and told her to sell it, so we could start fresh some place else when I was free again. They gave me two years on the rock pile."

The words seemed to choke Hutton. He upended the water pail and drank from it. "In the quarry I was paired with a hard case named Dugan. We worked in ankle chains under the eyes of a shotgun guard. Dugan was always bragging about how tough he was, about jobs he'd pulled, about policemen he'd beat up. I didn't believe half what he said. One day I was cracking rocks with a sledge and Dugan was prying with a crow bar. The guard got careless and let Dugan get too close. And Dugan cracked his skull with the crow bar. I was ten paces off when it happened."

"Did he kill the guard?" Doug asked.

"It looked to me like the guard was only stunned. The rest of the guards and prisoners were out of sight, in another part of the quarry. Dugan took keys from the guard's pocket, unlocked his leg chains and then mine. He told me to run and I did. Then he picked up my sledge and hit the guard with it. It left blood on both tools—like we'd both taken a hand in it. I was too scared to look back. And I was already running. I ran to a freight yard and hid in a boxcar. The boxcar took me to Omaha."

"You had on prison clothes?"

"I got rid of them in the dark at Omaha and found some more. Stayed there a month working on a levee. Then I saw my name in a paper. They'd caught Dugan at St. Louis. The guard was dead, so there was a first degree murder charge against both of us. Dugan swore I was as guilty as he was and blood on both tools proved it. So I climbed another freight and my next stop was Cheyenne."

"This was in 1880?" I asked.

"Yes. Seven years ago. The *Cheyenne Leader* told me about Dugan's trial. He was convicted and hanged. They'd do the same with me if I was caught. So I hit for the loneliest country I could find and ended up on the Crazy Woman, a few miles above where it joins Powder River. Changed my name to Hutton and filed a homestead. You know the rest."

"Not quite, Jim. How did you get in touch with Mary?"

"Let's call her Joan. I wrote to her. Told her my address was James Hutton, Buffalo, Wyoming. She answered and so did my sister. They both knew I was innocent but they warned me to stay away. I wrote my sister and she sent most of my money to me. I bought cows and had five good years."

"We'll never have another five years like them," I said. And any stockman will agree to that. 1881 to 1886 was the golden age of the open range cattle business. Just late enough in history to miss the Indian wars and just early enough to miss the overstocking of the range. Cattle fortunes mushroomed, those five years, all over Wyoming.

"Last fall I sold out," Hutton said, "thanks to Johnny Beaver. When I bought this place I wrote Joan to join me. By then her aunt had died and Joan was nursing at a Des Moines hospital. I told her it was the most beautiful spot in the world—this valley of the Goose above Beckton—close up under the pines of the Big Horns with a clear trout creek riffling by. Then I contracted for a herd of Texas cows. While they were trailing this way I drove to Douglas to meet Joan's train."

"What happened in town yesterday?" Doug probed.

"LaSalle braced me in the post office. He called me Prather and showed me clippings from an 1880 Ohio paper. Would I give him a bill-of-sale for a hundred cows? Or would I rather he'd call the sheriff?"

"Only a hundred?" Doug puzzled. "Why didn't he ask for two thousand?"

"He will," I predicted, "before he's through."

"I tried to bluff him," Hutton said. "Told him I'd never heard of Prather. Then Kincaid and Shonts joined us. They put on the pressure. Swore they'd let me off for a hundred heifers, which would still leave me nineteen hundred. All I could think of was Joan. Which would hurt her the least? This penalty or the one paid by Dugan?

I sweated blood over it, then finally agreed to sign the bill-of-sale."

"Did you do it right there in the post office?"

"No. They were too smart for that. They made me go with them down to the Ace of Diamonds and to a card room at the back. We went through a mock poker game there. Four-handed. LaSalle, Shonts, Kincaid and me at a table, with chips in front of us. I never once picked up my cards. But they made me sit there till after midnight. Every time I tried to go Kincaid would say, "Okay, call the sheriff, Shonts.""

"People saw you from the barroom?" I suggested.

Hutton nodded. His tired, dead voice went on. "Every time the door opened they'd see us sitting there, and it looked like a game. A big man in a cowskin coat was with us. He didn't play. He just brought in a new round of drinks now and then. Every time he opened the door LaSalle would say: 'You're called, Hutton. That makes another ten heifers you owe me.' "

They'd played it smart, all right. It would explain to the public why Hutton failed to bank any money after transferring title to a hundred cows. Extortion wouldn't be evident, since witnesses would swear they saw Hutton lose live stock in a card game.

I could understand, too, why for a starter LaSalle only demanded a hundred head. If he'd demanded the entire H Bar layout, land and cattle, Hutton might not give in so easily. He might choose to sacrifice his life rather than hand over Joan's complete heritage. Also the poker story was more convincing with only a hundred head in the pot. Later they could come back for more, and more, whittling away till Hutton didn't have a hoof or an acre left.

"You better put everything in Joan's name right now," I advised.

Hutton spread his hands helplessly. "They warned me against that. They say if I try any dodges, or if I claim a shakedown, they'll tell the law about Ohio."

A high Scotch rage climbed Doug's face. "Look. If you say so Harry and I'll go take it away from 'em. That paper you signed. And smoke the whole pack of 'em out of Wyoming."

Hutton said it was no use. And he was right. A gunplay like that would only bring his secret into the open. His neck was at stake and we mustn't forget it a minute.

"Besides," he said, "there's only my word it wasn't a real poker game; only my word they forced me to sign a paper. My word against theirs."

"You told Joan all about it?"

"She guessed it the minute she saw how beat up I looked. We've been dreading something like this all along."

Doug asked gently, "What does she want you to do?"

"She wants me to light out and hide, like I did before. To California, Oregon, Canada—anywhere. If I'm not here they can't blackmail me. Any tales they tell won't hurt me after I'm gone."

It was worth thinking about. Later Joan could sell the ranch and stock, then again slip away to join her father in a new life.

"But I won't do it!" Hutton's jaw clamped hard on the decision. "I'm through running. I won't let Joan spend the rest of her life running after me." Desperation gleamed from his eyes. "Before I do that, I'll wade into them with a gun."

I knew what he meant. A sort of sacrificial suicide. If he went at them with a gun they'd shoot him down. But it would save a fortune for Joan.

"It's a bum idea," I said. "What shooting there is, let Doug and me do it. Meantime better go to bed. We'll sleep on it and try to figure out something."

He got up and walked slowly to the house. A light came on in his bedroom. We waited till the window was dark again before going to the bunkshack.

We sat on the steps there and made cigarets. Neither of us felt like turning in. It was after midnight, and moon-bright, with the whole Big

Horn range climbing pine-black and steep to the stars. That high pink rage was gone from Doug's face. But some new strength and purpose was there to take its place. We didn't say anything. We just sat there looking at the shapes of the night—the sheds and the creek trees and the mountains. Riffles from Big Goose made murmuring music—the only break in the stillness—and a smell of clover came from the meadow.

After a while Doug got up and walked about ten steps to a window of the main house. It was partly open with the shade drawn. He took a coin from his pocket and tapped on the glass.

I wanted to call him back. He had no business tapping on a girl's window at two in the morning. Before I could say anything the shade went up. No light came on but the moon was bright enough to show the outline of Joan's face. She'd thrown a wrap around her and her dark hair hung loose.

"I didn't think you'd be asleep," Doug said softly.

"How could I sleep?" Her voice had the dead despair of Jim Hutton's.

"Your Dad told us everything, Joan, and fretting won't help any. Things'll come out all right—don't look at me that way! Like the world has come to an end!"

"Hasn't it?"

"No. And it won't. You're not going to give

up. You're not going to quit just because a cheap crook like Clanton makes a threat."

"Clanton? What does *he* have to do with it?"

"He's behind the whole dirty business. But it won't last." A commanding earnestness came into Doug's voice. "I had an old Scotch grandmother who used to say, 'Trouble never lasts forever.' "

"Ours will."

"No it won't. Things balance up. You should have seen this country last winter, Joan. Thirty below zero. Drifts ten feet deep and every coulee full of dead cows. The whole range froze up and every hope dead. And look at it now! Listen to it now! Can't you hear the creek riffling? Can't you smell that clover meadow? Wildflowers everywhere and grass stirrup high! No trouble ever was worse than Wyoming's, five months back. And look at it now!"

I wished the moon was brighter so I could see her face. There was bound to be a change in it because I caught a change in her voice. Some of the deadness was gone out of it. "You sound just like the governor." I knew she was trying to smile.

"And like my own grandma," Doug said. "Now you go back to bed. In the morning Harry and I'll take a ride to town."

CHAPTER XV

AS WE JOGGED through the downcreek gate in the morning, Jim Hutton was driving his spring wagon through the upcreek gate and heading for the forks with his load of salt. At breakfast he'd kept a stiff lip and so had Joan. Neither of them had asked why we were riding to town.

I didn't even know myself.

When we came opposite the c in a C meadow we saw Dumb George beyond the fence. The big fellow had on gum boots and was spading water into a lateral. Clanton's house showed no sign of life. As far as we knew the only ranch help Clanton had, just now, was George.

"Cal's probably in town," Doug said.

"Either there or up at the forks gloating over the heifers he slickered Jim out of. Wonder if he aims to leave 'em right there all summer."

"Why not, Harry? He might as well let 'em get fat there. It's government grass and he's got as much right to it as anyone else. Besides, he figures to take over the whole bunch, sooner or later."

"When I woke up you were writing a letter, Doug. Who to?"

"To Bob Otis at Lander. He ought to be home by now. I got a hunch Clanton's afraid of him."

"It's the other way around," I argued. "We doped it that Clanton blackmailed Otis out of a horse and saddle."

"That was a year ago. Otis left the country. But lately he came back and stood right on the main corner in Sheridan. He took in a speech and a banquet. It was Clanton who ducked 'em and kept under cover in his room."

"So what?"

"So trouble never lasts forever. Whatever trouble Otis had, it's ended. It's squared and he don't need to hide from Clanton. It's Clanton who needs to hide from Otis."

The Big Goose riffled along at our right and beyond it, through the cottonwoods, I could see the little schoolhouse where Carrie Gordon hoped to teach next winter. A little further on we came to a road junction, one fork crossing a timber bridge and pointing southeast toward Big Horn City, the other fork following on down the Goose to Sheridan.

It was after nine o'clock when we got to Sheridan and left our mounts at Dillon's barn. Then we stopped at the post office to mail Doug's letter. "I'm telling Otis a right good friend of ours is getting the screws put on him," Doug said.

194

"And I'm asking if he knows any way to build a nice hot fire under Clanton."

We walked up Main to the hotel corner and were about to turn in at the Windsor when Doug stopped suddenly and gripped my arm. His other hand slapped to a grip on his gun. When I followed his eyes I wasn't sorry to be wearing my own.

For right across the street, in a rocker on the Sheridan House porch, sat Bruno.

I could hardly believe it. Why didn't Malcolm lock him up? There he sat, in the most conspicuous spot in town, big as life! His boots were propped against the very porch post which, from the dark, he'd splintered with a bullet aimed at Doug McLaren. His dark, Spanishy face had an impudent smile and a tall-crowned gray sombrero was cocked on the back of his head. Apparently he wasn't armed. A cigar tilted upward from his lips and he had an air of owning the town.

"The nerve of him!" Doug seethed and went striding that way with me at his heels. "What does he think he's getting away with?"

"He looks kind of different," I said. "But he's Bruno all right."

By the time I got to the east walk I saw why he looked different. He'd gotten himself a new haircut. The deep, shaggy sideburns were gone. His hair was clipped short on top and the curly cowlick wasn't there. It was parted on the opposite side of his head.

I remembered seeing Clanton at the post office, the last time I was in town. Clanton with a new haircut which made him look less like Bruno! And now Bruno had spoiled it all by making the same change himself.

Bruno had done even more than that. When last seen, he'd worn a flat, low-crowned black hat after the style of a New Mexican hidalgo. Now his hat was gray and high-crowned with a single dent in front, cowman style. Just like Clanton's!

As we faced him he waved an idle hand. "We meet again, gentlemen." It was the same derisive politeness he'd used at the Powder River store. Otherwise he'd dropped the pose of a Spanish dandy. Was that, too, to make him seem more like Clanton?

Doug opened up bluntly. "Last time I was here, you gunned me from the dark."

"Did you see me?" Bruno gave us a gentle smile. "How could you see me in the darkness? I have asked Mr. Fallon that. He admits no one saw me. No witness, no case!"

He was laughing at us but what could we do? You can't take a punch at a man when he's sitting in a rocker. You can't shoot him when he isn't wearing a gun.

There was something back of it. "We'd better

find out what's goin' on, Doug," I said, "before we start roughing him."

"An excellent idea!" Bruno purred. He held out the cigar and daintily flicked ashes from it. "Why don't you have a talk with Mr. Fallon? He has a room right across at the Windsor."

"Who the devil *are* you?" Doug demanded. "A letter in a dead man's pocket says you're Rosa's husband and Clanton's brother."

"You shouldn't believe all you hear."

"Then who *are* you?"

"I'm a guest at this hotel. Why don't you look on the register?"

We went inside for a look at the book. The last name signed was Bruno LeFevre, Sheridan, Wyoming.

It hinted, but didn't prove, that he was Rosa's husband. Doug looked as confused as I was. "We better go see Mike," he decided.

As we crossed the street I saw a face at an upper window of the Windsor Hotel. It was Cal Clanton's. He was staring across at the Sheridan House porch with as black a look as you'd see anywhere. A sort of frustrated fury. I turned and saw Bruno gazing obliquely upward at that same window. There was a laugh on his face, like he was taunting Clanton.

"He's a flea in Clanton's hair, Doug," I said as we went into the Windsor.

We found Mike Fallon in the dining room

taking a late cup of coffee. He had a carnation in his buttonhole and looked spruce as a race horse. He waved a hand. "Come join me, cowboys."

We joined him and ordered coffee. "What's going on up the creek?" he asked.

"*You* ought to know!" Doug said. "Seein' as you've been sparkin' a gal up that way. What's this about you opening a law office in Sheridan?"

"It's a fact," Fallon grinned. "Just sent in my resignation to take effect right away."

Ordinarily we would have kidded him a little about Carrie Gordon. It was plain as the nose on your face that she was the attraction. Else why would he quit a good county job to get forty miles nearer to her?

But Doug had something more serious on his mind. A bee was buzzing under that sandy hair of his. I thought it was about Bruno but I was wrong.

"Look, Mike," he said. "Somewhere I heard that when a man hires a lawyer, everything he tells the lawyer is confidential. I mean if he's in a jam, the lawyer won't let it out."

Fallon gave us a searching look. "You fellows been branding the wrong calves?" he asked shrewdly. "Or maybe you just drygulched a sheepherder."

"It's not about us," Doug said. "It's a friend of ours."

Fallon sipped his coffee. "Anything a client tells me would be confidential."

"In that case," Doug said, "I got an idea who your first client'll be." I knew he meant Jim Hutton.

"Bring him around," Fallon invited. "My office'll be upstairs over the post office."

Naturally Doug couldn't follow through any further. First we'd have to persuade Hutton that he needed a lawyer and could trust Fallon. To change the subject I brought up Bruno. "He's in town, slick and sassy," I said. "Why haven't you tossed him in jail?"

Fallon smiled wryly. "I talked it over with the prosecuting attorney and we decided it's no use."

"But hell! Everybody knows he's an outlaw . . ."

"Everybody knows it but no one can prove it. Nobody saw him take a shot at Doug, the night of the dance. In court that charge would fall flat on its face. The best case against him is the same one we had against Gomer—the N.P. train robbery near Miles City. It's so weak that we had to release Gomer at Buffalo. Gomer's now back in Sheridan. The minute Bruno heard about it he rode into town, bold as brass. He knows we can't hold him if we can't hold Gomer."

"He broke jail, didn't he?"

"Not exactly. He walked out of an open jail door. Before that, he resisted arrest at the Potter cabin. But the arresters were just two cowboys without badge or warrant. No one can prove he had loot, there or anywhere else."

"Looks to me," Doug offered, "like he's playing cat-and-mouse."

Fallon gave a narrow-eyed nod. "Struck me the same way. Notice his new haircut?"

"Yeh, it's like Clanton's."

"So's his hat. If I had to bet on it, I'd say Clanton's the mouse and Bruno's the cat. We've got more to gain by letting Bruno worry Clanton than by picking Bruno up on some weak charge. You boys got any ideas?"

"Just one," Doug offered. "I think they're blood brothers just like it said in the letter from Gomer to Tuttle. The hitch is that Clanton's respectable and Bruno's not. Clanton's a stockman in good standing with the W.S.G.A. He can tip his hat to nice ladies. So it's kind of embarrassing to have an outlaw kid brother staring him in the face."

"Clanton's annoyed by it," Mike agreed, "and Bruno's rubbing it in."

"Bruno," I suggested, "first thought it was Doug who snatched the money from Rosa. So he cut loose at Doug from the dark. Right after that Rosa must've told him it was Clanton who grabbed the money. She knew by the scratch on Cal's face. So now maybe Bruno's pressuring Clanton to make him give back the money. And maybe to cut in on . . ."

I broke off, because as yet we couldn't tell Mike about the blackmail play against Hutton. But I had a feeling Bruno knew about it and wanted to cut in.

"It adds up," Fallon admitted. "By just sitting over there on the porch looking as much like his big brother as he can, Bruno can make people wonder about Clanton. Wonder if he's on the level; wonder if after all he's not just what the letter said—a clip-joint owner and brother to an outlaw. A form of subtle, silent blackmail. That taunting smile of Bruno's says to Clanton, 'If you want me to get out of your life, Brother Cal, just pay me off.' "

A couple of forty-five slugs would do it, I thought. One for Bruno and one for Rosa. Shooting a troublesome brother shouldn't bother Clanton too much. And Rosa probably knew as much as Bruno. Then it occurred to me that while Bruno had come back to town, Rosa *hadn't*. As far as we knew, Rosa was still hiding somewhere. Maybe she was Bruno's defense against Clanton.

We heard boot thumps come down the stairs and cross the lobby. They stopped at the dining room door and when I turned my head I saw Clanton standing there. The harassed look was still on his face. He'd intended coming into the dining room but sight of us made him change his mind.

Turning abruptly, he went out to the street.

"We'll see you later, Mike," Doug said. Quickly he steered me out of the room and on the trail of Clanton.

Clanton was half a block down the walk and we were just in time to see him turn into Leaverton's. "I guessed wrong," Doug admitted.

"Yeh, you thought he'd head for the Ace."

"Sure. To warn Martie he saw us huddling with an assistant county prosecutor. He doesn't know Mike has quit his county job. So he figures Jim Hutton told us about the shakedown and we hustled right in to see the law about it."

"But he didn't go to the Ace. He went to Leaverton's."

Doug mulled it over. "He was bare-headed, Harry. A cowman hardly ever goes outdoors without a hat on. Which gives me an idea. Come."

We went on to Leaverton's store and stopped in front of it. Looking in we saw Clanton trying on a hat. It was a black hat with a creased crown— Congressman style and a lot different from the tall gray cowman's sombrero he usually wore. Doug grinned. "It's as simple as that. Got his hair parted back on the other side too, I notice."

"Won't do him any good," I chuckled. "Every time he changes his hat and hair, Bruno can copy him. He'll be nuts before he's through. Let's wait across on that bench and see where he goes next."

We angled across Main to the stage bench in

front of Conrad's. "Rosa was sitting right here," I remembered, "when she spotted Clanton's scratch. Seems to be healed over now."

We waited for Clanton to come out of Leaverton's. It was still a fair bet that he'd keep on to the north end for a word with LaSalle.

"You wanted to probe for his weak spots, Doug. Already you've found two. Bob Otis and Bruno. Maybe Rosa'll make three."

Fifteen minutes passed and Clanton didn't come out. "Takin' him a long time to buy a hat," Doug said. "Wait a minute." He crossed to Leaverton's and went in.

Right away he came out and beckoned me over there. "Clerk says he bought a hat and left by the back door."

It meant he'd seen us waiting on the bench and so had given us the slip. He could get to Martie's place by the alley as easy as by the front walks. So we lost no time heading for the north end.

"We've got to think of Hutton," I warned. "We don't dare let 'em know Hutton told on 'em."

A shrewd gleam sparked Doug's eye. "We won't tell 'em a thing, Harry. We'll just pop 'em with one simple, natural question." When he told me what it was I agreed it wouldn't hurt Hutton any. And there was a fair chance it might pull the mask off of Clanton.

At the Ace we found the barroom almost empty.

One of the house girls was accepting a drink from a Lodge Grass sheepman.

Doug and I walked right by them to a door at the back. Low voices from beyond it made me pretty sure who we'd find there. Clanton in a powwow with LaSalle and Kincaid.

The barkeep came alive and yelled at us. "Hey, where you goin'? That's a private room."

He was too late. We opened the card room door and walked in.

But the three we found there didn't include Clanton. They were LaSalle, Kincaid and Shonts—the same three who'd posed in a fake game with Hutton.

Shonts and Kincaid jumped to their feet and they were both armed. LaSalle, who wasn't, kept his seat. A slight shake of his head warned the others they weren't to start a fight.

"Morning. What's on your mind?" LaSalle's voice was cautious and polite.

"Where do you want 'em delivered?" Doug asked.

LaSalle delayed his answer, exchanging cagey looks with Kincaid. "Where do I want what?" he countered.

"The hundred heifers you won from our boss," Doug said easily, his fingers twisting a cigaret. "Where do you want 'em delivered?"

Our hope was that they'd say the c in a C ranch. If they did it would tie the whole play to Clanton.

LaSalle owned no ranch at which he could receive live stock; neither did Kincaid or Shonts. They weren't expecting Doug's simple, natural question and it might catch them off guard.

But again we were disappointed. "You don't need to deliver 'em anywhere," Martie said. "They're on government grass, I understand. So leave 'em right there and when I want 'em, I'll send for 'em."

It stymied us. Our natural question had drawn the same kind of an answer. All we could do was walk out.

At the street walk Doug said, "Maybe Clanton came and went before we got there."

"He'd go in from the alley and leave the same way," I said, remembering he'd left Leaverton's by the back door.

So we circled to the back of the saloon on the chance of finding a witness. There was a shed with four saddle horses in it. The rest of the block was vacant and weed-grown.

A hundred yards west, in the yard of a shanty facing Brooks Street, a woman was hanging out wash. We sauntered over there. "Notice anyone come out of that saloon," Doug asked her, pointing to the Ace's alley door, "in the last fifteen minutes or so?"

"Yes sir," the woman said promptly. "A man came out of there and went thataway." She pointed west up Grinnell Street, which beyond

Brooks had no houses except an old hay shed where the street came to a blind end on the bank of Big Goose.

"A tall, good-lookin' guy, was he, wearin' a brand new black hat?"

"No sir. He was heavy-set and bare-headed. He had on a red and white coat—cowskin, I think."

Frank Gomer! The outlaw recently turned loose at Buffalo who'd stood looking on at the fake poker game. "Thanks, lady."

We hurried west along the weedy ruts which extended creekward from Grinnell Street. "Since Frankie's on foot and bare-headed," Doug reasoned, "he's not going far."

"The only place he could go down this way," I said, "is that hay shed by the creek."

Cottonwoods shaded the shed and just short of it we had to jump a brimful irrigation ditch. Doug made it easy but my own short legs let me land with a splash. As I scrambled out with a bootful of water Doug clapped a hand to my mouth, in case I felt like cussing. Then we edged a little closer to the shed and heard voices inside.

Two men were in there and one of them had to be Gomer. No saddle horse was in sight, so the other man had come on foot too. We slipped a step or two nearer, water squashing in my boot, and stopped to listen.

"Your job's to find her!" the voice had a brittle

snap and sounded like Clanton's. "Until she's found we can't lift a finger."

We waited for the other man to answer and when he didn't I knew something had made him suspicious. Maybe he'd heard my splash at the ditch. There was a minute of dead silence.

Then a bull-shouldered man appeared in the doorway. He wore baggy pants and a cowhide coat and his name was Frank Gomer. After a quick look at us he went for his gun.

CHAPTER XVI

IT WAS natural enough considering our last meeting. For he hadn't seen us since the gunfight in Suggsby's corral, on Powder River. We'd gone at them through smoke, that day, two against four, and a slug from Doug's carbine had cut this one down. Since then he'd likely put in a lot of time planning to get even.

So he drew on sight; but Doug, expecting it and shooting from the hip, bounced the gun from his hand. From the yell he gave I thought he'd been drilled through—but it was only the pain of a wrenched hand. The bullet went richochetting on and the gun flew wide. Frank Gomer stood there livid, bellowing like a bull and nursing a stung hand.

Then we saw Clanton peer over his shoulder from the shed. "What's the idea?" he demanded, but his voice had a false crack in it. His eyes looked scared and his face was three shades too pale.

It wasn't hard to guess why. He didn't know how much we'd heard. Actually we'd heard nothing we could hang him for. "Your job's to find her. Until she's found we can't lift a finger!" Only that much.

As we walked toward them they backed into the shed. Passing, I picked up Gomer's gun and threw it into the ditch. Then we followed them into the shed. One end had baled hay in it. The floor was dirt and cobwebs hung from the rafters. We didn't say anything. Gomer was sucking his stung hand and Clanton was sweating it out, wondering how much we'd heard.

We waited till Clanton's off-key voice repeated the question, "What's the idea?"

"The idea," Doug told him, "is that we were taking a walk when we heard talk in a shed. Talk about Rosa! About how you can't lift a finger against Bruno till Gomer takes care of Rosa! You oughta be ashamed of yourself, Cal, plotting against your own sister-in-law and sweet little brother!"

Clanton wasn't wearing a gun. Gomer's was in the ditch, so Doug put his own back in its holster.

I think Clanton guessed we were bluffing because his color came slowly back. "I haven't any brother," he said. "And I haven't the least interest in Rosa. It happens a mare of mine was stolen and I can't lift a finger against the thief till the mare's found. So I hired this man to find her."

It gave Doug a laugh. "And just to do that you sneaked off to a creekbank hideout?"

"After first sneaking out an alley door," I put in, "with a new hat!"

He looked me over from head to foot and his lip quivered. "You talk big, Shorty, with a gun on!"

So I took off my gunbelt and hung it on a wall nail. Then I edged toward him, half expecting to get what I'd got before. At the Sheridan House hitchrack he'd knocked me cold with a clip on the chin. "If I do it again," he predicted, "your pal here will gun me."

"I'd be tempted," Doug admitted. "So let's make everybody equal." He hung his gunbelt beside mine. Then he came over to stand elbow to elbow with me. "Take your pick, Harry, and I'll take what's left."

When I walked into Clanton's left it felt like a stone hammer. But I kept my feet. Next time I dived under it and got my head in his stomach. It bounced him back a little. Before I could get set the stone hammer banged into my chin again.

"Get under it, Harry," Doug urged, "and butt hell out of him. What's holding *you* up, Gomer?"

Gomer hugged his bullet-stung wrist. "If I had two hands I'd break your neck!" he swore.

Clanton didn't come at me. He just took off his jacket for a freer arm play and tossed it on a hay bale. Then he waited for me to bore in. When I tried it his reach was too long. His knuckles raked my cheek and drew blood. Again it was like stone rather than flesh. Then I saw the ring. It was a big heavy ring on a finger of his left hand. It had a pale red stone in it, like a signet—a square, pink stone with sharp edges. It slashed me every time I got close.

And naturally Doug couldn't help me. Two-timing a man wasn't his code. I'd picked Clanton and I had him; Gomer wouldn't fight. All Doug could do was keep one eye on Gomer while his other eye watched Clanton chop me down.

He hit me a dozen jolts and each time it was his left, the big, pink ring-stone smacking me like brass knucks. I felt the end coming so I made a last desperate dive, got inside his punch and clinched. I had two handfuls of his shirt when he bounced me back. The last thing I remembered was the rip as half his shirt came off in my hands.

I was out maybe a couple of minutes and then Doug was pouring cold water on me from his hat. When the stars cleared I saw we were alone in the shed. "How you feelin', fella?" Doug grinned as he swabbed my cut face.

"Like I let you down," I said. "Where did they go?"

"Home, I guess. Nothing I could do but let 'em walk out. But you didn't let me down, Harry. Fact is you did all right."

"Don't rub it in. The guy beat hell outa me and we both know it."

"He didn't tear off your shirt, like you did his."

"What's a shirt? He's got plenty more."

"You showed him up, Harry. He's got a scar on his chest. I got an eyeful when you tore off his shirt."

I blinked. "What kind of a scar?"

"A hot iron scar. The same kind cows wear. Only his is the shape on a dangling noose."

"A noose? Who put it there?"

Doug winked. "It's a cinch *he* didn't. I've heard tell of vigilantes doing that, though, when they warn a guy to leave the country. Looks like Cal wasn't popular on his last range."

When I mentioned the pink-stoned ring Doug said he'd noticed it too. "Clanton always wears that ring but this is the first time I took a good look at it. It's shaped like the pip on an Ace of Diamonds."

We buckled on our gunbelts and walked toward town. At Main and Grinnell we turned south and passed LaSalle's saloon. "But since he denies owning this dive," I puzzled, "why does he advertise himself with an Ace of Diamonds ring?"

It stumped Doug too. "Maybe Chuck Young knows," he brooded.

"Who's Chuck Young?"

"A bum who usually hangs out at the Cowboy Bar. But in his better days he had a job, remember?"

I remembered vaguely. "Didn't he use to be

night bartender at the Ace? The one LaSalle fired last winter?"

We went into the Cowboy Bar and found a bleary down-and-outer waiting for some generous customer to come along—the kind who'd stand treat to all present. Doug and I ordered drinks and then Doug beckoned for Chuck Young to join us. "What'll you have, Chuck?"

He came up, fawning. His eyes watered greedily as he ordered the same. "Let's take 'em to a table," Doug suggested.

At the table we let Chuck take a few sips. Then Doug said: "By the way, ever notice that big red solitaire ring of Cal Clanton's? Harry and I were arguing about it. He claims it's agate and I say moonstone. Which is it, Chuck?"

Chuck Young shook his head. "Search me. Calls it his luck ring, Cal does. Claims as long as he wears it the cards always fall his way."

Doug cocked an eyebrow. "That so? Didn't know he was that much of a gambler."

"He ain't now. But they say he used to be. Got his start on a Mississippi steamboat. I heard Martie tell Monk about it one time." Chuck drained his glass. His rheumy eyes looked at us hopefully and Doug ordered him another. "Yeh?" I prompted.

"On his last trip up the river, the way Martie tells it, Cal made a cleanup on one big pot. He drew one card to a King, Queen, Jack and Ten o'

Diamonds. And filled with the Ace! Made him a Royal and he cleaned up with it. So he figures it's his luck card. Had himself a ring made with a diamond-shaped stone."

"Gamblers are superstitious that way," I said. "He owns Martie's joint, don't he?"

"Not that I ever heard," Chuck said.

"Is Bruno his brother?"

"Search me."

"You know anything else about him?"

If the ex-bartender knew he wouldn't tell. As we left the place Doug said: "It's good enough for me, Harry. The whole set-up belongs to Clanton. LaSalle's just a front. Let's find Mike and bring him up to date."

We found Fallon in the IXL eating with the gaunt, Scotch deputy, Roy Malcolm. "Two more orders of the same," I said as we joined them.

Malcolm squinted at my bruised face. "Who beat you up, man?"

Doug answered for me. "We sort of broke even." When the waitress was out of hearing he gave details, being careful not to mention the threat hanging over Jim Hutton.

"Say that again, lad," Malcolm cut in when Doug told about the order given Gomer by Clanton.

Doug repeated the words. " 'Your job's to find her. Until she's found we can't lift a finger.' "

"Find who?" Mike Fallon asked.

"A stray mare, he claims. But I'll stake my saddle he means Rosa LeFevre. Looks like she knows too much. And she'll spill it if anything happens to Bruno. That way Bruno can laugh at Cal—he knows Cal can't lift a finger against him as long as Rosa stays out of reach."

Roy Malcolm looked thoughtful. I could see that for the first time he was beginning to doubt Clanton. "You ken that little schoolhouse at Beckton?" he asked suddenly.

"Sure," Doug said. "It's ten mile up the Goose and we pass it on the way to the ranch. What about it?"

"There's no school going on now," Malcolm said. "But when I looked in the other day I saw a fresh apple core and a crust of bread—and an empty paper bag."

"What's that got to do with Rosa?"

"The last seen of her," Malcolm reminded us, "was at nightfall of the day news came in of the gunfight at Big Horn City. She bought two sandwiches and an apple at a restaurant. Put them in a paper bag and disappeared."

"If she started up the creek afoot," Doug figured, "the Beckton schoolhouse would be about as far as she'd get that night."

We all agreed that ten miles would be a long tiring walk for a woman at night. "So she hid in the schoolhouse all the next day," I reasoned.

"When night came she went on again. Or maybe Bruno met her there with a horse."

"Aye," Malcolm said, "she ate her paper bag lunch there. She's hiding from someone, but I canno' believe it's Cal Clanton. LaSalle and Kincaid and Shonts, yes. But surely not Clanton."

His stubbornness rubbed me the wrong way. "Then why does Clanton sic Gomer on her?"

"He didn't mention her name, man."

Doug fixed a stare on the deputy. "You mean you still think he's on the level?"

"I'm beginning to have doots," he admitted uneasily. "But he's well thought of around here. We must be fair and not jump at conclusions. Maybe the shape of the scar is an accident. Or belike someone with a grudge put it there."

"You admit he looks like Bruno?"

"A little. But I canno' be sure."

Doug tried to be patient. "Look. Begin at the beginning. Clanton hit town two years ago in a cowskin coat. The same coat turns up later on a toughie named Gomer. Next we know of Gomer he's running fast from a train holdup with a boy who looks like Clanton. Then a letter from Gomer turns up in a dead man's pocket. It as good as says Clanton owns the Ace and is Rosa's brother-in-law. Before we can ask Rosa about it she runs away in the dark and hides. Clanton tells Gomer to find her. Top of all that . . ." Doug broke off suddenly and clamped his lips. Just in

217

time he remembered we didn't dare tell about Clanton writing letters to Ohio.

"Top of all what?" Mike Fallon broke in keenly. He looked searchingly at us. "Are you fellows holding back something?" Mike was a lot shrewder than Malcolm.

"There's a hatful of missing money," Doug said, covering up.

Malcolm smiled tolerantly. "Aye, lads, there is," he admitted. "You're likely right about Rosa making a midnight ride for cash loot hidden by Bruno. And about someone snatching it away from her on a dark walk. Someone like Kincaid or Shonts. But hardly Clanton. He's no man for a footpad job like that."

To change the subject I said, "Let's go see if Bruno's still posing on the porch."

Doug took the cue and we got out of there. At the bank corner we crossed diagonally to Conrad's. As we passed the big store I looked in and saw Monk Kincaid at a counter. He was pricing a rifle. At another counter a clerk was wrapping up cartridges for Shonts. "Get ready to duck," I said.

Doug grinned. "They wouldn't need that many shells just to snipe us from a gulch. Looks to me like they're stocking up for a long, slow fight."

We went on up the walk. At the entrance of Hickey and Weaver's feed and livery place we bumped into Martie LaSalle. He was just coming out. "You're in the wrong end of town, Martie," I said. "They don't sell poker chips up this way."

He gave a nervous laugh and looked a little scared. Like I might be referring to his gyp poker game with Hutton. "Okay," he said. "I'll try the drugstores." He moved on and we watched to see where he'd go. Kincaid and Shonts came out of Conrad's and joined him. Kincaid had a brand new rifle and Shonts a wrapped package. "They're loaded for bear, Doug," I said. The three went on toward the north end of town.

Doug looked curiously into Hickey and Weaver's. "Wonder what that buzzard wanted in there. I better go in and find out, Harry, while you check on Bruno."

When I got to the Sheridan House Bruno was no longer in the porch rocker. He wasn't in the lobby but I found him dawdling over a steak in the dining room. He gave me an impudent grin and I let it go at that.

Ten minutes later Doug met me at Dillon's barn. We on-saddled and rode for the ranch. A preoccupied look shadowed the sand and freckles of Doug's face. "They're going after the whole bunch, Harry."

"Whole bunch of what?"

"Hutton's heifers. All two thousand of 'em."

I cocked an eye at him. "You got somethin' new on it?"

"They figure on winterin' 'em," Doug said.

"That way they'll get a calf crop next spring and summer."

"What makes you think so?"

"What's the usual stockman's hay formula for winterin' cows?"

"Half a ton a head," I said.

"Okay. LaSalle just asked Hickey to price him a thousand tons of roughage in the stack, for November delivery."

"It figures," I said. "A thousand tons—two thousand cows."

CHAPTER XVII

AT THE RANCH we waited till after supper before starting to work on Hutton. He sat by the kitchen stove with an empty pipe in his mouth. Joan washed the dishes while Doug dried them.

"You've got to have a lawyer," I said after Johnny Beaver left us. Then I told about Mike Fallon quitting his county job to start a private practice. "Anything you tell your lawyer, Jim, is confidential. Like telling a priest."

"What good could he do me?" Hutton muttered.

"*Quien sabe*? But he's a lawyer and maybe he can build a backfire under Clanton. Anyway he could advise you what to do."

"What kind of a backfire?"

"In a way Clanton's being blackmailed himself. By his kid brother Bruno." I told the Huttons what we'd seen and done in town.

Doug summed it up. "Rosa's hiding out somewhere. It's a fair bet she knows things about Clanton—maybe just where and why he got branded by vigilantes. She'll tell the law if Clanton hurts Bruno. Meantime Bruno poses on Main Street. Our slant is he'll keep it up till Cal gives him back the money—plus interest, maybe. So Clanton can't lift a finger till he finds Rosa."

Joan stared at us, big-eyed and shocked. "You mean he'll kill her?"

"He isn't hunting her," I said, "just to play tiddly-winks."

"It only proves," Hutton said bitterly, "that he'll stop at nothing. I don't see how a lawyer can help any."

"Neither do I," Doug said. "But we got to try something."

"Doug's right, Dad," Joan decided. "We can't just sit here and wait." She turned to me. "You're sure we can trust Mr. Fallon?"

I was certain of it. In the end Hutton said: "We have to wait till the county accepts his resignation and he opens an office. That'll take two or three days. Meantime we got a clover stand to put up."

Three days hard work in the meadow at least served to make Hutton tired enough to sleep. But he was haggard and the ordeal was aging him fast. The whole thing looked futile. Even this long, fat haystack we put up. It was winter feed for cows which by then would be Clanton's. In fact Clanton could just as easily demand the hay itself, and the ranch to boot!

Hutton mowed and Johnny Beaver raked. Doug and I shocked, taking time off for a ride upcanyon to look at the heifers. The third day we worked fifteen hours with a hay rick and made the stack.

It was dark when we put up the teams. Doug and I went to the house to wash. Jim Hutton was the last to leave the barn and as he passed the well a voice hailed him from the dark. We waited for him but he didn't come.

Supper was getting cold and Joan said, "Won't you call him, please, Doug?"

Doug had to call twice before Jim showed up at the kitchen. His feet dragged. He sat down by the stove, gray, haggard and licked. Joan guessed right away what had happened. She went to her father and stood back of him, took his head between her hands. "Dad!" she said softly. He twisted to look up at her, his lips tight and grim. Then he let out a burst of bitterness, "If it wasn't for you, honey, I'd strap on a gun and walk into them."

"Who was it?" I asked. "LaSalle?"

"It was Kincaid," Jim told us. "Invited me to a stud game at the Ace. It'll give me a chance to get even, he said."

"And if you don't show up?"

"If I don't show up by noon tomorrow, and sit in with them, they sic the law on me. They'll spill the works if I try to duck out, or if I bring someone with me, or cross them in any way."

What I wanted to say made cotton in my

throat. It was the same with Doug and Joan. The kitchen clock gave slow loud ticks, like time was mocking us.

"How many cows do they want this time?" Doug asked.

"They didn't say. The whole bunch, maybe."

They'd be smarter, I thought, if they took only one or two hundred at a time. Because if in the end we accused them in court, their only defense would be to claim a series of voluntary, witnessed poker games. They'd want those games to sound convincing to a jury. So they might overreach themselves if they tried grabbing everything at one session.

"I got three choices," Hutton said dully. "I can disappear and leave Joan to face the music. Or I can stay and let them pick me clean. Or I can go back to Ohio and face the music myself."

Joan pleaded with him to choose number one—a fadeout to some new country.

"Never!" Hutton said doggedly. "I'm through running. Wherever I'd go, for me it'd be just another forbidden valley." He looked at me with his face contorted. "That's what they called this one, you said. A Forbidden Valley at the end of a Forbidden Trail! Every fort abandoned and burned! . . . For me it's still that way."

"You forget one thing," Doug said gently. "The ban didn't last forever. Only for ten years. Then it was lifted and the trail was opened wide."

It was my turn. "Look, Jim. Let's don't throw in our cards yet. Let Doug and me ride in to see Mike Fallon. He'll be ready to take his first case now."

"Please do," Joan begged.

Hutton gave a sigh. "Might as well. I'm at the end of my rope anyway. Tell him I'll be at his office at ten in the morning."

When it was all agreed, Doug and I went out and saddled up for Sheridan.

But as we rode out through the gate a thought stopped me. "Look, Doug. There's a chance Mike's over on Soldier Creek sparking Carrie Gordon. He's there about every other night, I hear. Suppose you ride on into town while I see if he's at the Gordons."

"If he is, bring him in. You'll find me at the Windsor."

Doug jogged on down the Goose while I turned north, riding steeply up to the divide between Goose and Soldier. It wasn't far to the Gordon place and from the ridge top I could see its lighted windows. I rode down to a pasture fence and went through a gate.

A dog barked when I got near the cabin. Likely the dog figured me for another beau coming to see Carrie. The cabin had a big cottonwood in the yard and was lighted back and front. Through a back window I saw Bruce Gordon sitting lonely by the kitchen stove with his pipe. The parlor shades were drawn and Carrie's light-hearted laugh told me she had a caller there.

A shame to drag Mike away from her, but it had to be done. I'd say it was an emergency. Lawyers were like doctors, I'd heard; they'd leave anything for a client in bad trouble.

I knocked at the front door and right away Carrie opened it. She looked pretty as a ripe peach and I couldn't blame Mike Fallon much. Only the man in the parlor wasn't Mike. He was Cal Clanton.

He was Clanton slicked up and looking plenty serious; like he knew right what he wanted here and her name was Carrie. He stood up when he saw me at the door. And Carrie smiled. "Hello there, Mr. Riley, come right in."

I had to think fast. I didn't dare mention Fallon in front of Clanton. Clanton of course knew all about Kincaid's call on Hutton, an hour ago; so if he caught me rushing right over here looking for a lawyer, especially one lately connected with the county prosecutor, he'd get the wind up right away.

"Just want to see your Pa, Miss Carrie," I said. "Is he in?"

Bruce Gordon himself heard me and came forward to the parlor. "Here I am, Riley. Come on back to the kitchen and I'll open up some cider."

"You know Cal Clanton, don't you?" Carrie said.

"We're old friends," Clanton said, smiling like a fox. "How goes it, Riley?"

"Not so good," I said, rubbing a hand over my still sore jaw. "Fact is I've been taking it on the chin lately. Let's see. Last time we met you were looking for a stray mare. Ever find her?"

"Not yet." The foxy smile faded and all at once he was on edge, wondering what I'd say next. So just to be mean I hung around a while, before letting Gordon take me to the kitchen.

"Where are the boys, Miss Carrie?" I asked.

"They're spending the night at the PK," she told me.

"I hear you figure on takin' a teacher's exam."

"That's right, Mr. Riley. If I pass I'll get the little school at Beckton."

"Joan says they let you see last year's questions. Do you know the highest mountain in Africa?"

She laughed. "That and lots else, Mr. Riley. 'I know the kings of England and can quote the fights historical, from Marathon to Waterloo in order categorical.' "

"Gosh!" I said. "That rhymes. Did you rhyme it on purpose?"

"No. But Gilbert and Sullivan did."

It went over my head. And Clanton's too. I kept him on pins and needles a while longer, him wondering if I'd slip out another hint about his looking for Rosa. Then I went on back to the kitchen stove with Bruce Gordon.

227

While he filled cups I said: "Just rode over to see if you'll need any help puttin' up your hay. We could lend you a mowing machine, if you want, and send Johnny Beaver over for a day or two."

"That's right neighborly," he said. "But the PK made the same offer and I took it."

I'd made my point, which was to give a reason for my call which didn't connect with Mike Fallon. By raising my voice I'd made sure of Clanton hearing me from the parlor. Now I could leave just as soon as I downed this cider.

Before I could finish it a rider loped up in front. We heard him dismount and knock. Likely it was some cowboy coming to make competition for Clanton. It might even be Mike Fallon.

Gordon gave me a half-wink and lowered his voice. "Only trouble with having a pretty daughter is you have to spend your evenings by the kitchen stove."

We heard Carrie open the front door. *"You?"* She let it out in a tone of surprise and shock.

That, and her failure to ask the visitor in, made me move a few steps so I could see into the parlor. Clanton was on his feet, his face reddening, and I could see he was a good deal more shocked than the girl. The man in the doorway was Bruno LeFevre!

Bruno with his hair cut and parted exactly like Clanton's. His hat and his jacket and his boots matched Clanton's; they made him look more than ever like a younger and slighter edition of Clanton. He smiled at Carrie and his voice had oil in it. "Excuse me. I'm taking a short cut to the Wheaton Ranch on upper Wolf Creek. Is there a gate at the top of your pasture? And do you mind if I cut through that way?"

He stood there polite as a lightning rod salesman, smooth as when Carrie had last seen him at the Powder River store. But what hit her hardest, and me too, was the fact that again he had his left arm in a sling. Just like it was broken, although of course it wasn't. His holster gun, I noticed, was a new and fancy one with a mother-of-pearl butt.

Carrie found her tongue. "You're quite welcome," she said, "to cut through our pasture."

"Thanks." Bruno's bow was like a Spanish cavalier's. Then he faded into the dark and we heard him lope off upcountry toward the Wolf Creek hills.

Bruce Gordon let me out the kitchen door and I took the opposite direction, toward Sheridan. *The sly little devil!* I thought. Bruno's call, of course, had been nothing but an act to plague Clanton. He'd picked the most embarrassing spot possible, with Clanton courting a girl. Deliberately he'd let the girl see them both at the same time, face to face. Bruno the outlaw and Clanton the gentleman rancher! He'd even faked the arm

229

sling to make sure she'd remember him.

All with Cal right back of her in the parlor, seething and wanting to wring Bruno's neck! "Please may I cut through your pasture?" It made me laugh. Outlaws like Bruno rode where they pleased. They never asked permission to cut through pastures. It was all a show to bait Clanton. Right now Clanton was burning up, his evening spoiled, sitting there with a girl's intelligent eyes searching him, and her wondering if after all he'd told her the truth about having no connection with Bruno.

One thing I could bet on. Bruno would keep at it. He'd keep plaguing Cal till Cal paid him off.

I angled across the ridge and struck the road at Beckton. From there I rode on down the Goose to meet Doug and Mike in Sheridan.

CHAPTER XVIII

I FOUND them in Fallon's room at the Windsor. Doug had already told Mike the sad tale of Jim Hutton. Mike made me go over it again. He sat puffing his pipe, his eyes clouded and his feet propped on the bed. "It's rotten!" he said. "A rotten deal clean through! Of course I'll take the case. You say Hutton's coming in to see me?"

"He's coming in," I said, "to play sitting duck at the Ace. It means his neck if he doesn't. Noon's the deadline. But at ten o'clock he'll slip up to your office for advice."

Mike knocked out his pipe. "I'll sleep on it. You fellows better be there too. Only don't come with Hutton. Slip up the back steps separately."

"Haven't you got any ideas?" I asked impatiently.

"What do you think I am? A magician? They've got Hutton over a barrel, all right. I could send LaSalle, Kincaid and Shonts to prison. But they'd take Hutton along with them. Even then we couldn't touch Clanton. Not with a ten foot pole."

We admitted there was nothing on Clanton. He

hadn't shown up at the shakedown. It's no crime to write letters to Ohio. "He just stays in the background," Doug said, "and pulls strings."

It was after midnight when Mike sent us to bed. In the morning we looked for him in the dining room but he wasn't there.

Cal Clanton was, though. He'd come in during the night and taken a room. His back was our way and all through breakfast he pretended not to see us. I was on my second stack of pancakes when Fallon looked in from the lobby. Then Mike went out to the street and turned north toward the IXL cafe.

I guessed why he hadn't joined us. "He'd rather not let Clanton see him in a huddle with us, Doug."

When we went outside we saw Bruno. He was across at the Sheridan House, again perched in his porch rocker and again looking like a cat sneaking up on a cream pan. We crossed over and I said to him, "Find your way through that pasture, Bruno?"

"No, I got lost in the dark." He grinned and drooped an eyelid. "So I gave my horse a loose rein and he brought me back to town."

Again I noticed the pearl-butted gun in his holster. There was no chance of prying anything out of him so we went on down the east walk to the bench in front of Conrad's store. From here we could watch the whole street. Pretty soon we saw Fallon leave the IXL, next to the bank, and walk a block north to Brundage Street. He crossed to the drugstore corner and disappeared up steps to the office floor. It was still an hour until his appointment with Hutton.

Editor Tom Cotton came along, fresh as the posey in his buttonhole, and turned at the Mills corner. His *Sheridan Post* print shop was in the back end of the Mills building, and opened on Brundage Street. And promptly at nine Mr. Alger passed our bench. He crossed to the Bank of Sheridan, where he was cashier, and opened it for the day. Doug gave me a nudge. "Look who's his first customer, Harry."

It was Cal Clanton. Clanton entered the bank less than a minute behind Alger. "What's on his mind?" Doug wondered. "Him riding in after midnight and Johnny-on-the-Spot when the bank opens! Stay here, Harry, while I go cash a check."

He angled over to the bank and went in. I knew he didn't have any check to cash. In less than two minutes he popped out again.

"Believe it or not," he reported, "that guy's drawing out money. A big wad of it, all in cash."

"How much?"

"Sixteen thousand, Harry."

I whistled. "Are you sure?"

"Dead sure. I heard Alger complain about shelling out that much without a warning. He started counting it out, though. Wonder what Cal wants with it!"

"It's double what he snatched away from Rosa," I remembered.

When Clanton came out of the bank he had a bulging dispatch case. The cashier must have loaned it to him to carry the money away in. "Hold your breath," I said, "till we see if he takes it to Bruno."

We watched Clanton walk south to the Windsor and turn in there. Across from it Bruno still posed in his porch rocker. "Guess again," Doug said.

But I could smell a pay-off. After last night's show at the Gordons', Clanton could be in a sweat to get rid of Bruno at any price. The price could be double indemnity—the snatched loot plus one hundred percent interest. "He wouldn't take it over there in broad daylight," I argued. "Not with us watching him."

Another half hour passed and Clanton didn't come out of the hotel.

"There comes Hutton," Doug said.

We saw him ride across Main Street toward the Dillon barn. Promptly at ten o'clock he reappeared on foot and went to the Brundage Street entrance of the Mills Building. He looked warily both ways before going up steps there.

Doug and I waited five minutes and then headed that way ourselves. At the top of the stairs a long narrow hall had the Masonic Lodge on one side and a row of offices on the other. At the front, in an office looking out on Main, we found Hutton telling his story to Mike Fallon.

Mike's law books hadn't come from Buffalo yet. Letters painted on the window pane, MICHAEL FALLON, LAWYER, were hardly dry. Doug and I sat on a packing box. Mike locked the door and went back to his desk, which was bare except for a tin can he used to knock out his pipe ashes. "Go right ahead, Mr. Hutton," he said.

Hutton told him what he'd told us, a few nights ago, on the well coping. Mike only interrupted once. That was when Hutton described the convict Dugan, who later had been recaptured at St. Louis and hanged in Ohio.

"You say Dugan was always bragging about how tough he was, about jobs he'd pulled, about policemen he'd beat up?"

"Yes. He always talked big like that."

"Go on."

When Hutton finished, Mike went to a window and stood staring down at the Main Street traffic. Time was ticking away. Only an hour was left before Kincaid's deadline at the Ace.

I was afraid Mike was as stymied as we were and that he'd let us down. When he turned back to us he said quietly: "Okay, Mr. Hutton. If you want my advice, here it is. First, meet their deadline and sit through their phoney poker game.

235

At the end of it they'll bring out a bill-of-sale for you to sign. If it's for more than a hundred heifers, don't sign it."

Hutton stared at him, confused. And Doug gave out with exactly what I wanted to say myself. "Hold on, Mike. Those guys play for keeps. The minute Jim says no, they crack their whip. He don't dare . . ."

"He doesn't dare say a total no," Fallon broke in. "But if he says yes to a hundred heifers and no to two hundred, they won't crack their whip. Why? Because they're realists and a hundred heifers are better than none. A week from now they can make him sign for another hundred. And so on till they clean him out. But the minute they sic the law on Hutton, they're through. Their power's spent. They get revenge but no more heifers."

"But that's just draggin' it out!" I objected.

"Exactly," Mike agreed. "At the rate of a hundred cows a week it'll take them four months to squeeze out Hutton's last drop of blood. Which gives us time."

"Time for what?"

"Time to work out two ideas I've got. A little idea and a big idea. The little one is Rosa LeFevre. We think she's hiding out and holding a whip of her own over Clanton. The whip's got such a sting that Clanton assigned Gomer to find and destroy her. So let's find her first."

"Finding her won't help," Doug said, "unless we can make her talk."

"We've got to try," Mike insisted. "Maybe she won't mind putting the skids under Clanton when we tell her about the murder order he gave Gomer in the shed. That stray mare skit may fool Roy Malcolm but it won't fool Rosa."

"Wonder what she could pin on him!" Doug brooded.

"Maybe she could tell us where and why vigilantes put a hanging noose on his chest. At the very least she can take away what he wants to keep most—his social standing in Sheridan." Mike smiled grimly as he filled a pipe and tamped it. "It goes up in a puff of smoke if people find out he's Bruno's brother and owns a dive like the Ace."

"Okay," I said. "We'll try to beat Gomer to Rosa. What's your other idea? The big one."

Mike held a match to his pipe. "It's for me to go to St. Louis and ask police there in what neighborhood Dugan was recaptured, six years ago."

We all three had confused stares. "Go on," I said.

"Dugan was there a month before they picked him up," Mike reminded us. "It was the month when Hutton worked on a levee in Omaha. We know Dugan was a braggart. Could he go a whole month, there in St. Louis, without shooting off his mouth? Maybe to impress a few underworld characters in some back-alley bar. He'd just beat up a cop, hadn't he? All by himself! A prison guard in Ohio."

Jim Hutton clutched at it, desperately, like it was a plank eddying toward him in a flood. "He was like that, always bragging . . ."

"If I can find someone he bragged to," Fallon said, "your troubles are over. Ohio won't convict you of a crime Dugan boasted of doing all by himself. At the worst you'd only have to serve out the last year of your manslaughter rap."

"I'd be willing to do that," Hutton said eagerly.

"I doubt if you'd have to," Mike said thoughtfully. "You were convicted of horse-whipping a horse-beater who happened to have a weak heart. Against that you've got a fine record of citizenship here in Wyoming. Where Tom Moonlight happens to be governor. And Tom Moonlight also happens to be an old cavalryman who loves horses and heartily dislikes horse-beaters. What the governor of Wyoming says to the governor of Ohio, when he sends along the extradition papers, can be awfully important in this case." Fallon stood up and his wide Irish grin seemed to light the whole dingy room. "So if I find a witness in St. Louis, we'll let Riley go to Cheyenne and have a talk with his old C.O., the governor."

"You make me feel a lot better," Hutton said.

Mike took his hand in a firm clasp. "We're with

you all the way. Doug, Harry and I. So at noon go on down to the Ace and play poker. With your chin up and your lip stiff. They want a game, you'll give it to 'em. Real poker—for stakes a lot higher than they think."

Doug and I put in the afternoon trying to get a lead on Rosa LeFevre. We covered every bar in town except the Ace. And both the livery barns. The only tip we got came from an OZ strayman who'd noticed smoke drifting from the chimney of a cabin that was supposed to be empty. But it was on Dutch Creek, east of town, and we knew Rosa had headed west because she'd holed up for a day at the Beckton schoolhouse. The OZ man promised to ride by the Dutch Creek cabin and take a closer look.

"Our best bet," Doug decided, "is to watch Bruno."

It made sense. Bruno was sure to know where his wife was hiding; most likely he'd taken her there himself from Beckton. "He might ride out to see her any dark night," I agreed. "Especially if Clanton pays him off." I couldn't forget that Clanton had drawn money from the bank.

Bruno had quit his porch rocker but was still at the Sheridan House. The clerk said he was in his room. Come nightfall we checked on his horse at the Hickey and Weaver barn. It was still there. "Let us know if he takes it out," Doug said

239

to the barnman. "We're bedding down over at the Windsor." The night man promised he would; it wouldn't trouble him much because it was only a few steps over to the hotel.

We'd seen nothing of Jim Hutton since noon when he'd gone down to LaSalle's place like a lamb to the slaughter. But we hardly expected him to get away from there before midnight. They'd kept him that late the other time. They could make their winnings look more convincing by having the game last all afternoon and half the night. We made sure Cal Clanton wasn't there. A dozen times between noon and midnight we saw him in the Windsor lobby.

"He's building an alibi," Doug guessed, "so he can swear he had nothing to do with what's going on down at the Ace."

We checked with Fallon right after supper. "When are you leaving for St. Louie, Mike?"

"On tomorrow's stage," he said, "unless something new crops up. I want to be here when Hutton reports on tonight's shakedown. Wake me when he comes in." He went up to his room and to bed, to be fresh for the twenty-six hour stage ride to Custer. After that he'd ride the cushions to St. Louis.

Doug and I went to our favorite lookout, the bench in front of Conrad's. From here we could see Hickey and Weaver's in case Bruno called for his horse. And we could spot Hutton when

240

he made his long sad walk from the north end.

Main Street went dark except at the saloons and hotels. By midnight the hitchracks were empty. A drunk reeled out of Zan's Place and fell off the sidewalk. He went to sleep right there in the dust.

Then we saw Hutton. He was walking slow, like an old man, and he got clear to the bank corner before we knew him. We crossed to meet him in front of Smith's drugstore. Doug laid a gentle hand on his shoulder. "How did they treat you, Jim?"

Hutton didn't need to answer. When he looked straight at us we saw a bruised and swollen face. "They beat you up?" Doug's voice cracked like brittle ice. He took out his forty-five and checked the loads. "There's a limit, Harry," he said in a choked voice. "And this is it. Let's go have it out with 'em."

"Please don't!" Hutton begged. "It'll mean my finish. Mine and Joan's. They've got a telegram all written out. If I stir up anything they'll send it to Ohio."

I was burning up, the same as Doug was, but I kept hold of myself. "How many cows did they want you to sign over, Jim?"

"Five hundred. But I said I'd sign only for a hundred and I wouldn't play with them again for a week. It made them mad."

"So they three-timed you? Kincaid, LaSalle and Shonts?"

"No. Only the big man in the cowhide coat. Gomer. He didn't play cards. He just stood by. He locked the door and hit me. He hit me four or five times."

"You gave in, then?"

"No. I did what Fallon advised. I said they could take a hundred cows or nothing. It was the stiffest bluff I ever made and it worked. When they saw I meant it, they made out a paper for a hundred cows and I signed it."

"What did they do then?"

"They said for me to keep my mouth shut. And come back in a week."

"Let's go tell Mike," Doug said.

CHAPTER XIX

WE ROUTED Mike out of bed and he listened to Hutton's report. "You've got guts," he said, and gave Jim a pat on the back.

He'd taken a room for Hutton and we made him go to sleep there.

Then Fallon began packing a bag to be ready for tomorrow's stage. "You work the St. Louis end," I said, "and leave Rosa to us. We've figured a way to find her."

"How?"

"By keeping an eye on Bruno. He's likely to join her. And the liveryman'll tip us when he takes his horse out of the barn."

It didn't occur to us that Bruno might leave town some other way than horseback.

After an early breakfast I crossed to the Sheridan House for a routine check. And got a jolt from the clerk there. "Bruno LeFevre? He's gone. Paid his bill and left about an hour after midnight."

I had a sold-out feeling as I joined Doug on the walk. We hustled half a block north to Hickey and Weaver's barn. The night man hadn't gone off duty yet. "Sure I seen him," he said when we asked about Bruno. "He came in with a suitcase 'bout a hour after midnight."

"You promised to let us know. Why didn't you?"

"I said I'd tip you if he took out his horse. But he didn't. He said he didn't need his horse any more. Or his saddle. He offered to sell 'em. Made the price so cheap I couldn't turn it down."

My mouth hung open. "You mean he left on foot, with a suitcase?"

"Yeh. All fancied up with a pearl-handled gun on his hip. He went out the back way and headed north up the alley."

We took off along that alley hoping to find sign that a mount had been waiting for Bruno somewhere in it. The alley passed back of Conrad's store and came out on Loucks Street. We crossed Loucks and kept on down the alley to Brundage. And there we ran into the town's other livery barn, Dillon's.

Then the truth popped at both of us and we lost no time getting over there. The day man had just come on duty. "Look at your tab book," I said to him, "and see if the night man did some business about half past one. See if he sold or rented a saddle horse."

The day man took a look at the office book. "Nobody took out a saddle horse," he said. "But a buggy outfit was rented at two A.M. It was

Bruno LeFevre and it says here he paid cash in advance."

I guess we looked like we'd been holding the bag at a snipe hunt. We walked back to Main and turned toward the hotel. The northbound stage was late this morning and hadn't gone through yet. So Mike Fallon was still in town. "Plain as the nose on your face," Doug said as we went into the Windsor lobby.

"It sure is," I agreed. "Bruno's drivin' to some hideout in the hills to pick up Rosa. Naturally he needs a buggy instead of a saddle horse to haul her away in—her and a suitcase full of duffle."

"Full of money, you mean!" Doug corrected. He gripped my arm and pointed. "Take a look."

Through the dining room archway I saw Clanton at breakfast. But Doug was pointing to a hat and a dispatch case on a lobby rack. It was the hat we'd seen Clanton buy at Leaverton's. And it was the dispatch case he'd borrowed yesterday at the bank.

Then the dispatch case had bulged with money. Now it was flat. The very carelessness with which he'd hung it unguarded on a lobby rack was proof that nothing of value was in it. Clanton had clearly left it there, with his hat, while he took breakfast.

"Like the nose on your face," Doug said again. "He pays off Bruno—and Bruno agrees to leave the country with Rosa."

Mike Fallon wasn't at the hotel. So we went down the street looking for him. As we passed Conrad's I noticed Shag Shannon sitting on the bench there. Shag didn't get in very often, being usually out on the road with a freight outfit. Sight of him made something tug at a corner of my mind. Last time I'd run into him was the night of the Governor's ball. The night I'd talked to Rosa on that same bench. Then Shag Shannon had come along and I'd asked him about her. "Wait a minute, Doug," I said.

I joined Shannon at the bench. "Right where I saw you the last time, Shag. Remember?"

"That's right, Harry." He grinned through his tobacco-stained beard.

"You told me somethin' about that singer down at the Ace. Rosa. You said she had some good in her, under the skin, because one time she took a runaway kid back to her folks."

"She did that, Harry. A slip of a country kid who got to hankerin' for the bright lights of Sheridan. Rosa slapped her in a buggy and drove her home."

"You say the kid has folks? Who are they?"

"Old couple by the name of Stacey. Her grand-parents, I reckon. You know that sawmill at the top o' Hurlburt Crik? It's shut down this season but Old Man Stacey stays there as caretaker. What's your rush, fella?"

I hurried back to Doug. A few quick words

with him and he was off to get our horses. I kept on looking for Mike Fallon and found him eating breakfast at the IXL. "Stage is late," he said. "So I can take my time."

"We can't take ours, Mike. We got to make a fast ride to Hurlburt Creek." When I told him about the Staceys he caught the idea right away.

"They'd be grateful to Rosa," he agreed. "Grateful enough to let her hide out there, later."

"So we're on our way, Mike, with Bruno seven hours ahead of us in a buggy." I told him about Bruno slipping out of town after midnight and about Clanton's flat dispatch case.

"I guess I'd better stick here a day longer," Fallon decided, "and catch tomorrow's stage instead of today's. If you're right I might get a chance to question Rosa."

"Bruno'll beat us to her," I said. "But in a buggy he can't very well leave the trail so we ought to meet him coming back. Maybe Rosa won't talk, now that Bruno's been paid off. But we know she hates Clanton. '*Sin verguenza*,' she calls him."

Doug came with the horses. Presently we were loping out of town, taking off up the Little Goose on the southbound stage road. It was the most direct route to Hurlburt Creek, which came into the Little Goose a few miles above Big Horn City. "If they're smart," Doug said, "they'll wait till dark before trying to leave this range in a buggy. Guys like Shonts and Gomer could be laying for them, to grab back that sixteen thousand dollars."

We made the eight miles to Big Horn in an even hour. At Sackett's barn we asked if a buggy had passed upcreek during the night. "Night's my sleepin' time," the barnman said. "But Nate Trumbo might know."

We looked up Trumbo, who was night man at the stage station. He nodded. "Yeh, a one-hoss rig went through just before daylight. It headed upcrik."

"Thanks." We changed to fresh horses and pressed on. Here the stage road turned southeast toward Banner. Our own route kept to the Little Goose and was now a dusty ranch trail too well-travelled to show separate tire tracks. Three miles of this took us to the mouth of Hurlburt Creek. Up Hurlburt we followed deep ruts made by lumber hauling from the sawmill. But there'd been very little recent travel so it wasn't hard to spot the fresh tracks of a one-horse buggy.

"They go both ways," Doug said.

"Looks like he's come and gone," I said, noting a shod hoofprint pointing downcanyon. "But why didn't we meet him on the road?"

It wasn't a long creek and before noon we were in pine timber at the top of it. A sawmill there still had its machinery but was shut down. In the caretaker's cabin we found only an old lady.

Doug tipped his hat. "We're lookin' for Rosa LeFevre, ma'am."

She eyed us cautiously. "Do you mean any harm by her?"

"No ma'am. We mean good by her. Who else lives here besides you?"

"Only my husband and our granddaughter. They're off in the woods berryin'."

"Rosa left here about daybreak, didn't she, in a buggy?"

The old lady looked steadily at Doug's frank young face and decided she could trust him. "Yes. A man came in a buggy. He was the same man who brought her here one night. Only then they were horseback."

"Which way did they go?"

"In a buggy, there's only one way you *can* go. Right back down the creek."

"What did the man say?"

"He said, 'We're getting out, Rosa.' Then he whispered something to her and she looked happy about it. The sun was just coming up when they drove away."

We rode back down Hurlburt Creek, wondering why we hadn't met them on the trail. At the fork of the Little Goose we lost the tire tracks in the dust of the road. Between here and Big Horn City the valley widened, the hills falling away on both sides. The buggy might have turned off almost anywhere. We inquired at three ranches: Ollie Hanna's, the Bard place and Jack Willet's Open 8. No one had seen Bruno's buggy.

At sunset we gave up and rode on into Sheridan. After putting up our horses we went looking for Mike Fallon. He wasn't at the Windsor. But Clanton was in the lobby there. Jim Hutton had checked out and gone home to the H Bar.

Clanton looked over his newspaper and met our eyes. "Our boss had some hard luck," I said. "He lost some cows in a card game. Hear about it?"

"No," he said, and there was a smugness about him which he hadn't had yesterday. Like things were breaking just right for him. I saw him saunter into the dining room and kid the waitress who took his order.

Doug noticed it, too. "By rights he ought to have a grouch on, Harry," Doug said as we went upstairs. "On two counts. Hutton bluffed the ante down from five hundred to a hundred cows; and Bruno, if we've doped it out right, made him cough up sixteen thousand dollars."

We washed the dust off our faces and took a walk down Main. We found Mike in Mills's drugstore. He was looking at a stagecoach schedule on the wall by the post office wicket. It showed that the north and southbound stages were scheduled to meet at Sheridan, at seven every morning. Trouble was they were likely to be from one to five hours late. This morning the southbound stage had been on time, but the northbound hadn't pulled in till noon.

"They flew the coop," we told Mike.

Over supper at the American Restaurant we gave him details. My own hunch was that the LeFevres were still in the county and had merely changed hideouts. But Doug didn't think so. "Bruno wouldn't sell his bronc and saddle if he aimed to stay here. My guess is they're heading for some place like Rawlins or Miles City." He mentioned those two towns because often they were called the "Cowboy Capitals of the West." One lay southwest in Wyoming and the other northeast in Montana. Either would make a good hunting ground for the talents of Bruno and Rosa LeFevre.

"We've lost them," Fallon decided. "So in the morning I'll catch the stage north. Soon as both stages are in, you fellows better call for the mail and then hit for the ranch."

The mail he meant was a possible letter from Bob Otis of Lander.

On our way back to the hotel I glanced into Mills' window and saw Martie LaSalle. He was looking at the stagecoach schedule posted on the wall. "Maybe he wants to meet one of the stages tomorrow," I said, nudging Doug. "Might be some new singer he's bringing in to take the place of Rosa."

We thought no more about it and went on to the Windsor. Clanton had finished supper and was playing solitaire in the lobby. It was something I'd never seen him do before. Then he did something else which wasn't like him. At the desk the clerk was telling a customer that every room was taken. It was Dave Dunnick of the Flying E. "Unless we can find someone willing to double up, Dave, you'll have to try somewhere else."

"He can double up with me," Clanton offered, looking up from his cards.

It was arranged that way. "Gettin' big-hearted!" Doug whispered. "Offerin' to sleep double."

All I could figure was that Clanton could be afraid of somebody. Maybe he'd double-crossed someone and didn't want a knife in his back. Which he might get if he slept alone. But he wouldn't be bothered if he had a husky roommate like Dunnick.

In the morning the northbound stage was on time. While it changed horses, the driver and his passengers came into the Windsor for breakfast. Mike, Doug and I had just finished ours. Mike's bag was out on the sidewalk ready to be loaded on the stage.

"I'll wire you," he promised us, "if I have any luck at St. Louis."

Just then the southbound stage pulled up in front. The driver came in alone for breakfast. "Where's your passengers?" a waitress asked him.

"I brought in three," Driver Bill Warshaw told her. "But they're Sheridan folks so they went

252

right home. Means I'll pull outa here empty, I guess."

Chug Downs, the northbound driver, was at the next table. "You won't be empty long, Bill," he said. "As I changed teams at Banner they was a couple waitin' there to board you. They're goin' clean through to Douglas."

"Anybody I know?" Bill asked idly.

"Maybe. Man and a girl. The girl looks kinda like a singer I seen one time down at the Ace o' Diamonds."

We were all ears. Banner was the next team-changing stop south of Big Horn City. It was just a piece this side of Massacre Hill. Mike looked at us and we both nodded. Bruno and Rosa! By cutting due east from the mouth of Hurlburt Creek Bruno could drive his buggy directly to the Terrill ranch at Banner. And by catching a southbound stage there he'd miss going through both Big Horn and Sheridan.

Mike stepped over to Chug Downs' table. "How do you know they're going clear through to Douglas?" Douglas, thirty-seven hours south by stage, was end-of-rails for the Fremont, Elk-horn and Missouri Valley Railroad.

"Because while I was changin' teams," Chug said, "they asked how good a connection the stage made for Omaha. I told 'em they'll pull into Douglas tomorrow evening and get a train east at 9.15 the next mornin'."

"Thanks." Mike beckoned and we followed him outside. Todd Swain was on the sidewalk, inspecting the two Concord coaches standing in front. Swain was Sheridan agent for the Northwestern Stage Company.

"Change my ticket," Mike said to him, "and make it read to Douglas instead of to Custer."

"Cost you ten bucks more," Swain said.

Mike paid him the ten dollars and the ticket was changed. Then he drew us aside. "Looks like I won't be lonesome, fellas."

"You sure won't," I said. "You're due for a long, cozy ride with Bruno and Rosa."

CHAPTER XX

SOON the two big Concords pulled out, one bound for Montana, the other for Big Horn City, Banner, Buffalo and points south. Doug and I stood on the walk and waved goodbye to Fallon.

"It's a break," Doug said. "After he rides all day and all night and all day tomorrow with the LeFevres, he oughta know plenty."

"And clear to Omaha on a train with 'em," I added.

We went to Dillon's for our horses and then stopped at the post office for mail. We had to stand around till it was sorted. The only letter was for Doug McLaren.

His face fell as he read it. "It's from Bob Otis at Lander, Harry. He says Clanton put the screws on him one time, just like we thought. But he says he'd rather not testify in court about it."

"Why?"

"Says he's about to marry a Lander girl. He's told her about a mistake he made one time, but her folks don't know it yet. And he'd rather they wouldn't."

We rode up to the Windsor to check out. As we

paid our bill Cal Clanton came out of the dining room and bought a cigar at the desk. "Thanks for letting me double you up," the clerk said. "Will you be needing the room again tonight?"

"Yes," Clanton said shortly. He sat down and began laying out solitaire again.

As we went out and got on our horses, I noticed an alert look growing on Doug's face. We rode a block to Loucks Street and I started to turn left for the ranch. But Doug stopped me. "Wait here a minute, Harry, while I check something."

Without explaining why, he loped another block down Main and disappeared back of the Ace of Diamonds. In ten minutes he rejoined me looking more alert than ever.

"We're suckers, Harry."

"Yeh? What did we overlook?"

"Think. Why does Clanton keep hanging around town? Playing cards in a public lobby. Sleeping with a reliable witness like Dunnick. Keeping right where he can be seen every minute."

"I'll bite. Why does he?"

"For an alibi. He's building an airtight one. Means something's on tap; a killing, likely. Last night we saw Martie LaSalle checking the stage schedule, remember? Just now I looked in the horse shed back of the Ace. Kincaid, Shonts and Gomer keep their broncs there. But right now the shed's empty."

I thought of something else; the smug look on

Clanton's face. Which wasn't quite natural after Bruno had made him pony up sixteen thousand dollars.

Not unless he expected to get it back!

"Let's go, Doug," I said. And off we went not up the Big Goose toward home but up the Little Goose in the wake of the southbound stage.

"How much start's it got on us?" Doug worried. He meant a stagecoach with Fallon aboard—the one due to pick up the LeFevres at Banner.

"A good half hour," I estimated. "It'll be pretty near to Buffalo before we can catch up."

Doug thought we could do better than that. Buffalo was the fourth stage station out of Sheridan. The first three in order were Big Horn City, the Terrill ranch at Banner, and Miller's at Lake DeSmet.

"They can shoot up the stage," Doug said, "and make sure the LeFevres don't do any talking."

"It'd cost 'em only two slugs," I said. "One for Bruno and one for Rosa. While they're at it they can grab back the money."

"And Clanton with a sweet alibi! Is that a buggy coming?"

A one-horse buggy met us and we stopped it. The driver was a teen-age Mexican who was chore-boy at Terrill's ranch. "That a Dillon rig?" Doug asked him.

The boy smiled lazily. "It is, señor. Do you have a cigaret?"

I tossed him the makings. "Bruno LeFevre told you to take it in, huh?"

"I do not know his name, señor. He arrives at dark with his wife and they stay all night with us. This morning they wait for a stage. And they give me a peso if I return their buggy to Sheridan."

"Where was the stage when you passed it?"

"As I pass, she is changing horses at Big Horn."

We rode on, certain now that the passengers waiting at Banner were the LeFevres. Which meant there'd be no attack this side of Banner. "The best place to pull it," Doug brooded, "would be at the Big Piney crossing. They'd have plenty of brush cover there."

A lump weighed on my stomach as I thought of Mike Fallon. A volley into the stage-coach, aimed at the LeFevres, could also mow down Fallon. "We're as dumb as Dumb George," Doug said bitterly, "for not figuring it in time."

A mile short of Big Horn City we left the stage road and forded the Little Goose on a bee-line short cut for Banner. A low gap beyond the Little Goose let us into Cruse Creek. This put us on the original Bozeman Trail as it was routed before Sheridan and Big Horn existed. There were a dozen deep ruts left by the old trail wagons and we followed them to the west fork of Meade Creek. Here the present stage road swung in to meet us again. We'd gained maybe ten minutes.

"If we catch up before anything happens," I said, "we'd better ride escort clean into Buffalo. We can let Sheriff Snider take over there." When we told Snider that a stage passenger had a bag of cash, and that three outlaws might be laying for it, he'd either hold Bruno for questioning or provide the stage with an escort to the south line of Johnson County.

After fording Pomp Creek the trail led between a butte and a pond on Terrill's ranch. And just beyond we pulled up at the stage station known as Banner. A hostler was loafing on the corral fence. "How far ahead is Bill Warshaw?" I asked him.

"Bill pulled out fifteen-twenty minutes ago," the man said.

"Did he pick up a man and a woman?"

"Yeh. A good-lookin' dame and the guy with her wears a pearl-butted gun. Whatsamatter? Anything wrong?"

"Plenty," Doug said. Time was too precious for talk so we pushed on, keeping to a lope till our mounts began blowing. We hit the head of Prairie Dog Creek and from there the trail climbed toward a divide between the Tongue and Powder River watersheds. The ruins of old Fort Phil Kearny lay just beyond that divide, on the bank of Little Piney.

Far ahead I glimpsed the stage. It was just disappearing over the crest. The grade slowed us to a walk. You don't get anywhere running a horse uphill. Doug looped a leg around his saddlehorn and made a cigaret. His eyes narrowed as he looked at the summit ahead. "What was it they used to call it, Harry? I mean before they began calling it Massacre Hill."

"Lodge Pole Ridge," I said.

"It was a kind of a deadline, wasn't it, that day?"

I knew the day he meant, and nodded. "Captain Fetterman had orders not to go beyond it. As he rode out of the fort the colonel said to him, 'Stay on this side of Lodge Pole Ridge, Captain.' But Fetterman had eighty men and I guess he felt like he could lick all the Sioux in Wyoming. So he rode right over the brow of that ridge we see ahead of us—and Red Cloud jumped him with four thousand warriors."

"It was the year I was born," Doug said. "I read about it in a book. It said what happened only happened two other times in U.S. history. Not a single survivor."

"Nary a one," I said. "Just like at the Alamo and at Custer's stand on the Little Big Horn. Fetterman and his eighty men lay dead and scalped, when the colonel found 'em next day. So now we call it Massacre Hill."

"Listen!" Doug cupped a hand to an ear.

Then I heard it too. Put, put! Put—put! Distant rifle shots. The sounds came from beyond the brow of the ridge. Right about where the stage would be now.

We slashed flesh with spurs and went racing up the grade. We had to get there, and fast, even at the risk of killing our mounts. It was a good two miles, mostly upgrade, and we wouldn't have heard the shots if the wind hadn't been right.

"The stage! They've cut loose on it, Harry." Doug snatched a carbine from his saddle boot and we pounded on, stirrup to stirrup.

It was the longest two miles I ever rode and just before the end of it my horse played out. As we topped the crest he went quivering to his knees. Doug's horse lasted forty jumps further, but to save it he had to get off and run afoot toward the stage. I ran after him, carbine cocked, but there was nothing to shoot at. The raid was over and the raiders were gone.

The stage was turned crosswise of the road, the four horses wild-eyed and trembling. The off lead horse had reared and come down astraddle its trace chain. Bill Warshaw was twisted around, face down on the driver's seat, his reins loose. The coach itself was still as a grave.

Doug got there half a minute ahead of me. When he looked inside his face took the color of a quarry stone. "Mike!" he said hoarsely. "Did you see them, Mike?"

Mike Fallon didn't answer. When I looked in I thought he was done for. He was on the back seat, his bloody head against the canvas wall of the coach. The two on the opposite seat had toppled toward each other, Rosa's arms clutching Bruno. There was a red hole at her temple and the same quick death had found Bruno.

But Fallon had life in him. "Take a look at the driver," Doug said. He opened the stage door to examine Mike.

I climbed a forewheel and right away saw nothing could be done for Bill Warshaw. A rifle bullet had drilled him heart high. Massacre Hill! After twenty-one years it had happened again— at the same place. I tried to cuss but it was like chewing dry cotton. I stared up a ravine which took off westerly from the road. A cabin-size rock there was the only cover from which killers could fire without being seen. "I'll see which way they went, Doug." It sounded foolish and futile, with me on foot and Mike sure to die unless we got him to town quick.

Bruno's suitcase had been snatched from the baggage boot and lay open in the road. It meant they'd gotten back the sixteen thousand dollars. "They took his gun, too," Doug said.

I walked to the big rock and sign there was plain. Three horsemen had waited under cover and nine empty rifle shells lay on the ground. No arrows this time, I thought crazily. Nobody scalped. Just a nice civilized massacre of whites by whites.

I went back down the road to Doug's horse. He stood head down, blowing, in no shape to be ridden faster than a walk. I led him to the big rock and mounted. At a snail's creep I followed the hoofmarks of killers. Doug's hollow voice yelled after me. "I'll take 'em to Banner, Harry."

Looking back I saw he'd righted the trace chains and was on the driver's seat. He turned the outfit to head north and began driving back toward Terrill's.

The sign took me to a bend in the draw and from there to the backbone of a ridge. Lodge Trail Ridge! Fetterman's deadline. From it I looked south across the cottonwoods of Piney Creek to the ruins of old Fort Phil Kearny, only a few miles away. The same fatal few miles up which Fetterman had taken his last ride.

From there the sign veered north and dropped into a swale at the head of Prairie Dog Creek where a bunch of Murphy Brothers cows were feeding. The creek wasn't bigger than a man's leg and there was a salting trough right where the killers had crossed. Then on over another rise with me walking and leading my spent horse; then down into another swale where cattle were grazing. Nelson Story's stuff, this time.

On a fork of Meade Creek the sign led me into a bunch of Open 8 range mares and from there on the trailing got tough. It looked like the killers had scattered—one to the right, one to the left, one straight ahead.

I followed the one straight ahead in the direction of Big Horn. At no place could I move faster than a walk. I figured Doug would have the stage at Terrill's by now. Men there would be sent to help. Some would take this same trail with fresh horses. Others would go for a doctor and a sheriff.

The sign of one horseman took me to brush along the Little Goose. A ranch road ran along the creek—the one we'd followed yesterday to the mouth of Hurlburt. It was a dusty, hoof-pocked road and I lost my sign there. I went one way, decided I was wrong, turned back and ran into two men from Terrill's. "Leave it to us, Riley," one of them said. "Doug wants you to meet him at Bard's in Big Horn."

CHAPTER XXI

I GOT into Big Horn and left my horse at Sackett's barn. A crowd was in front of Skinner's store and they had fifty questions. But most of them knew as much as I did. The story had spread here from Banner.

Bard's hotel was right across from Skinner's and I found Doug in a ground floor room with Mike Fallon. A Terrill buckboard had brought Mike here. Bert Bundy, the local doctor, had treated Mike's wounds and put him to sleep. "We sent to Sheridan for Kueny," Doug said.

"How bad is it?" I asked.

"Not as bad as we thought, Harry. He was hit twice—but not hard. A hole through his arm and a crease down his scalp. Lay him up about two weeks, Bundy says."

We went into the dining room for supper. "That means we got to wait two weeks," I gloomed, "before he makes the trip to St. Louie."

Doug shrugged. "No help for it, Harry, unless you go yourself."

I didn't feel up to it. Sleuthing around a big city wasn't my line. Nor Doug McLaren's. Especially

265

since we couldn't ask police to help us. Hutton's secret couldn't go an inch further than just the three of us—Mike, Doug and myself.

We couldn't even tell Roy Malcolm, who'd be showing up pretty soon with Doctor Kueny. All we could tell Malcolm was about Clanton paying off Bruno—and then sending the Ace gang to grab the money back. And that was just a suspicion we couldn't prove.

Horsemen drew up as we finished eating. Malcolm came in with Kueny at his heels. We left the doctor in Mike's room and went out on the porch with Malcolm. There we explained why we'd chased the stage in a try to head off what had happened.

A messenger from Terrill's had already told Malcolm about the raid itself. "So I checked on Clanton," the deputy said grimly. "He's at the Windsor and hasn't left there for twenty-four hours."

"To make sure you'd know it," I fired back, "he even slept with Dave Dunnick last night."

My charge of a planned alibi disturbed but didn't convince Malcolm. He was still willing to swear by Clanton. "LaSalle," he admitted, "is a duck of another color. I checked at the Ace and found him at the bar with Kincaid, Gomer and Shonts. Been there all day, they say, except for a nap they took upstairs."

"Why didn't you look in the shed?" Doug

266

argued. "You'd've found sweaty saddle blankets and hard-run broncs."

"I *did* look in the shed. And you're wrong, lad. The saddle gear was dry. So were the horses. They hadn't come on a hard run from Massacre Hill."

"They turned their broncs loose," Doug guessed, "and put fresh ones in the shed to fool people. And dry blankets."

"Aye, perhaps they did. But we've no proof of it."

We went in to Mike Fallon. He was awake and in no great pain. Malcolm had only one question. "Did you see the killers, lad?"

Mike shook his head. "Something burned down my scalp," he said weakly. "Next I knew I was riding the wrong way—back toward Banner."

"I have to meet Sheriff Snider there," Malcolm said. "He's on the way from Buffalo with the coroner."

Kueny stayed all night with us. In the morning he consulted with Bert Bundy. They decided we could take Mike into Sheridan after another day of rest here. "Or you could take him home with you to the H Bar, if you had anyone to look after him."

When Kueny was gone Doug and I talked it over. "Mike's a lawyer and Hutton needs his advice," Doug said. "Why not featherbed a spring wagon and haul him to the ranch?"

"He'd have four nurses," I said. "Us and Jim and Joan."

We knew the Huttons would welcome Mike. He'd been shot while on an errand in their service. So I went to Sackett's barn to see about a spring wagon for day after tomorrow.

When the day came I drove it slowly toward Beckton. Not on the stage road, which went around through Sheridan, but along the old original Bozeman Trail which cuts straight from Big Horn on the Little Goose to Beckton on the Big.

Mike lay on a feather mattress and I tried hard not to jolt him. Ruts were deep and it wasn't easy. Many a cavalry cart had passed here in the early days, hauling supplies to Fort C. F. Smith in Montana. As we crossed Beaver Creek, we stopped to rest at the Menor cabin on the shady bank there.

The roughest spot was Jackson Creek where there was no bridge. Beyond that we passed Tony Yentzer's place and then the tall mill on the near bank of the Big Goose. The mill wasn't running and everything was as quiet as noon in dog days. Upcreek a little way I saw the schoolhouse where Carrie Gordon hoped to teach next winter.

Then I crossed the Goose on a log bridge and hit the Sheridan-Beckton road. Doug was waiting for me there. He'd ridden ahead on his own horse, leading mine. A Terrill hand had picked up our horses and brought them to Sackett's barn. A rest and a feed had put them in shape again.

At the Beck ranch we left the county road and kept on upvalley along the trail which served the Hutton place and Clanton's. I saw a man on foot ahead of us and Doug said: "He looks big as a mountain. Is that a Jersey cow he's wrangling?"

It was Dumb George walking behind a milch cow, hazing her homeward with a stick. He milked her morning and evening, turning her loose by day to graze along the creek. Sometimes she strayed as far downcreek as the school.

We caught up just as the giant halfwit got his cow to the Clanton gate. There he turned to gape curiously at our makeshift ambulance. "Is he sick?" the man asked.

I nodded. "He bumped into a couple of bullets, George."

"A fight with guns? Where does it happen?" Dumb George had clearly heard nothing about the stage killings. He was too simple and direct to try fooling anyone.

"Someone shot up a stagecoach," I said, "and our friend happened to be riding it. How's things at your place? Clanton home yet?"

"He came home last night," George said. He drove his cow through the gate while we kept outside the fence in order to follow the trail around the Clanton meadow. "He hasn't heard a thing," Doug said.

"And why should he?" I said. "He can't read or write. So newspapers mean nothing to him. He never goes to town. He hardly ever talks to anyone except Clanton. And Clanton's not likely to talk about what happened to the stage."

"Just like a big ox," Doug said. "Or like a big dumb watch dog ready to bark or bite if you get funny with Cal Clanton."

We got past the Clanton ranch and went through Hutton's lower gate. Joan was drawing water at the well when she saw us. She set the dripping bucket on the coping and ran toward us. One look at our passenger and she called to her father. "Hurry, Dad. They've brought Mr. Fallon and he's badly hurt!" Mike waved her away and got out of the wagon on his own power. He'd lost a lot of blood and had to hang on to Doug for balance. "Nobody's going to coddle me," he said.

When we got him to the house he insisted he was going to bed down in the bunkshack with Harry and me and that he was perfectly able to take care of himself. Jim Hutton came out, his face still showing bruises. "We heard all about it, Mike," he said.

Joan looked at Doug and said gratefully: "I'm glad you brought him home with you. Now I can help. Now I won't feel so useless."

Doug took Mike's right arm and steered him

toward the bunkhouse door. The left arm was in a sling and Doug quipped: "Looks kind of like Bruno. Let's tuck him in, Harry."

Hutton followed us inside with something on his mind. He let us in on it after we got Mike in bed. "Joan doesn't know they worked on me," he told us, touching his black-and-blue chin.

"What did you tell her?"

"The truth except about Gomer slugging me. I said there was a fight in the barroom and someone threw a bottle."

We could understand why he didn't want Joan to know. In five days he had another date at the Ace. "You better figure out something else to tell her next time," Doug advised. "The flying bottle story won't work twice."

Just thinking about it made me boil. "Look, Doug," I said, "why don't we have a heart-to-heart talk with Gomer? We can say if he lays a finger on Jim, we nail his hide to the barn."

Doug was willing enough. But Jim vetoed it. And Mike, from the bunk, backed him up. They were right. A play like that would let out that Hutton had told us about the blackmail. And they'd sworn to blow the lid off if he told anyone at all.

We made Mike comfortable and went out to unhitch. Johnny Beaver rode into the corral and told us the heifers were doing fine. He'd been up to the forks looking them over. "Tomorrow,"

Hutton said to him, "you can take this rig back to Big Horn."

"Have they caught the outlaws?" the boy asked.

"Not yet," Doug said, adding curiously, "Who told *you* about it?"

Hutton answered for him. "One of the PK men came by. I guess everybody in the county knows about it by now."

"Everybody but Dumb George," I said.

In the morning Doug and I jogged up to the forks and things looked good there. I don't think I ever saw a more contented bunch of cows. "They're puttin' on tallow," Doug said. The feed was dewlap-high and pretty soon would be coming to a head, like grain.

Everything was peaceful as Sunday morning. The Goose made sweet music and birds chirped in the brush. Two hundred of these cows belonged to Cal Clanton, held in proxy for him by LaSalle. In a few days he'd take title to a hundred more. In the end, unless Fallon pulled something out of a hat in St. Louis, he'd get all of them. But no one from the Clanton gang came to look the stock over. At least not today.

"Why should they?" I brooded. "They've got us to do the herding and it don't cost 'em a cent."

"Suppose they showed up right now," Doug said, "and wanted to cut out their stuff. Which two hundred would we let them take?"

I saw what he meant. Milk has its cream and so does a bunch of cattle. "They'd want their pick," I said. "And when they began cuttin' 'em out I'd go for my gun."

Doug shook his head sadly. "No you wouldn't, Harry. You'd just sit on your tail and let 'em drive off the biggest, sleekest, curliest-maned ballies in the bunch. You'd chew your tongue off, cussin' 'em out. But you wouldn't fire a shot."

When I thought it over I knew he was right. Whatever happened, we didn't dare do anything that could make them crack down on Hutton.

We rode home and learned that a visitor had called at the bunkhouse. One look at Mike told us that much. He'd done a one-handed shaving job and was propped up in bed, whistling like a spring robin. "Only two things could cheer you up like that," Doug surmised. "Either Clanton dropped dead or Carrie Gordon dropped *in.*"

"Clanton didn't drop dead," Mike said, grinning.

"Did Carrie bring this?" I asked. Some late magazines lay nearby.

"She thought I'd need something to read," Mike said.

"And something to smell," Doug added. Wild flowers in a vase hadn't been there this morning.

"And something to eat," I complained. A plate had crumbs of chocolate cake. "Why didn't somebody shoot *me* up?"

"Did she say Clanton's still buzzing around?" Doug asked.

"We didn't talk about Clanton. And she could only stay a minute. Had to get back home and study for that exam."

The Huttons, by contrast, were tense and uneasy when we met them at supper. The days were slipping by, bringing nearer Jim's next date with LaSalle. When Johnny Beaver left us Joan asked nervously: "Do you think he'll come out here again? Like he did last time?"

"No reason he should," Hutton said. "He made it plain enough when I'm to show up. I promised I would. And if I don't . . ." He broke off with a helpless gesture.

"Mike's picking up fast," Doug said. "Seeing Carrie Gordon did more for him than a ton of medicine. Don't forget he's going to take off for St. Louis the minute he's in shape."

After supper Jim and I left Doug to dry the plates for Joan and went over for a talk with Mike. "Cheer up, Jim," Mike said, "and look at the bright side."

"What's bright about it?" Hutton puffed grimly on his pipe.

"I've been thinking. And I've figured they won't throw any punches next time, when you cut their take down to a hundred cows. They'll just let you sign the paper and walk out."

"What's to stop 'em?" Hutton countered.

"The fact that a sheriff and coroner from Buffalo have been asking them a lot of questions. About three killings on Massacre Hill. Sure they've got alibis and won't be arrested. But I've been in court and I know how criminals act when they slip off a hook. They get careful. They play nice for a while. The less attention they get the better. Cleaning a sucker and then kicking him out won't look too good, even if the victim doesn't tell tales. What I mean is, they know they're on trial in a court of public opinion; so they're not likely to beat anybody up just for the fun of it."

It made me feel a lot better. But Jim himself took small comfort from it. At best his herd would dwindle at the rate of a hundred head per week, and gone would be the future he'd hoped to build here for himself and Joan.

In the morning Doctor Kueny drove out from Sheridan. "You're mending fast," he said after treating Mike's head and arm. "Keep him quiet till Sunday," he told Joan. "After that I wash my hands of him. Here's your mail, Miss Hutton."

Fallon waited till Kueny drove off down the creek. Then he let out a whoop. "Sunday! Did you hear that? St. Louis, here I come! I'll catch Monday's stage at Sheridan."

To prove his strength he dressed and came over to the main cabin to eat with us. Later he took Hutton aside for an earnest coaching. "You'll have to go through two or three more sessions with them before I get back. Stand up to them, Jim. They can take a hundred a week—or nothing at all."

I took this week's *Sheridan Post*, which Kueny had brought along with the mail, and went out to the front stoop with it.

The main headlines were about the killings on Massacre Hill. Every angle was hashed over, including the theory Doug and I had offered Roy Malcolm. But the paper said it didn't hold water. The accused men had tight alibis. Their horses hadn't been ridden that day. And as for Clanton paying money to Bruno, the paper's only comment was a quote from Clanton himself. "Ridiculous! Why should I hand over money to Bruno? I didn't even know the man, except by sight. Or the woman they call Rosa. The whole thing was trumped up by Riley and McLaren. All because I had to take a punch at Riley one day, in front of the Sheridan House."

The sting of it was in knowing that more than half the county would believe Clanton.

I turned to an inner page and saw the Brevities column with the line:

"A chiel's amang you takin' notes,
And faith, he'll prent it."

The first item he'd 'prented' this week was about Carrie Gordon.

Miss Carrie Gordon rode in from Soldier Creek and is spending the night with Superintendent and Mrs. Gridley. Tomorrow she takes the examination for teacher in Johnson County School District #7. Be warned, Miss Carrie. Gridley's a fiend for asking tough ones. The *Post* wishes you good luck.

So did I. I hoped Gridley would go easy on her. And privately I hoped something else: that her teaching career would be brief and that next spring at the latest would find her keeping house for a certain rising young lawyer of Sheridan.

What I didn't know or even dream, as I read that item about Carrie's exam, was that it held the key to more destinies than her own; that the miseries of Jim Hutton hung on it, either to be worsened or healed—and that in fact every single one of us would be saved or doomed by Carrie's trip to Sheridan.

I wasn't with her when she made it. So it can only be told as it came out later, from Carrie herself, after the smoke had cleared and the blood-letting was all over.

CHAPTER XXII

IT WAS early Friday afternoon (as everyone who read the *Sheridan Post* found out later) when Carrie started home from town. She wore denim pants and was astride a pony. A bag tied back of her saddle had the skirt and blouse she'd worn as an overnight guest of the Gridleys, and at the examination this morning. An examination she'd passed with flying colors. There'd been twenty questions and she'd missed only part of one. Gridley had promptly graded her paper and given her 98%.

Which meant she'd get the Beckton school when it opened in September. The prospect thrilled her. It would be the first money she'd ever earned. Fifty dollars a month! More even than was earned by top hands—men like Douglas McLaren and Harry Riley.

The road led up the north bank of the Big Goose. Carrie loped a mile, then let the pony walk. Hay smells filled the air. A gentle snowfed breeze blew down from the Big Horns and the world looked beautiful. Lupine grew riotously at the roadside.

She thought again of the two cowboys, Riley and McLaren. She liked them—yet common sense made her sure they were all wrong about Cal Clanton. Personal enmity must have warped their judgment. The terrible things they said about Cal just couldn't be true.

She wondered why they'd taken Mike Fallon home with them to the H Bar. Did it mean the Huttons were in trouble and needed a lawyer? She'd sensed something wrong at the Huttons. Lately Joan had been a bundle of tight nerves.

Carrie's pony shied as a pair of sagehens whirred from a meadow and sailed gracefully over Goose Creek. From cottonwoods came the mourning of doves.

Presently Carrie came to a fork where the road from Big Horn City joined this one. It bridged the creek at her left—the same bridge she'd need to cross herself every school day next winter. For the schoolhouse was on the other bank of the Goose, in the trees a little above here.

On an impulse Carrie reined to the left and crossed the bridge. A tall grim mill loomed just ahead of her, deserted now, and through a cottonwood grove at her right she could see upstream to the school. She rode curiously to it and dismounted in cool shade there.

What was it like inside? Was there a blackboard? Back of it she saw a pile of cut stovewood. Carrie tried the back door and because this was a public place, it was unlocked. She went inside and raised a window shade.

It was much like she'd expected. A schoolroom with seats for twenty pupils, a teacher's desk and a blackboard. Two tiny cloakrooms, one for girls and one for boys. In one corner a barrel stove. A shelf of schoolbooks, mostly primers. A few tattered hymn books on another shelf told her that upon occasion, when a circuit rider came along, Sunday church service was held here.

The blackboard had chalked figures left by the last teacher. It was a numbers problem for beginners. Carrie took a woolen eraser and rubbed the board clean. Then she picked up a stick of chalk. Had she forgotten how to write on a blackboard? Could she make neat, level lines as a teacher should?

She could write something and find out. Why not write the correct answers to the five-part question she'd slipped on in the exam? After grading the paper Gridley had told her the right answers. It was a question about the Bozeman Trail and Carrie had missed parts *a* and *e*.

  a. On what date did the President of the United States order the abandonment of the three Bozeman Trail forts?

Carrie wrote on the blackboard, March 2nd, 1868.

b. Name and locate the three forts abandoned.

Carrie wrote: Fort Reno on Powder River; Fort Phil Kearny on Little Piney; Fort C. F. Smith on the Big Horn.

c. In addition to abandoning the forts, what else did our government by official treaty promise the Sioux?

Carrie wrote: That all whites would thereafter be forbidden to pass through or settle in an area of about 22,000,000 acres, extending from the Big Horns to the Black Hills, and from the North Platte to the Rosebud River.

d. For how long was the ban generally obeyed?

Carrie wrote: For about ten years, 1868 to 1878.

e. After the Bozeman Trail was reopened, what four towns sprung up along it?

Carrie wrote: Buffalo in 1879; Big Horn City in 1881; Sheridan and Dayton in 1882.

She stood back and looked at her neat, level lines. Pleased, she decided to leave them there.

Let it be the first problem her pupils would see when they assembled in September.

She went to the teacher's desk, dusted it, then sat down to sift through odds and ends in a drawer. A roster of last year's children; a note or two from parents; a few graded spelling papers. Carrie looked through them, childishly curious, too absorbed to hear a footstep outside—or to notice a big, brutish face pressed against a window.

Dumb George had no doubt who she was—this girl hiding in the schoolhouse. She'd hidden here before and her name was Rosa! That much he knew. His master and his master's friends had gone into a worried conference about it, one night at the ranch. For hours they'd talked about Rosa, while Dumb George kept the beer mugs full. It had embedded in his bovine mind certain basic facts.

First, that Rosa hated his master and had once clawed his face; that she knew things which could destroy his master and so must be caught and destroyed herself.

And second, that Rosa after running away by night from Sheridan had hidden all the next day in the Beckton schoolhouse.

Now here she was again, back at the same hiding place! Dumb George couldn't doubt it. When night came she'd again slip away. He could see her pony tied in the creek brush. She'd slip off in the dark as she had before, unless he, George, made sure she didn't.

Like many big men he had the gift of a light step. He moved soundlessly to the back door and went in there; like a monster with the feet of a cat and the strength of a gorilla he slipped up behind Carrie Gordon.

She had no idea he was there till his hands had her throat. One frantic twist let her see his face—a wide, fleshy face not savage but inhumanly stupid. Her scream was less than half out when his fingers stifled it. She saw his face and felt his strength and then dizziness, a nausea of terror came over her like a tawny flood and swept away her consciousness.

For a moment George thought she was dead. His hands came away and she fell to the floor. He hadn't meant to kill her. At least not here. What a weak thing she was to die so easily!

But when he kneeled by her he found she'd only fainted. So what should he do next?

Always when in doubt he had but one answer. He must ask the master. The master was in town today.

George squatted there on his haunches like a bear hovering over a lamb he'd just pawed down. Then an animal cunning came into his eyes. The first thing was to get her away from here. They were too close to a public road.

So the big man picked up the girl, tucked her under his arm and walked out. He went to her pony and hung her across the saddle. Then he led the pony up the creek bank, where cottonwood and alder gave him a thick screen. There was no chance for anyone at the Beck ranchhouse, on a knoll beyond the creek, to see or hear him.

The milch cow he'd come looking for would have to wait. First he must dispose of Rosa. He looked over his shoulder, saw her hanging limp across the saddle, and pushed on through the brush. Rapid Creek came in from the south and he waded across it, continuing on up the Goose. Soon he was well away from the Beckton road. Even if Rosa screamed she wouldn't be heard now.

He came at last to the fence of the Clanton land. Here in the creek timber there was no gate. So George simply pulled on the wires till a dozen staples came out. He pressed the wires to the ground and led the pony over them.

Still keeping to the brush, George continued on till he came opposite the Clanton corral. Here he forded to the north bank and was about to enter the corral when a terrified cry made him whirl about. The girl had come to her senses and the shock had toppled her from the saddle. She was scrambling to her feet when George grasped her arm. "Come, Rosa," he said.

As he tried to lead her on her struggles made

it awkward. And now she really screamed. So again George took her under an arm and walked into the corral with her, his free hand leading the pony. Her legs kicked frantically and again she screamed. In the corral he set her down. "A cry will not help, Rosa."

His hand clamped over her mouth but she twisted away. "I'm not Rosa!" she gasped. "Are you mad?"

Again an animal cunning leaked from his eyes. Of course she'd claim she wasn't Rosa! She'd use any trick to make him let her go. If he let her go she'd destroy his master. "We will go inside, Rosa." He picked her up, kicking and screaming, and walked into the house.

The house had five large rooms and a small, private den. Because George had to keep the house clean he had keys for every door. The stoutest lock was on the door of the small den, where Clanton kept his private papers. More than once he'd held other secrets there, such as stage and train loot brought here for safekeeping by Gomer and Shonts.

For that reason the den's one window was small, high up and barred. George unlocked the den and pushed the girl inside. She fell in a sobbing heap. "Wait there, Rosa," George said.

He closed the den door, locked it and left the house. At the barn he saddled a big, sixteen-hands horse and hit the trail for Sheridan. It wasn't often he went to town. He hated the town because people there made fun of him. But now he must find the master. How proud the master would be of him for catching Rosa!

With light from only one small, high window, the den was dim. In the dimness Carrie saw a roll-top desk with an oil lamp on it. She found the match box and lighted the lamp. A wall clock told her that half an hour had passed since hoofbeats had faded down the valley.

Gradually she'd sensed that she was alone in the house. As her wits came back she knew it was Cal Clanton's house. A book on the desk had his name in it. She'd heard about a slow-witted giant who worked for him. Why had the brute mistaken her for Rosa?

Whatever the reason, she must get out of here before he came back. She stood on a chair and tried the window bars. She called through them but only an echo came back. She banged on the locked door.

The desk had drawers. Maybe one of them had a tool of some kind. A chisel or hammer or something to pry with. Frantically she began going through the desk drawers.

There was no tool she could use. But a name on a paper caught her eye. The name James Hutton. What connection could Mr. Hutton have with Clanton?

Then she saw it was a bill-of-sale for chattel. It was signed by James Hutton and conveyed one hundred cows to Martin LaSalle of Sheridan. Another bill-of-sale was pinned to it. The two papers were alike except that they were dated a few days apart.

Carrie brushed them aside and went on rummaging for something to pry or pound with. Deals in livestock didn't concern her now; nor had she time to puzzle over why titles belonging to a Sheridan saloonman were kept in Clanton's locked, private den.

Then, looking through another drawer, she again saw James Hutton's name. It began a letter. "Hutton ain't his real name. It's John Prather . . ."

Carrie glanced at the heading and date. The letter had been sent from Ohio. ". . . and he's on the dodge. Joan ain't the girl's name either. She's Mary Prather."

The full impact hit Carrie when she remembered an air of tension at the Hutton household—certain shadows of fear she'd glimpsed in Joan. On the dodge? Was that why they had a lawyer at the ranch? But why should it concern Clanton?

Carrie read further. "Looks like you hit a jackpot, Cal. I went to the morgue of the *Toledo Blade* and here's what I dug up."

A six-year-old news story was outlined. About two convicts escaping from a quarry after the murder of their guard. Convicts named Dugan and Prather. Then a later clipping about Dugan's recapture at St. Louis and his speedy execution in Ohio.

For a moment Carrie almost forgot her own peril. Joan was the closest friend she'd made in this new country. Mike Fallon and Cal Clanton seemed to be in it too. Mike as a lawyer and Clanton as . . . as what? What jackpot could Clanton expect to win out of the blight hanging over James Hutton?

There was still a paragraph of the letter and Carrie read on: "But you better not waste any time, Cal, shaking him down. Because a break came only a month or two ago. Seems this Dugan was a blow-hard. Always blowing off about how tough he was. And he blew off to his landlady in St. Louis, at the joint where he was hiding. Swore he did it all himself. Said the guy Prather didn't lift a finger. Said all Prather did was run. Said he picked up Prather's sledge and finished off the guard. After six years the landlady softened up and told the cops. Which don't leave much of a rap against Prather. So you better grab what he's got fast, Cal."

The signature meant nothing to Carrie. But a phrase in the last line did. "Grab what he's got." She looked again at chattel bills-of-sale— hints that two hundred cows had already been "grabbed." Not by Clanton but by LaSalle. Yet the titles were in Clanton's desk. Was LaSalle only a pawn? Carrie remembered the sensational theory offered by Riley and McLaren—that Clanton had bribed an outlaw brother to leave the country, and then had conspired to recover the bribe by murder on Massacre Hill.

It had seemed preposterous! But how could she doubt it now?

Frantic, she again went to the locked door and pounded desperately. If she could only break out! She could race up-creek to the Hutton place. Mike Fallon was there, crippled. But he was a lawyer and he'd know what to do with this Ohio letter—and with this fruit of blackmail at Sheridan.

She went back to the desk and again rummaged for a tool.

And at the bottom of the last drawer she found one. Not a pry or a hammer but a gun. A fancy gun with a mother-of-pearl butt.

It was loaded with bullets. Five in the cylinder and one in the chamber. Carrie Gordon picked it up gingerly and went to the door. Both of her small hands gripped it as she pressed the muzzle against the lock. She shut her eyes, held her breath—and pulled the trigger.

The roar deafened her and the kick was like a sword slapping her wrists. A chip of metal flew from the lock and bit her face. But she held tightly to the gun and stepped back with it, trembling, ready to shoot if the giant halfwit or anyone else came charging in. She wasn't sure how far he'd gone, or if she was alone on the ranch. Anyone within half a mile would hear the shot.

No one came. Nor was the lock shattered. There was a hole through it but when Carrie tried the door it still held. So again she gripped the pearly butt with both hands, shut her eyes and fired. Again the boom deafened her and a stench of burned powder fouled the room.

But this time she'd smashed the lock. When she pulled on the door it opened. Beyond, nothing but a silent, empty house challenged her. Carrie turned back to the desk, picked up the letter and the bills-of-sale. With these and the pearl-butted gun she ran—ran for the corral to get saddled and away.

At the corral she didn't need to saddle. Her pony stood hipshot there, where the big man hadn't bothered to unsaddle it. Carrie climbed on and rode out of the corral. Then a drum of hoof-beats made her look downvalley. Terror surged back when she saw men and horses. Six men were riding hard toward the house.

Carrie wore no spurs. But she managed to heel her pony into a run. Wagon ruts led toward a gate at the upper end of the meadow and she raced that way—raced for her life, a slight, frightened girl on a small brown pony. She knew who those men were. And she couldn't forget they'd killed Rosa!

At the gate she slid off the pony, fumbled with the gate chain and lost half a minute unhooking it. Looking back she saw that the six riders had stopped at the house. Relief swept over her as it seemed they'd come no nearer. She led her pony through the gate and didn't waste time closing it.

Still clinging to the pearl-butted gun, she scrambled up into the saddle and rode on. It was past sunset. A deer, watering at the creek, broke from the brush and went bobbing toward the hills. Then Carrie looked back and panic came again. One of the six men had gone into the house. Now he rushed out and she saw he was Clanton. He swung to his saddle and waved an arm upvalley. Right away all six men broke into a gallop toward the upper gate.

Again Carrie heeled her pony to get it running. But it was a small, fat pony and the men behind were sure to have faster mounts. Yet when Carrie looked back they didn't seem to be gaining. If they'd raced all the way from Sheridan their horses couldn't be fresh. She saw them streak through the gate she'd left open.

Then a bullet zinged over her head and she heard the crack of a rifle. Another bullet splashed dust under her stirrup. It was still more than a mile to the Gordon gate. Doves mourned from the cottonwoods and a big, awkward crane went flapping up the creek. Another bullet zinged close. Carrie leaned low over the pony's mane and rode on.

CHAPTER XXIII

WE WERE ALL at supper when I heard the shooting. Six of us—the Huttons, Doug, Mike, Johnny Beaver and me. Johnny had brought in a mess of native trout and Joan had fried them a golden brown. Mike was telling a funny story to keep Hutton's mind off of tomorrow—when he must face LaSalle in Sheridan.

"Bunch of roundup hands," I guessed, "potting at rocks and rabbits."

The shooting came nearer and Doug got up for a look. He went to the front door and stepped outside. In half a second he was back in and reaching for his gunbelt. We always hung our side arms on a rack before sitting down at the table.

I made a jump for mine and followed Doug outside. A yellow-haired girl was making dust this way on a pony. About two furlongs back some hard-riding men were throwing lead. Rifle lead! It didn't make sense. Why would anyone want to shoot gentle little Carrie Gordon?

She was almost to the well when a slug caught up with her pony. It stumbled, squealed, then hit the dirt nose-down. Carrie flew over its head and landed in a sprawl. Doug ran to her, his gun out and blazing. But Carrie wasn't hurt. She got up and dashed for the house. As she passed me I saw that she had a gun herself. We didn't have time to ask questions. Bullets were snapping at us. "Get inside, Carrie!" Doug yelled.

Neither of us was using his head. It caught us too much by surprise, so we just stood there like dolts and emptied our six-guns at men riding at us with rifles. They were out of our range and it's a wonder they didn't cut us to ribbons.

Fallon's yell snapped us out of it. "Duck for cover!" he shouted from the porch. I turned and saw him there, his bad arm in a sling and his good arm pushing Carrie inside. Doug made a run for the door and I wasn't more than a jump back of him. But it was the wrong door and we both knew it a second too late. Our rifles were in the bunkshack. We should have made a dash for them the instant we heard the shooting.

Window glass crashed as we dived into the main cabin. Carrie was there, half hysterical and with Mike's arm around her. She'd had more than she could take—running a race with those bullets. Johnny Beaver slammed the door shut, his coppery face flaming with the light of battle. He'd taken Jim Hutton's shotgun from its wall pegs. Jim himself stood there with his Winchester, an old model rimfire .44.

"Keep away from the windows," he said hoarsely.

A bullet splintered the door and plunked on brass. It crashed an oil lamp from the table. "They're playing for keeps," Doug said. Right then I'd've given my left eye for a saddle gun. All I could do was reload my belt gun and duck below a sill with it. The shooting stopped and I peered out. Clanton and five men had pulled up about two hundred yards away, beyond pistol range.

Then they scattered, deploying to circle the house. "Cover the back side, Doug," I said. "Mike, take the girls into Joan's room and make them sit in a corner."

Carrie had dropped something and Mike stooped to pick it up. It was a .45 hip gun with a mother-of-pearl grip. It looked like the one Bruno had left town with!

"Where did you get it, Carrie?" Mike asked gently.

She was still too upset to explain coherently. But when Mike asked again she gave out five words . . . "At Clanton's . . . and this too."

She held out some crumpled papers and Mike took them. Then Joan put an arm around Carrie and led her to a bedroom. "Johnny Beaver," I said, "take your shotgun in there and cover the window. Whang away if anyone tries sneaking up."

Doug was in the kitchen, whose window faced

upvalley. Here in the parlor we had windows on two sides. Hutton took the one which fronted toward the hillside and I took the downvalley window. When I looked out I saw Monk Kincaid. He was prone behind a ditch bank and out of my range. Only his head and shoulders showed. Further along the same ditch I saw a black slouch hat that looked like Shonts'.

So I traded guns with Hutton and took a shot at Kincaid. He fired back and came closer to a hit than I did. The difference was that he had a new model centerfire rifle which could shoot twice as far and twice as accurate as a rimfire. Again I wanted to trade an eye for my own 44-40.

"How long till dark, Jim?"

"There won't be any dark," Hutton said. "And it's already moonrise."

He was right. A full moon rises when the sun sets. "No clouds," Jim added. "It'll be light enough to shoot by all night."

Right now the twilight was about an hour old. I heard Doug shoot from the kitchen. I looked into Joan's room and saw Johnny Beaver crouched under its window with a shotgun. The girls sat on the floor with their backs to a log wall. The logs were full-bole and about fifteen inches through. "That's the ticket," I said.

Mike Fallon looked in on them. His free hand held a pearl-butted gun and some papers. And his eye had the flash of a lawyer who'd just won the biggest case of his life. "You say you found this stuff in Clanton's house, Carrie?"

"In his private desk," Carrie said, "in a locked room." She wiped a tear-streak from her face and tried to smile. "Have I been acting like a baby?"

"You acted like General Sheridan," Mike said, "at the Battle of Winchester." He looked at her proudly and then spoke to Joan. "If we ever break out of this trap, your troubles are over." He waved the papers and the pearly gun. "Here's clearance for your dad, Joan. And enough else to hang the pack of 'em a mile high!" His voice had a lilt of triumph. Then a storm of bullets from four sides kept him from telling us more.

We manned the windows but didn't shoot back. "Just make sure they don't rush us," I yelled. "Kincaid and Shonts are on my side. Who've you got, Doug?"

"LaSalle," Doug called from the kitchen. "He's behind a stack of cordwood and out of my range."

"And you, Jim?"

"Gomer," Hutton said. "He's on the hillside back of a big boulder."

Fallon reported from the bedroom window which faced toward the creek. "We've got Clanton and Dumb George. They're in the creek brush." But a minute later he corrected this. "I hear someone in the bunkhouse. I think it's George. He could get in there from the creek, easy enough."

The bunkhouse was about thirty paces creek-ward from the main cabin. By using it as a screen George could get into it without our seeing him. "There he goes!" Fallon yelled a minute later. "He's back in the creek trees with an armful of rifles."

There went my saddle gun and Doug's. So all chance of rearming ourselves was gone. It made the odds six to five against us, with all the long range weapons on their side. Six to four, really, because Mike with his bandaged arm and head, and an indoor man by trade, wouldn't count for much in a gunfight.

The shooting stopped and I knew the last fusillade had been mainly to cover George's raid on the bunkhouse.

"Listen, everybody," Mike said. He stood in an open inner doorway where we could all hear him. "Listen to what Carrie dug out of Gentleman Cal's private desk. First, the gun Bruno had when he was killed. Which ties Clanton in a hard knot to the raid on the stage. Next, the cattle titles Jim gave to LaSalle. Which ties Clanton to the blackmail. Last and most important—get ready to cheer, Joan—a letter Clanton got from Ohio."

Mike read the letter aloud to us. As he finished, Joan came running from the other room. She threw her arms around her father's neck, too choked up even to sob. Neither of them said a word.

"It means," Mike told us, "that at the worst Jim'll only have to serve out the last year of a manslaughter term. And maybe not even that. Harry, soon as you get out of this trap grab the first stage to Cheyenne. Make a plea to your old horse-loving colonel, Governor Moonlight. Tell him a top Wyoming citizen needs a kind word from him to the governor of Ohio."

"Leave that end of it to me, Mike," I said. "But first we got to get out of this wagon-box." The last word slipped out because I couldn't help thinking of the Wagon Box Fight back in '67, not far from here, where a detail of troops got boxed up and besieged much like we were now.

Nobody said anything for a little while. For now we could see the situation from Clanton's angle. His neck was at stake. His and Kincaid's and Shonts' and Gomer's. And maybe even George's and LaSalle's. If a single one of us survived the truth would come out. The truth about murder on Massacre Hill! The truth about blackmail. The clear proof that Clanton owned the LaSalle deadfall and every thug in it.

"Okay, Harry," Doug said finally. "We've got to get out of this box. You're the one who served under Moonlight in the old Fort Laramie days—the only one of us who ever soldiered any. So you might as well be captain and start giving orders."

"That suits me," Hutton said. And Mike echoed him.

I peered over my sill and dimly I could still make out Shonts and Kincaid. They ducked out of sight in the ditch as I poked the old rimfire over the sill. An hour-high moon, bright and full, hung over them. Twilight had faded but moonlight and starlight made up for it. I'd never seen a clearer sky.

"First," I decided, "you go back to Carrie, Joan, and both of you stay low in a corner. Mike, keep an eye on them and keep Bruno's gun loaded. Everybody else stay alert at his post. Don't waste a shot till they come within range."

"Okay," Doug said. "Then what?"

"Time's on our side. There's always a chance someone might happen along. What about your dad, Carrie? Won't he worry about you not coming home and go looking for you?"

"I'm afraid not," Carrie said. "There's a taffy pull in town tonight. I was invited and said I couldn't go. But when I don't get home Dad will think I changed my mind."

So I shrugged that chance off. Well, maybe the doctor would come out in the morning for a look at Mike. Or somebody from Beck's might come fishing up the creek. Or a PK strayman might ride by.

"Sir, I have a thought." The voice was Johnny Beaver's.

"Shoot, Johnny."

"It is a night of full moon but high mountains

300

rise to the west. The full moon will hide behind the mountains an hour before the east gives a sun."

I caught what he meant. There'd be a moonless hour just before dawn. At this spot moonset would precede sunrise because of the Big Horn range just west of us. "Go on, Johnny."

"In that hour," the Indian boy said, "they do not see me if I slip out and crawl to a horse. Then I am gone. If they chase me you are free. If they do not chase me, I will bring men and guns."

"Bull's-eye!" Doug applauded from the kitchen. "Only it's me who oughta do the Portugee Phillips act. What about it, Harry?"

It was Portugee Phillips who'd done exactly what Johnny Beaver volunteered to do now. The night after the Fetterman massacre, with four thousand Sioux besieging Fort Phil Kearny, Portugee had slipped out to ride a killing two hundred miles in subzero weather to get help from Fort Laramie. As if I didn't know! Wasn't I on sentry duty myself, that blizzardy Christmas Eve, when Portugee's spent horse dropped dead under him right at the gate?

"Johnny's the man to go," I decided.

Doug didn't argue about it. Maybe he saw my two good reasons for picking Johnny. The job meant crawling in the dark to creek brush, from there slipping like a shadow to the nearest horse, from there a hard bareback dash down the valley. For that who would be better than a slim, quick Hunkpapa boy? My other reason was even sounder. The men surrounding us meant to wipe us out. It was their only chance to cheat the gallows. So they were sure to come at us, either to gun us or burn us out with a torch. For that their best time would be the hour of darkness, just before dawn. The same hour Johnny must pick for his dash to Sheridan.

So in that hour I couldn't spare Doug McLaren. In a gunfight he'd be worth two Johnny Beavers.

The twilight had completely faded which made it a lot darker inside the house than out. Here there was no direct moonlight and Jim Hutton, guarding the other window of this same room, was only a dim shape to me. It gave us an advantage and proof of this came when a rifle bullet missed my window at least six feet. Yet I saw a flash in the ditch and knew it came from Shonts. If he tried crawling this way he'd make a moonlit target. It would be the same on the other three sides of the house.

"Doug," I said after a minute, "trade places with Johnny. And trade guns with me as you come through."

I could barely see them as they passed by, Doug changing from kitchen to bedroom and the boy from bedroom to kitchen. Doug gave me his forty-five as he passed and I let him have the rimfire rifle.

It put Doug in the same room with the girls. Maybe it would make them a little less frightened. But that wasn't my main idea in posting Doug there. "Clanton's your man now, Doug. He's in the cottonwoods with George."

"Yeh," Doug called back. "It's just like that bird to deal himself the best shelter."

"Now get this, Doug. Clanton's the leader. If you can pick him off, the others might do a fade-out. I mean they might light out for Idaho, or somewhere. They're not anchored here like Clanton is. They don't own real estate like he does. They're just a pack of rats and if you pick off their leader, they might scatter."

That was why I gave Doug the rifle. Even a rimfire rifle is better than a six-gun if your target is more than eighty yards off. It was six hours till the moonset deadline and in that time Doug might get a chance at Clanton.

An occasional shot came at us from one side or another. Usually it was a wide miss. With no candlelight in the house, our windows didn't even make black squares for them to shoot at. "They're just trying to draw fire," I said. "So don't shoot back."

Mike was the only man who didn't have a shooting post. So I called him to me. "Take over my post, Mike, while I inspect the guard."

As he stooped by the window the white shapes of his arm sling and head bandage stood out in the dark. "Keep low, Mike. Just peek about once a minute to see if they're behaving."

I stepped to Hutton's window for a look. The moonlight out there showed me a hillside sloping up from the valley floor with rock outcroppings and a few scrub junipers. "Gomer's back of that biggest rock," Jim said. And just then a flash of gunfire came from it. Another wide miss. "Let him shoot, Jim. But sing out if he comes any nearer."

Groping into the kitchen I bumped into the table where we were eating when Carrie Gordon raced up. The supper things were still on it. I felt my way around it and found Johnny Beaver at the upvalley window. A stack of cut wood was about two hundred yards away on this side. Beyond it the Big Horns made a sky-high wall against the night. "Is LaSalle still out there, Johnny?"

"Two times he shoots at me," the boy said.

"Shoot twice at *him,* Johnny, if he comes within shotgun range. Give him both barrels."

When I went to the bedroom Doug heard me and reported with mock discipline. "All quiet on post number four, corporal."

The bunkhouse and sheds were on his side, with the creek brush a little beyond them. Clanton and George might be in an outbuilding or they might be in a thicket. "Not a peep out of 'em since I've been here," Doug said. "What does the clock say, Harry?"

"Never mind the clock," I said. "Look at the moon. When you can't see it any more it'll be half past three in the morning. And time to stand off boarders."

"Can't *we* do something?" Joan spoke from the darkest corner. All I could make out was her white apron. Carrie, beside her, had on the jacket and Levis in which she'd ridden from town.

"Did you ever shoot a double-barreled shotgun?" I asked.

Joan, fresh out from the east, hadn't. But Carrie Gordon was farmbred and had hunted quail with her father. "I'm all right now," she said. "If there's another shotgun let me have it."

"When Johnny leaves at moonset," I told her, "take his shotgun. And blast away with it if they try to rush us."

I went back to my post and relieved Mike. "Carrie didn't have any supper," I said. "There's a coupla trout left on the platter. And a pitcher of milk. Take her in there, Mike."

It turned out to be the smartest order I ever gave.

Because when Mike took Carrie into the kitchen, they stayed there. Which left Doug alone with Joan. A chill came on as the night got older, as it always does in Wyoming. Supper coals were still alive in the kitchen stove and they gave a little warmth. Also the stove was the only piece of iron furniture in the house, and would stop a bullet. Also there was a wood-box back of the stove and if a girl sat on it she had a stove between her and the window, in case a slug came zinging in.

So the next time I made a round of inspection, which was when the full moon was more than half across the sky, I found Mike and Carrie sitting on the wood-box back of the stove. "Getting along all right?" I asked.

"Yes," Carrie said. Her voice was easy and relaxed.

"Don't give us a thought," Mike said.

"How about you, Johnny?"

"I am good," the boy said. "When the moon goes, so do I."

I went to Doug's post and this time he didn't hear me come in. Again I made out Joan by her white apron. She was standing near the window and Doug had an arm around her. "Corporal of the guard!" I announced sharply. "Inspecting post number four."

Doug stepped back and took a crouch under the window. "All clear, corporal," he reported. I couldn't see his face but his voice had a grin in it. "Where's Mike and Carrie?"

"Holding hands in the kitchen," I said. "Which is okay with me because I remember something I heard Colonel Moonlight say one time, down at Fort Laramie."

"What?" Joan asked curiously.

"He said in a siege the main thing you need is morale. He said if your garrison's in high spirits, you'll never get smoked out."

I let them think it over and went back to the parlor. Hutton had been watching both windows there. "It won't be long now," I said.

But it seemed long. The next two hours were like ten. By then you had to look out the west window to see the moon. It inched along toward the piney wall out there, the Big Horns, the west fence of our forbidden valley. "Slip away the minute she drops out of sight, Johnny," I said. "Leave your shotgun with Miss Gordon. You couldn't crawl with it anyway."

"I have a deer knife," Johnny said. "It is all I need."

He stood pat on that, so we didn't try to make him take a six-gun. His only chance was to sift through them unseen. If they saw him they'd kill him, whether or not he had a gun. He was an Indian and Indians have never liked short guns. They use long guns, held with two hands against the shoulder, or no gun at all.

Mike and Carrie were still back of the stove. "I'll take over," Mike said, waving Bruno's forty-five, "soon as Johnny leaves."

"*We'll* take over," Carrie corrected, her voice steady and calm.

On this round, to tease Doug and Joan, I knocked before going in. But they didn't move an inch. They were kneeling side by side at the window, eyes level with the sill. "How long till moonset?" Doug asked.

"Call it an hour," I said. "Then look out for tricks. There's a can of kerosene in the bunkshack and they might use it to fire the house."

I heard Joan catch her breath. But she said nothing. Doug's free arm went around her. This life-or-death crisis had bridged time—had brushed aside all restraints and brought them quickly together. It made me remember something Doug was always citing from a Scotch grandmother. "Calamities, like as not, turn out to be blessings." Whatever happened, they were having this one blessed hour.

So it was, too, with Mike and Carrie. So it was even with Jim Hutton, born John Prather; for if the calamity of Dumb George hadn't seized a girl by the throat, he'd never have known about the evidence in Clanton's desk.

I went back to my post and waited. Kincaid had fired a few shots while I was gone. During the next ten minutes a shot came from each of the other sides of the house. So they were still out there, waiting for total darkness and a chance to destroy us all.

As the last minute of moonlight slipped by I went back to see Johnny off. We saw the big yellow circle ride the Big Horn divide; then a piney peak cut it in half and it sank slowly out of sight. It left only a thin starlight. I opened the back door and Johnny Beaver, with a deer knife at his belt, slipped out into the night.

"Good luck, Portugee!" I called after him.

CHAPTER XXIV

AS THE MOON dropped deeper behind the Big Horns the night got even darker. From my east window I could see barely a dozen yards. Ears were better than eyes now. I strained mine for the sound of crunched gravel or the crackling of a dry stick.

I raised my voice so that all posts could hear me. "When one comes they'll all come. All six of 'em. Maybe from four directions at once. Let's have a report about every five minutes."

It was too dark to see a clock. A prickling suspense made the minutes creep. Then Mike Fallon sang out, "All quiet on my side, Harry."

"Same here," Hutton echoed. Joan reported for Doug: "I can hear my heart beat—and an owl hooting at the creek."

"Keep looking. Keep listening," I said. "Cut loose at any close-by shape or sound."

More minutes dragged by and then Hutton said hopefully: "Johnny must've slipped through. Anyway they didn't shoot at him. Not a shot fired since he left."

That didn't prove anything. If they grabbed

Johnny Beaver there'd be lots of ways to kill him without shooting. But two reports later Doug said the same thing. "No shots since Johnny left, Harry. Might mean they're chasing him."

I didn't think so. Pursuit would be mounted and I'd heard no hoofbeats. Still, it was odd that they'd stopped shooting after keeping up an intermittent fire on us all through the night.

Maybe they were trying to lull us into a feeling of security just before the attack. Hoping to make us less alert. "They may jump us any minute," I warned. "You girls got good ears. Use 'em."

Joan used hers a minute later. "I heard a faint sound in the bunkhouse—like a board squeaking."

"Might be George," I said. "Maybe they sent him for the kerosene. Keep listening, Joan."

For a while we held our breath but she heard nothing more. Doug gave a nervous laugh. "Bet it was a pack rat, Harry. There's a sack of oats under my bunk. They go for it any night nobody's around."

Another tight silence was broken by Fallon. "If Johnny got through he ought to be at the Beck place by now. Who'll he find there?"

"No tellin'," I said. "Beck himself's not there." We knew George Beck was in politics and was accompanying Governor Moonlight on his tour of the territory. "The saddle help's off with the stock," I remembered. "That only leaves the old couple who run the Beckton post office. Likely

312

Johnny'll leave word with them and go tearin' on to Sheridan."

It was thirteen miles to Sheridan. Which meant that no relief could arrive from there until at least four hours after Johnny Beaver had slipped out of this house.

Carrie must have had the same thought for suddenly she asked, "How long did it take Portugee Phillips?"

"Believe it or not," I said, "he made it in seventy hours with half a sack of oats on his saddle. Two hundred and thirty miles through snow and sleet and a thousand blood-hunting Sioux! Had to hide in the willows by day and ride like hell in the dark. Compared to his, Paul Revere's ride was a cakewalk. He got there right while a Christmas Eve dance was goin' on at the Fort Laramie officers' club."

"He must've had a good horse," Hutton suggested.

"A better one than Johnny's got," I said.

I strained my eyes but couldn't see any glimmer in the east. Would dawn never come? Why didn't they rush us? Why the cold, dead quiet out there? I listened so hard I heard Doug's subdued talk with Joan. "I'd sure like a cup of coffee," he told her. "I'll sure make you one," she promised, "when morning comes."

"Make me one too," I said, just to loosen everybody up.

The next sound was about the sweetest I ever hope to hear. It was a rooster crowing from his roost in the shed. Not a streak of pink in the east yet, but that rooster knew it was soon due there. He crowed and Mike Fallon echoed with a cheer.

And still no attack. Not a shot fired for nearly an hour!

In a few minutes I could see it wasn't so black outside. The dark got grayer and thinner and let me see the outline of the well. From that moment a wave of confidence began building up in all of us.

Every new shade of daylight added to it. We heard the peeps of poultry coming out to forage, a swallow twitter under the cabin eave, the mooing of the milch cow in the corral and a dozen other intimate sounds of daybreak on a farm.

But no gunfire. "I can see the cordwood again," Mike reported. "No one's behind it."

"How do you know?"

"Couple of magpies on it," Mike said.

"No one's back of Gomer's rock, either," Jim Hutton announced. "That Bessie mule of yours just came down the hill to water at the ditch. Passed right by Gomer's rock without shying."

Bessie watered at the ditch and then grazed on down its bank.

I saw her nibble at sweet clover right close to the cover used by Kincaid and Shonts. Nothing disturbed her, so I knew they weren't there now.

"Either they've pulled out," I said, "or else they're all bunched at the creek."

As daylight brightened Joan went to the kitchen and fired the stove. She put coffee on. "Stick to your posts," I told the men, "till we're sure."

Joan was already sure. She came buoyantly to her father and hugged him. "We made it, Dad!" she whispered.

I began to feel fairly sure myself when sunup came without any trouble popping up with it. Just the same it didn't make sense. Why would they lay siege to us till four in the morning and then pull out, right when they had the best chance to mop us up?

"Keep manning the ports," I said, "till we know what's going on."

Assured by the magpies that no one was to the west of us, the girls moved boldly about the kitchen and made breakfast. They brought a plate to each man at his post.

I watched the hands of the parlor clock move from six to seven. And at half after seven we heard what sounded like a low wail or moan. Like someone in bad trouble down by the creek. My first thought was Johnny Beaver. "Maybe they cut him down," Doug said. "I'm going to find out."

He took the rimfire rifle and stepped out the back door. I joined him and no one took a shot at us. So we made a run for it and got in the bunkhouse. From there we again heard a moaning at the creek.

We dodged on that way, dashing first to the stock shed, then into the corral, from there to cottonwoods along the creek.

"It's Dumb George!" Doug exclaimed. "And gosh! There's Johnny Beaver! And Clanton!"

Of the three, only George was alive. We didn't need to throw down on him. His rifle lay off to one side, where he'd dropped it to mourn by the body of his master. Once I'd seen a sheep dog mourn like that, with an occasional heart-wrenched growl, by the still, cold form of its only friend the herder.

Under the same cottonwood lay Johnny Beaver. The deer knife wasn't in his belt. We saw it on the ground near Clanton, the blade red. Doug looked at me and we both knew what had happened. Johnny Beaver, crawling in the dark, had run into Clanton. He'd knifed Clanton. And Dumb George had reached out with bare hands to break the boy's neck.

That was why we'd heard no shooting.

"Like you said, Harry," Doug reasoned. "Clanton was the leader and with him dead the others quit cold and ran for it. All but George!"

And George, with no master to fight for, had simply dropped his rifle to mourn. He gave us no trouble. Driving him to the saddle room was like leading an ox to its stall.

• • •

The aspens hadn't turned yellow when I got back from Cheyenne. The stage was right on time, a breakfast gong ringing in the Windsor Hotel as we drew up there.

Joan and Doug were on the walk to meet me. It was a Joan I'd never seen before, all the pressure of fear gone from her. She threw her arms around my neck, kissed me till Doug had to pull her back. "Hold on there!" he complained. "You're *my* girl, remember?"

She laughed and cried and laughed again. Then she showed me a telegram just in from Ohio.

JIM AND I CATCHING FIRST TRAIN WEST stop HOMICIDE CHARGE DROPPED stop MANSLAUGHTER TERM SUSPENDED stop TELL HARRY INTERCESSORY PLEA FROM CHEYENNE BIG HELP.

MIKE.

We went in to breakfast and they wanted to know how I'd managed it. "All I did," I said, "was hang around till Tom Moonlight got back from his thousand-mile buggy trip. Folks were ten deep waiting for him by that time. All I ever got with him was half an hour on the capitol steps."

Doug chuckled. "You must've laid it on pretty

317

thick. Because Mike said he wrote a peach of a letter to the governor of Ohio."

"What about Clanton's playmates?" I asked. "Did they get away?"

"Two did and two didn't. They nabbed LaSalle and Kincaid as they boarded a train at Miles City. But Shonts and Gomer lit out for the lower Big Horns. Roy Malcolm says they joined up with the Hole-in-the-Wall gang down that way. Whatever happens to the Hole-in-the-Wall gang will happen to Shonts and Gomer."

"It won't be good," I predicted. "A bullet or a rope, one or the other. Did you backtrack Clanton any?"

Doug nodded. "His boots had the trademark of a bootmaker in Sacramento. So we checked up and found out the year gap in Clanton's life, between New Orleans and Sheridan, was spent in the California goldfields. Bruno was with him there and met a California Mexicana named Rosa. Vigilantes ran Clanton out, about that time, for shaking down some of the best people."

"Speaking of best people," I said, "what about Carrie Gordon? Has her school started yet?"

"Not for a week yet," Joan said. She hesitated, looked at Doug and then lowered her voice. "And when it starts, Carrie won't be teaching it. She asked them to get someone else."

"What?" I exclaimed. "After answering all

those tough questions! What's the matter with her, anyway?"

Joan leaned excitedly toward us, all the wildflowers in Wyoming in her cheeks. "Nothing—except she and Mike are getting married!"

"And so are we!" Doug chimed in before I could catch my breath. "A double wedding at the Beckton schoolhouse. What's more, you've got to double as best man."

My eyes were still popping when Joan followed up quickly: "But we haven't announced it yet. Carrie can't set a date till Mike gets back. She hasn't seen this telegram. We have to take it out there right now. Please don't say anything about it until . . ."

"Sh!" I whispered, looking past her at an extremely alert man at the next table. He was Editor Cotton of the *Sheridan Weekly Post*, scribbling fast in a notebook and with a reportorial eye cocked shrewdly our way. "Sh!" I warned. " 'A chiel's amang us takin' notes, and faith, he'll prent it.' "

Books are produced in the United States using U.S.-based materials

Books are printed using a revolutionary new process called THINKtech™ that lowers energy usage by 70% and increases overall quality

Books are durable and flexible because of Smyth-sewing

Paper is sourced using environmentally responsible foresting methods and the paper is acid-free

Center Point Large Print
600 Brooks Road / PO Box 1
Thorndike, ME 04986-0001 USA

(207) 568-3717

US & Canada:
1 800 929-9108
www.centerpointlargeprint.com